Reyn's Redemption

Beth Cornelison

SAMHAIN
PUBLISHING

Samhain Publishing, Ltd.
577 Mulberry Street, Suite 1520
Macon, GA 31201
www.samhainpublishing.com

Reyn's Redemption
Copyright © 2011 by Beth Cornelison
Print ISBN: 978-1-60504-962-5
Digital ISBN: 978-1-60504-943-4

Editing by Bethany Morgan
Cover by Tuesday Dube

First Samhain Publishing, Ltd. electronic publication: March 2010
First Samhain Publishing, Ltd. print publication: January 2011

Dedication

To Paul and Jeffery—I love you guys!

And thanks to my brother-in-law, Kyle Beeson of the Athens/Clarke County Fire Department, for his assistance with questions regarding firefighting.

Chapter One

Reyn Erikson wrapped his sweaty hand around the church's cross-shaped door handle and steeled himself with a deep breath. He'd known coming back to Clairmont, Louisiana, would be difficult. So many ghosts lived here. But walking back inside this small country church could well be the hardest test of all.

The last time he'd darkened the door of Clairmont Baptist Church had been his mother's funeral twenty years ago. That day, as a guilt-ridden ten-year-old, he'd only wanted to run as far and as fast as he could. Away from that church. Away from Clairmont. Away from the fingers pointed at him.

And never come back.

If not for the message from his grandmother's friend, he wouldn't be back now. He wouldn't be standing on the stoop of the aged sanctuary with his heart thumping like a trapped animal trying to escape. The merciless July sun baked down on his back, and the oppressive Louisiana humidity stuck his dress shirt to his clammy skin. But he could only blame dread for the sense of suffocation that squeezed his chest.

Of all the places where Gram's friend could have asked to meet him, why the church, damn it?

Open the door, coward. What's wrong with you? Just go in.

When he tugged the door open, it squeaked a loud protest,

drawing the gaze of the man in the pulpit as well as most of the congregation. Reyn stepped inside and caught the door before it banged closed.

"As I drove through Arkansas last week," the minister continued, despite Reyn's late arrival, "I saw a church billboard that read, 'So you think it's hot *here*?'"

With another glance at Reyn, the minister waited for the soft stir of chuckles to quiet before he continued.

The man's voice faded to a muted drone when Reyn turned his attention to the stained-glass windows that had glared down at him through his mother's funeral. Angels in flowing robes condemned him from the brightly colored glass. Saints and prophets stared back at him with contempt and censure.

You let your mother down. You let her die, the figures shouted at him. *Coward.*

His mouth grew dry. His feet seemed rooted where he stood. Like dense, acrid smoke filling a burning house, guilt and resurrected grief billowed in his chest. He struggled to suck air into leaden lungs. Out of habit, he reached down to adjust the flow of oxygen into his breathing apparatus, only to remember he wasn't wearing his turnout gear.

A tug on his shirtsleeve yanked him back to the present. Glancing down, he found a freckle-faced boy grinning at him.

"...to have a seat, sir?"

He realized belatedly the minister was talking to him, and he snapped his gaze to the pulpit. Scanning the curious faces turned toward him, he recognized a few members of the aged congregation. Obviously Principal Horton remembered him too, judging from the scowl that darkened the man's face. Mrs. Skinner directed a suspicious glare toward Reyn, and her lips thinned and frowned. No Clairmont Welcome Wagon for him.

He hadn't expected a warm reception. At least not from the

people who remembered him. These same people had accused him, judged him and driven him out of his tiny hometown.

Reyn stepped to the back pew and folded his large body onto the hard bench. At ten, the narrow wooden seats had been uncomfortable. For a thirty-year-old man of his considerable size, the pew promised nothing but stiff muscles.

The minister continued his sermon, despite the growing buzz as more people recognized him and whispered to their neighbor. Had he really thought he could come to town, see Gram and make arrangements for her care, then quietly leave Clairmont without the rumor mill catching wind of it? He wouldn't care what the people of Clairmont said about him if not for Gram. He hated to think of his grandmother being subjected to the pettiness of this small town. With his return, the Clairmont gossips would breathe new life into the embers of old fires. His name would be vilified again. He couldn't deny that he'd earned his reputation as a troublemaker. So why should they have believed in his innocence when it mattered most?

When the sermon ended, Reyn rubbed the tension building at the back of his neck, and the choir stood to lead the last hymn. A flash of color caught his eye, and he focused his attention on a young woman in the choir loft. As if her youth in this elderly congregation didn't already make her stand out, a bright sunbeam shone through the stained glass, spotlighting her heavenly face. The ray of light set her thick halo of red hair on fire and made her ivory skin glow.

The young woman raised her eyes and caught him staring. Before he could awkwardly look away, a lopsided grin tugged the corner of her mouth. Her seductive mouth. Her extremely hot, kiss-me-you-fool mouth.

Intrigued, Reyn held her gaze and lifted one eyebrow,

acknowledging her grin. Before his eyes, the angel with the flaming hair and the sexy mouth transformed into a full-fledged temptress. A come-on in a choir robe. Her lopsided grin melted into an alluring, come-hither invitation. Her eyes glittered and danced with mischief.

"Hi," she mouthed.

In response to her none-too-subtle flirting, liquid heat pooled in his belly and spread through his veins. He shoved his hands in his pockets and jerked his gaze away when he recognized the heaviness collecting in his groin.

He drew several deep breaths and shook himself from the siren's spell. Though *he* no longer cared what got whispered about him, Gram didn't need to hear that her grandson had become aroused at church.

After the minister dismissed the congregation with a benediction, the pianist played another verse of the last hymn. The congregation filled the aisles, and Reyn sighed his relief, eager to get out of the church that held so many bad memories. A few of the people who knew his history sent him disapproving looks, and he clenched his teeth.

To hell with them. They couldn't hurt him now. He was no longer the frightened boy they'd run out of town.

He searched the crowd, wondering which of the white heads or beehive hairdos belonged to Gram's friend, Olivia Crenshaw. He knew the name, since Gram mentioned her friend from time to time in their Sunday phone calls. But like most everything else about Clairmont, he'd forgotten the face that went with the Crenshaw name. All he had to go on was the message Mrs. Crenshaw left at the fire station when she'd called about Gram's broken hip and asked him to meet her at the church.

Mrs. Crenshaw had been Gram's friend for several years

now, keeping tabs on her as his grandmother became frailer. She'd been the one who found Gram on her bathroom floor, unable to walk and in desperate pain.

Reyn's gut clenched thinking of Gram laid out on the cold tile floor and suffering. While he worked in Atlanta, fighting the enemy fire week after week, praying for redemption, Gram was alone. Though he'd urged Gram to move to Georgia, had flown her to Atlanta every Christmas and Easter for years, he still worried about Gram living alone. He owed Mrs. Crenshaw, whoever she was, a tremendous debt for her attentiveness to his grandmother.

He searched the milling congregation, the townsfolk apparently in no hurry to get home, and noticed the redheaded seductress from the choir making a beeline for him. She'd removed her choir robe and draped it over her arm. Without the robe to hide her figure, he discovered she had dangerous curves to match the promise of trouble glinting in her eyes.

Reyn groaned. Tempting as she was, the last thing he needed during his brief stay in Clairmont was trouble. He couldn't do anything to cause tongues to wag and leave another scandal to haunt Gram.

He turned to leave through the back door of the church, hoping Miss Trouble would take the hint and find another target. But the press of bodies clogging the doorway, where people waited to shake the minister's hand, blocked his path.

The redhead came up behind him and gripped his arm. "James Reynold Erikson, better known to his family and friends as Reyn, lieutenant with the Atlanta Fire Department and Mr. August of the Firefighters Association's charity calendar."

Stunned, Reyn turned to the beauty with the flaming hair.

She stuck her hand out for him to shake. "It's a pleasure to finally meet you."

After staring at her outstretched hand for a moment, he gave her a polite smile and wrapped his fingers around hers. Her hand was small, but her grip was strong.

He cleared his throat. "How did you know—?"

"Oh, puh-leeze. Your grandmother can't stop talking about you and your heroic deeds with the fire department. I've heard about every cat you've rescued and every blaze you've put out. She loves to brag on you. Why, she talked for six months about the little girl you pulled out of the burning car."

A prickling suspicion crawled through him. "You're—"

"Olivia Crenshaw. I called you a few days ago about your grandmother. My car's outside, and I'm headed to the hospital to visit Lila now if you want to ride along." She gave him another lopsided grin.

His focus dropped to her mouth, riveted by the wicked allure of her full lips. The idea of being alone in a car with the loquacious flirt tantalized him, but his conscience reared its head. *Better not play with fire.*

"Um...yeah. Sure. But I can take my truck and fol—"

"Leave it here. I'll drop you back here after we visit Lila and maybe grab a bite of lunch at Burdeaux's."

"How is Gram? She was asleep when I called the hospital last night, and I haven't gotten a chance to call again this morning. I left Atlanta at three a.m. and drove straight through."

Her expression modulated. "Physically she's doing quite well, considering. But her spirits have been low lately. I know having you here will do her a world of good. She misses you."

Did he detect a note of censure in the woman's tone?

With a short, wry laugh, he dragged a hand along his jaw. "*You're* Mrs. Crenshaw? I was expecting an old biddy. Someone with gray hair and support hose."

"Ah." Her smile brightened again, and laughter sparkled in her eyes. "Sorry to disappoint you. And it's *Ms.* Crenshaw, not *Mrs.* Furthermore, I don't wear pantyhose of any kind, especially not in the summer. The things are too dang hot."

Reyn battled the urge to check out her legs and confirm what she'd said. Instead he locked his gaze on her face, studied the parade of freckles across her nose and cheeks, the shimmer of peach lipstick on her lips.

She cocked her head to one side and caught her bottom lip in her teeth. "Hmm. Your pictures don't do you justice. Well, that calendar shot does maybe, but—" she picked a loose string off his shirt at the shoulder, "—with that shot, who's looking at your face, huh?"

She gave him another devilish grin, echoed by the gleam in her eyes.

No doubt about it. The woman was a mistake waiting to happen. He'd made enough mistakes to last him a lifetime, thank you. And she clearly had misconceived notions about him based on his grandmother's boasting and the damn calendar picture.

He wasn't surprised to learn Gram bragged on him. She always gushed about how proud she was of him when he called her. She'd always had a blind faith in him, even when he was a kid. Even when the rest of the town condemned him and his penchant for trouble. Guilt rose up to prick him again. Gram refused to see the truth, which was just as well. She didn't know the whole story about the night of the house fire that killed his mother. He hadn't had the guts to tell her what had happened, hadn't wanted to hurt her any more than his inaction already had.

Reyn ran a finger under his collar to loosen the tie that

threatened to strangle him. "Can we get outta here? This place is starting to close in on me."

"Sure. Follow me." Olivia pivoted gracefully on her toes and sauntered up the center aisle of the church. Her hips swayed beneath her short, flouncy skirt, and heat coiled inside Reyn as he watched her walk away. Recklessness and curiosity overrode the voice of caution, and he peered down to check out her legs. Long, sleek and sexy. Just as he'd expected.

It would have been a hell of a lot easier if Olivia Crenshaw had been old and arthritic. But when had anything in his life ever been easy? The sooner he took care of Gram and got out of town the better.

"'Livia, wait!" A girl, who looked to be about five years old, waved to Olivia from the pews. "I wanna ride with you."

Olivia stopped and waited for the girl who, Reyn realized with a second look, wore braces on pencil-thin legs. Tucking a wisp of dark hair behind the girl's ear, Olivia shook her head.

"I'm not going home yet, sweetie. I'm taking Lila's grandson up to the hospital to see her." The girl pouted, and Olivia tugged her ponytail. "Reyn, this brat is my sister, Katy. Katy, this is Reyn."

Katy turned wide eyes to Reyn. "The fireman?"

Reyn held his hand out to Olivia's sister and gave her a friendly smile. "Nice to meet you, Katy."

Katy shook his hand with hero-worship in her eyes. The girl's awe caused a funny catch in his chest, his usual discomfort with receiving undeserved adulation.

"Ride with your dad, Katy. I'll see you at home later, and we'll play Clue. Okay?"

Her sister nodded and plodded down the aisle toward the crowd near the exit. Turning, Reyn followed Olivia to a side door. When he stepped out of the church and into the blinding sun, he slipped on his shades and glanced around the parking lot. Gravel crunched under his feet, and the fresh scent of cut grass perfumed the air. Olivia headed to a rusty sub-compact parked in the shade of a live oak.

"I'm gonna have to move some things off the front seat before you can get in." She dangled her keys from one finger while she opened the driver's side.

"If you'd rather take my truck, I don't mind—"

"It'll only take a second. I just have to move a few books. I take a night class at ULM, finishing my degree in pharmacy."

"ULM, huh? That's a long commute. You go every night?"

"Naw, just Tuesdays and Thursdays this semester." Her short skirt rode higher when she bent and stretched to clear a seat for him. He looked away from the tantalizing view and watched the family parked beside them pile into their van.

"Reyn? Reyn Erikson, is that you?"

He turned to the middle-aged woman with graying black hair who addressed him as she approached from the opposite end of the lot. He searched his memory to place the familiar face.

"I'm Hannah Russell," she said. "Your mother was a dear friend of mine for years."

"Was she? Well, then it's a pleasure to meet you." He offered his hand, but she bypassed his proffered handshake and gripped his shoulders. "My goodness, look at you. All grown up and handsome as the devil."

He fumbled for a response to the compliment, but before he could reply, Hannah added, "You must be home to see your grandmother. I heard she was in the hospital."

"Yes, ma'am. A broken hip."

Hannah clapped a hand to her chest. "Oh, the poor dear. Give her my best, will you?"

"We sure will. That's where we're headed now." Olivia stepped up beside him, and he cut a sideways glance to her.

Reyn detected a slight shift in Hannah's mood. She greeted the younger redhead with cool reserve. "Olivia. How're you?"

"Never better. And you?"

"Hannah, what the devil's keeping you?" A tall man wearing a straw cowboy hat stalked up behind Hannah and scowled at Reyn.

"Just sayin' howdy to Reyn, George. You remember Claire Erikson's son, don't you?"

"Remember him?" George scoffed and gave him a dark glare. "Course I do. I lost a perfectly good barn and several thousand dollars worth of equipment thanks to him and his arson. Not likely to forget a thing like that."

Reyn tensed. He sensed Olivia's curious gaze, but he kept his eyes trained on the man across from him. Animosity radiated from the farmer like the heat waves rippling from the pavement.

He remembered George Russell. The farmer had been one of his accusers, one of the men who'd convinced the sheriff that the town wasn't safe with Reyn in it.

Hannah faced her husband and planted her hands on her hips. "George, that's ancient history. Leave it alone."

"Arson?" Olivia took a step toward George, her stance combative. "He's no arsonist. I'll have you know, Reyn's a lieutenant with the Atlanta Fire Department. He's been honored several times for his valor and job performance."

Reyn gritted his teeth and took Olivia by the arm. "Don't. Let's go."

Geez, the last thing he wanted was a showdown with George Russell. He'd only been in town a couple of hours, and already the trouble had started.

"How would you know, missy? You were too young to know Reyn back then, to know the trouble he caused." George shot Olivia a stern glance. "Your daddy let him get by with it too. Didn't do his job like he oughta."

Olivia drew a sharp breath. "Don't you dare malign my father! He was a good man, and if he believed in Reyn and gave him the benefit of the doubt, that's good enough for me."

George narrowed a menacing scrutiny on Olivia, and Reyn tightened his grip on her arm, tugged her back from the man challenging her.

"Olivia, don't," he repeated tightly. "Let's go."

"It don't surprise me none that this boy'd take up with the likes of you soon as he hits town. Billy told us plenty about the kind of Jezebel you are. You and this boy...y'all are birds of a feather."

Reyn felt Olivia stiffen and saw a flicker of emotion in her gold eyes. A vulnerability or sadness. Instantly his defenses came up. The slam against Olivia grated his nerves. He had no respect for a man who'd harass a woman. He faced George, drew his shoulders back, and balled his hands in fists at his side.

His instinct to protect her rivaled his need to protect himself—from her. He didn't want to identify with her hurt, couldn't afford to drop his guard around those wounded gold eyes.

But almost as quickly as the pain had clouded her eyes, a spark of defiance lit them.

George aimed a finger at Reyn. "You best not make trouble while you're in town. Hear me? I'll be watching you, boy."

"I'm not here to make trouble." Keeping his tone even, Reyn met the man's icy glare. "And I haven't been a *boy* for many years."

When her husband turned and stalked away, Hannah gave them an apologetic look before following.

Reyn sighed and rolled the tension out of his shoulders.

"Welcome to Clairmont," Olivia said with a wry sideways glance.

"Maybe it'd be best if I went to see Gram by myself. I don't want to make any problems for you."

"Don't be silly. That old windbag doesn't intimidate me." She tossed her mane of fiery hair over her shoulder and climbed behind the wheel of her Chevette. "Shall we go?"

Reyn watched George cross the parking lot, the farmer's back stiff with hostility. He'd have to be careful to avoid George. He didn't want to cause any more grief for Gram. Or Olivia.

Across the parking lot, George approached Principal Horton. Horton wore the same dark scowl he'd given Reyn inside the church. The two men conferred, cast glares back at Reyn, then parted ways.

"Reyn? You comin'?" Olivia called.

"Yeah." He rounded the back end of her car, wondering whether the men genuinely thought he posed a threat or if they simply bore a grudge after so many years.

Popping open the passenger's door, he stared down at the tiny front seat and contemplated how to best fit his long legs in the limited space. Ducking his head, he lowered himself onto the ripped seat and slowly tucked his feet inside. He bit back a curse when his knees bumped the dashboard.

"Maybe we *should* have taken your truck." Olivia's eyes sparkled with amusement.

He shrugged and gave her a wry smile. "Too late now. I'm not sure I could get back out if I wanted to."

She laughed as she put the Chevette in reverse and backed out. "I just need the old jalopy to make it until I finish school. I can't afford a new car now. It runs—usually." She quirked a sexy, crooked grin and cut a quick glance toward him. "And that's what counts."

"I suppose." Reyn stared with an eerie detachment out the side window at the aged town. He noted a few changes along Main Street, but everything largely remained the same. Still, time had faded enough of his memories that even what he recognized seemed like echoes of a dream.

He glanced at Olivia, studied her sun-lit profile. She had a radiant quality that fascinated him, an inner spark evident in the confident way she carried herself.

"What did George Russell mean about your father? That he didn't do his job and let me get by with stuff?"

She gave him an unlady-like snort. "Just sour grapes, I imagine. Don't worry about it."

"I mean...who was your father? Should I remember him?"

She met and held his gaze. The smoky depths of her eyes, the intelligence and energy glittering there, mesmerized him. Without wanting to be, he found himself intrigued by and drawn to this woman.

"My father was Ray Crenshaw. He was the sheriff here until he died in a hunting accident when I was five."

A vague memory of a lawman coming by their house after the incident at the Russells' barn lurked in the back of his mind. He dredged up a slightly clearer memory of the same lawman talking with Gram before he was sent to Georgia to live with a relative. But the most vivid memory was of a kind man with strong arms who had restrained him from running to his

21

mother as her draped body was wheeled from their smoldering house.

Reyn tamped the surge of guilt and grief that particular memory stirred.

"Did you know him?" Olivia's voice cut through his daze, held a wistful note that stabbed at him.

"I think so." He didn't elaborate, even though he could tell from her expression she wanted more about his memories of her father. But recalling memories of her father would mean opening the door to events he'd long ago locked away where they couldn't hurt him. He had no intention of opening the past and all its painful memories while he was in town.

She turned her attention back to the road, and he heard disappointment in her sigh. Wearing a thoughtful expression, she wet her lips with the tip of her tongue. He followed the erotic movement of her tongue and stared at the glistening moisture left in its wake. Desire pumped through him and wound in his gut. He wanted a taste of those lips, but he knew better than to act on his urges.

Starting anything with Olivia would be a mistake. Starting something would raise her expectations—expectations he couldn't meet. Starting something would inevitably hurt her, and he'd caused enough pain in this town.

"Answer something for me now." Olivia's auburn eyebrows drew together. "Did you really burn down the Russells' barn when you were a kid?"

Reyn hesitated a beat then lifted an eyebrow. "You just told George Russell I wasn't an arsonist. Don't you believe what you said?"

"I... He was just being so ugly to you that I had to say something. Knowing what I do about you, it just seems so ludicrous that you would have—"

"Well, I did." His admission drew a startled look from her. "And as much as I appreciate your vote of confidence, you're wasting your breath defending me in this town."

She stopped for a red light, one of the few traffic lights in town, then cast him a curious glance. "I just—"

He held up a hand to stop her and shook his head. "I'd rather not go into the reasons why. Just know I earned the reputation I have, and I'm not proud of it."

"I know more than you think. Lila tells me a lot."

His chest tightened, but he covered his unease with an embarrassed grin. "All of it glowing, I'm sure."

He scratched his chin, telling himself he had no reason to worry about what Gram might have revealed to the red-haired spitfire. Even Gram didn't know the whole truth. "Don't judge me based on what Gram has told you. She has a distorted version of reality."

"Reyn, I—"

"Light's green."

Her sly smile, one that said she knew a titillating secret about him, triggered alarms in his head. He looked out the passenger's window, signaling he was through discussing himself.

Before long, she turned in at the visitor parking lot of the small hospital and took the first available spot. "I guess while you're home, I'll have the chance to see for myself who's right about you, won't I?"

Reyn faced her, and her eyes glittered with anticipation, as if rooting out his deepest secrets was an exciting challenge.

"Clairmont has never been my home...even when I lived here." He released a sigh, full of his regret and resignation. With that, he pried his legs out from under the dashboard and levered himself out of her tiny front seat.

He'd have to be careful. A woman like Olivia Crenshaw could be dangerous. She could sneak past his carefully erected defenses and discover things he'd kept hidden for years—things best left locked away where they couldn't hurt anyone. For her sake, as well as his own, he couldn't let that happen.

Like standing too near a fire, if Olivia got too close to him, she would get burned.

Olivia followed Reyn to the hospital entrance, musing over his last statement. Obviously, he wanted to keep her at arm's length with his brusque manner. But she saw much more than he probably realized. She sensed an underlying bitterness—and yearning—in his comment about Clairmont.

Everyone needed a place to call home.

She studied the flesh and blood man whose calendar picture had ignited numerous steamy daydreams over recent months. The summer sun highlighted his golden tan and made his short, wheat-colored hair appear more blond than light brown. He moved with a controlled power, and the muscles under his shirt told her he kept his body in top form. He was taller than she'd expected, and he exuded a magnetism that photographs couldn't capture.

Until that moment, she hadn't realized how eagerly she'd been anticipating the chance to meet Reyn. Now, finally, she had the opportunity to see for herself if he was everything Lila said and match a voice, a smile, a soul to the two-dimensional calendar image that had fascinated her, mesmerized her. She desperately hoped the real man was as beautiful inside as out. Not only did Lila deserve a worthy grandson, but thanks to her own disastrous relationship with Billy Russell, Olivia had already had her fill of handsome men with little other redeeming characteristics.

She'd reserve judgment on Reyn's character until she learned what was inside the man with the athletic body and GQ face. She sensed a sadness, a distance in Reyn that puzzled her. His remoteness resounded inside her like a lonely echo and cautioned her to stay away. She didn't need to be disappointed, broken-hearted again.

When he held the front door for her, she rewarded his thoughtfulness with a smile. The brisk chill of the air-conditioned hospital nipped her skin, and she rubbed her arms as they headed to the elevator. "She's in room three-eleven."

He nodded again and stepped into the elevator. "I appreciate your being there for Gram."

"I'm glad I could help. Lila's certainly been there for me enough times. She's very dear to me."

His gray gaze slid over her, seeming to size her up, lingering on her lips. She'd noticed his focus on her lips earlier, and his continued interest in her mouth left her feeling decidedly self-conscious. She'd never given her mouth much consideration, other than to slap on a bit of lipstick. Why did it intrigue him so? Curious, she studied his mouth in return.

His smooth lips weren't too full but looked soft and skilled. No doubt Mr. August had plenty of practice kissing. The idea unsettled her, and she jerked her gaze away. She may have kissed him plenty of times in her calendar-driven fantasies, but she had no intention of tangling herself up with a man she knew so little about.

"Did Gram need surgery?" He shot her a worried glance.

Olivia nodded. "They operated yesterday, replaced her hip joint. I'm sorry you couldn't be here then, but when I couldn't reach you at home, I had a hard time tracking down the phone number for the right fire station."

Looking away, Reyn pulled his broad shoulders back, leveling them as if squaring off to face a challenger. She watched him wipe his palms on his pants and fill his lungs with a deep breath as the elevator shuddered and creaked.

Was he nervous about visiting Lila? Or could his jitters have anything to do with his reason for staying away from Clairmont for so many years? She wanted to believe he had a good reason for his absence, that he wasn't just selfish.

Olivia found it hard to reconcile the heroic firefighter, who risked his life to save others, with someone self-centered enough to ignore his family's needs. Although Reyn arranged for Lila to visit him regularly in Georgia, he couldn't seem to be bothered to come to Clairmont. Didn't he know how lonely Lila got? Didn't he care that his grandmother needed him? He was the only family Lila had left, and Olivia had been raised to believe family always came first. Family mattered most. No matter what.

Yet he was here now, despite his nerves, whatever their cause. That said a lot.

He glanced toward her. "Did you tell Gram I was coming?"

She shook her head. "I didn't want her to be disappointed in case something happened and you couldn't make it."

His eyes darkened like the sky before a storm, and a muscle in his jaw jumped. "Like me backing out and not showing?"

She raised her chin defensively. "I didn't say that."

"But you thought it."

When the elevator doors slid open with a ding, she stepped in front of him, blocking his path. "What I thought was that you might not be able to get away from the fire station, might not be able to find someone to work your shift on such short notice."

His steely eyes drilled into her. "My grandmother will always come before work."

She matched his hard look with one of her own. "Then why is this your first trip back to Clairmont in twenty years? Do you have any idea how much your grandmother misses you?"

Dark emotions flashed in his eyes. "My reasons are my business."

He stepped around her and headed down the corridor toward Lila's room. His defensiveness intrigued her. What nerve had she touched to set him off?

Clairmont has never been my home...even when I lived here. Maybe by the time he left town, she could root out some answers. For herself. For Lila.

She watched him stalk down the hall and wondered how he'd react when she told him about the papers she'd found in her father's files. Apprehension tightened its grip on her stomach. She couldn't help but wonder if Lila's distress over the mysterious documents hadn't contributed to her fall. Olivia had been distracted the past few days herself, wondering what the strange notes her father had made about Claire Erikson could mean for Reyn and Lila.

As she usually did when she thought of her father, she ran her fingers over the ladybug pendant dangling from a gold chain around her neck. It might not be fine jewelry, but to her, the necklace was priceless. The ladybug—her father's pet name for her—had been his last gift to her before he died.

Merry Christmas, ladybug.

Then fifteen years later, during Olivia's sophomore year in college, an aggressive tumor had claimed her mother. Her stepfather, Hank, had been left to raise Katy, barely one year old, by himself. Olivia had put college on hold and become Katy's mother as well as her sister.

God, she missed her parents. As much as she cared for Hank, her parents' deaths had stolen a piece of her soul.

She shook herself from her memories and had to jog to keep up with Reyn's long-legged strides. When she knocked on Lila's door, they received a weak, "Yes? Come in."

Lila's face registered shock, then sheer delight when she spotted her grandson. "Oh, Reyn, you sweet boy. What are you doing here?"

"Question is what are *you* doing here?" Reyn crossed to Lila's bedside and leaned down to gently hug her. "I thought I asked you to give up bungee jumping. Now look at you."

Olivia moved to the opposite side of the bed, noticing the tears welling in Lila's eyes, despite her chuckle at his joke.

"I wish I could claim it was something as exciting as bungee jumping. No, it was a wrinkle in my throw rug that tripped me. Dratted thing." Lila clung to her grandson's broad shoulders and patted his back.

When Reyn pulled out of the hug and gazed down at his grandmother, the warmth and affection in his eyes stole Olivia's breath. He took Lila's hand and clasped it between his. The man that stood before her, greeting his grandmother, bore little resemblance to the stony, withdrawn man she'd ridden with in the car. More proof that Reyn Erikson was a complex and multi-faceted man. A man she wanted to learn more about.

"Olivia, dear, did you go and call my Reyn? You shouldn't have done that. I'm fine." She shook a finger at Olivia then turned back to her grandson with a satisfied sigh. "But I'm glad you did."

"Tell you what, Gram. We'll get rid of your rugs. I'll put in wall-to-wall carpeting for you before you leave the hospital, if you want."

She noticed that Lila had yet to release Reyn's hand. Or

vice versa. So the tough guy had a soft spot for his granny? Interesting. And encouraging. But puzzling too. Something didn't add up.

"Oh, darling, you don't need to do that. It's just that I'm getting old. I'd trip over something else if not the rug." Lila shook her head and patted Reyn's hand.

"Old?" Reyn scoffed. "You don't look a day older than thirty. In fact, the guys at the fire station all want to know when you're coming back for another visit. You have several admirers in Georgia."

He winked, and Lila hooted with laughter.

"I can still turn you over my knee for lying, young man." She lightly touched the covers near her injured hip. "Well, maybe I can't at the moment, but I'll have Olivia tan your backside for me."

Reyn's gaze darted to Olivia's, and his slate-gray eyes grew warm. "Promise?"

A lusty rasp deepened his voice, and prickly heat skittered over her skin as she held his gaze. She couldn't help but conjure up the image of Reyn from the firemen's calendar, the image that had starred in her sexual fantasies since she'd first seen it. In the photo, Reyn wore nothing but his bunker pants and suspenders. He stood beside a gushing fire hydrant while he poured water from his cupped hands onto his upturned face, down his hard chest, inside the loose bunker pants.

Olivia's mouth went dry thinking about the picture, and she had to swallow hard before she could speak. "Hey, if Lila thinks you need a spanking, I'm perfectly willing to dole it out."

In response, Reyn lifted one light brown eyebrow, just as he had at the church when she caught him staring. The gesture held a hint of mystery...and a lot of potential.

Her pulse raced at the prospect, while a nagging voice in

her conscience reminded her what had happened the last time she'd fallen for a pretty face. In Billy's case, beauty was indeed only skin deep.

To distract herself from the sensual track of her thoughts, Olivia reached in her purse and pulled out the hairbrush she'd brought from Lila's house. She held it up for the woman to see. "Shall I?"

Lila patted her head. "Please, dear. I'm afraid I look a fright. Do you have a lipstick in there for me?"

"Absolutely. Plum Passion."

"Wonderful," Lila said with a sigh.

Reyn gave Olivia an inscrutable look before turning to his grandmother. "If you don't want carpeting, is there something else around the house I can take care of while I'm here?"

Olivia pulled the brush through Lila's fine white hair, coiling the thin wisps around her fingers and patting the curls in place. The older woman closed her eyes as she worked. Olivia waited for Lila to mention her father's mysterious papers. Reyn had just given her the perfect opening, yet Lila said nothing.

"What about your medical care after you leave the hospital?" Reyn pressed. "I need to line up a physical therapist and perhaps a home health nurse to help you at first."

"Don't bother with the nurse. Olivia can help me."

Reyn glanced up at Olivia and scowled.

"Unless I'm mistaken, Olivia's not a nurse. I'm glad she's been able to help you in the past, but now you'll need—"

"I want Olivia. The nurse can show her what to do." Lila peered up at her as if seeking confirmation and agreement.

"I'll be glad to do what I can. You know I will, but I think Reyn is talking about—"

"Good. It's settled." Lila closed her eyes again and waved

her hand to say Olivia should continue brushing her hair.

Reyn met Olivia's gaze and shook his head, indicating nothing was settled. He silently watched Olivia brushing Lila's hair with a peculiar knit in his brow. One by one, he bent his fingers down with his opposite hand until each knuckle popped. The nervous habit intrigued her. Clearly he loved his grandmother. So why did visiting her make him so anxious?

"There is something you can do for me while you're home, Reyn." Lila's voice was little more than a whisper.

He stopped fidgeting and leaned forward. "What is it, Gram? You name it."

Olivia held her breath and waited, her heart tapping an expectant rhythm.

"I've recently learned some things that concern me." A sad, tired quality tinged Lila's normally cheerful voice.

A glance at Reyn's face confirmed that he heard the difference too. His thick eyebrows drew together, and his lips pressed in a thin, grim line. "What...kind of things?"

"Things about your mother's death. About the fire. I won't have any peace until I have answers—" The old woman's voice cracked, and Olivia's heart twisted.

She hated stirring up this worry for Lila, but what else could she have done with the troubling information she'd found?

Lila's eyes fluttered open and held a blaze of purpose. Her gaze found her grandson's and held. Olivia saw the color drain from Reyn's face.

"Olivia was cleaning her attic the other day and found some old files in a box of her father's things. He was the sheriff once, you know."

Reyn's gaze lifted to Olivia's, suspicion narrowing his eyes.

31

"She showed me the files, because they mentioned the fire that killed your mother, my Claire. It seems he wasn't satisfied with the coroner's findings. He still had questions about Claire's death. Things that were never mentioned to me."

Reyn squeezed Lila's hand. "What did the papers say?"

"Nothing concrete," Olivia volunteered when Lila faltered. "Just lots of speculation and a handwritten note mentioning questions he had about the coroner's report."

Lila found her voice again. "I want you to find out everything you can about the fire that killed your mother, Reyn." Lila raised a gnarled finger and aimed it at him to punctuate her point. "Ray Crenshaw had decided the facts didn't add up, and I want to know why. I'm betting you'll find that your mother's death was no accident."

Chapter Two

"I want to help," Olivia said, breaking the tense silence that had filled the car since they left the hospital.

"Help with what?" Reyn spoke in a quiet voice and narrowed eyes the color of rain on her, eyes with a sensual intensity that pierced straight to her feminine core.

She grunted her disbelief that he didn't understand what should have been obvious. "I want to help find out what happened to your mother. Lila is my friend...no, more than a friend. She's like family to me. If finding out more about the fire will give her some peace of mind, I'm in."

Reyn turned toward the passenger's window, his brow puckered in a frown. "I don't need any help. And until I see those papers you found for myself, I'm not promising that I'll do anything either."

"But you promised Lila you'd do your best to find out what really happened."

"To appease her," he said then fell silent. The brooding loner was back. If she hadn't seen his warmth when they first met, his kindness to Katy and his teasing with his grandmother, Olivia would not have believed this was the same man. But which was the real Reyn? The discrepancy bothered her, left her off balance.

"Then you didn't mean it?" she asked warily.

He sighed. "I didn't have the heart to tell her no."

She squeezed the steering wheel tighter in frustration. "Why would you tell her no? Her daughter is dead, and she deserves to know why. Especially if foul play was involved like my dad suspected."

He glanced at her again, and his eyes flashed with determination. And some other emotion she couldn't pinpoint. "Leave it alone."

Olivia's heart sank. Surely he wouldn't shirk his promise to Lila, would he? The man who'd stayed away from Clairmont for twenty years might, but the man who'd held such love in his eyes when he greeted Lila wouldn't. That warm and caring man was the one she had to convince. But how did she reach him when he kept himself so distant? For Lila's sake, she had to find a way.

He drew a deep breath, and she watched him flex and curl his fingers into fists. His body vibrated with palpable tension equal to her own frustration and confusion. She wanted to ease whatever anxiety had him strung so tight. But not only did she sense a pat on the back or comforting stroke from her would be unwelcome, she knew her reasons for wanting to touch him weren't purely altruistic. His chiseled features begged to be touched, to be explored by curious fingers. But to do so would be asking for trouble. She reached for her ladybug pendant instead, rubbing the smooth metal and taking a bit of solace from it.

When they arrived at the church, she pulled her car alongside a silver Sierra Z71. Considering it was the lone truck in the gravel lot and bore a bumper sticker reading "My other truck is a Tiller Rig", she knew it had to be Reyn's.

While he unbuckled his seatbelt, she gave her argument another shot, working to keep her tone calm. "Don't you think she has a right to know the truth?"

He shook his head. "Not if the truth will hurt her. She's been hurt enough, and I don't want her to suffer anymore. So leave it alone, all right?"

When he faced her, a haunted expression darkened his eyes and stirred a response inside her that sliced to the bone. She longed for some way to help him fight the ghosts he was battling. He clenched his teeth so tight, a muscle in his cheek jumped. Again, the urge to touch his cheek, to soothe his tension spun through her with a stunning force. She lifted her hand to trace the hard line of his jaw, but he pulled away. Without another word, he opened the door and climbed out.

Leaving her engine idling, Olivia hopped out and scurried around her Chevette to catch him before he could drive away.

"Wait. What do you mean, 'The truth will hurt her'?" She grabbed his arm, absently noting that the muscles under her fingers were hard and tight, his body in peak condition for the demands of his job as a firefighter. "You can't drop a bomb like that and walk away."

Sighing, he faced her. "Olivia, this doesn't have anything to do with you. As much as I appreciate everything you've done for Gram, you need to butt out of this."

He turned to unlock the door of his truck, and she squeezed the muscles of his arm tighter to stop him again.

"Tell me why. Why would it hurt her?"

"Goodbye, Olivia. Thanks for the ride, but next time we'll take my truck." He climbed onto the front seat and cranked his engine. The truck rumbled to life, and when he tried to close the door, she stepped in the way.

"I'm going to do this. Lila is the closest thing to a mother I've had in years, and I won't let her down. My father had questions. Lila needs answers, and I intend to find them. With

35

or without your help."

Reyn gave her a sharp glance, cursed bitterly and jumped from the front seat with an angry thrust. When he faced her, she backed against his truck, making room for his wide shoulders. She looked up to find frustration blazing in his eyes.

"What is it with you?" He ran his hands over his short-cropped hair, leaving it enticingly mussed, then exhaled a harsh breath. "Why do you want to stir up trouble? Hasn't my mother's death caused enough pain in my family without rehashing the details? She's gone, and nothing we could learn now will bring her back."

Olivia jutted out her chin and met his fierce gaze with her own. "I'm not trying to cause trouble. I'm trying to give Lila some peace. Doesn't it bother you that there could be more to the fire that killed your mom than the authorities are telling?"

He growled and braced his arm on the side of the truck near her head. Rather than quashing her desire to find out more about the long-ago fire, his defensiveness fanned the spark of her curiosity. Was he protecting secrets? Or running from them?

With his gaze drilling into hers, he stepped closer, trapping her against the sun-baked side of his truck. She became keenly aware of every inch of his muscled body aligned so intimately with hers.

"Let me take care of what to tell my grandmother. You stick to bringing her lipstick and fluffing her pillow, okay?"

Sticky heat wavered through the thick July air. Yet with his body pressed close to hers, a shiver raced through her. His scent, a combination of soap, sun and sensual man, surrounded her, teasing her imagination. The picture of him from the calendar, water droplets clinging to his bare chest and slicking his hair, flashed in her mind and sent rivers of desire coursing through her.

She cupped her palm on his cheek, and this time he didn't withdraw. Slowly she dragged her hand along the stubble-roughened line of his jaw, smoothed her thumb across his lips. The intensity in his eyes softened, the muscles in his face relaxed a degree, and she felt him shudder. She rewarded his eased manner with a half smile, noticing that his gaze zeroed in on her lips again when she did. Just by lifting her head an inch or two, she could kiss him, could discover how those unsmiling lips tasted. Tempting, yes. But a fling with a man who was so closed and mysterious wasn't what she needed in her life.

He caught her hand with his larger one, swallowing her fingers in his warm grasp. The calluses on his palm gently chafed her skin and caused a flurry of sensation to dance along her nerve endings.

"What happened back then, Reyn? What are you protecting your grandmother from?" she whispered.

His grip on her hand tightened, and he pushed it away from his face. The sadness had returned to his eyes. "Some things are just best left alone."

She shook her head. "Not good enough. What are you hiding?"

He stiffened. Wariness flickered in his eyes. "Please, don't interfere, Olivia. I'm warning you."

"And if I don't heed your warning?" She raised her eyebrows and cocked her head, challenging him. "What will you do?"

He clenched his teeth and glared at her. "Are you always this aggravating?"

She smiled unrepentantly. "Yes."

He stepped back, grunted and kicked the gravel with the

toe of his dress shoe. When he looked up at her again, he gave her an exasperated sigh. "Get in the truck. If you insist on discussing this, can we at least go somewhere it's not hot as hell and quite so public?"

The idea of being alone with him, for whatever reason, appealed to her, kicked up her pulse. "Promise you'll tell me what this is all about?"

"All I'm promising is to look at your dad's files. Now get in the truck. Please."

"Let me get my keys." She moved around him, cut her engine and hurried back to the driver's side of his Sierra. He put a hand on either side of her ribs to help her climb onto the front seat, and the heat of his fingers burned through the thin fabric of her dress.

She smiled her thanks to him, but his answering nod did little to relieve his closed, guarded expression. Disappointment plucked at her. She wished he'd lower the wall he had put between them, that he'd share whatever was troubling him and holding him back.

With a sigh, she reminded herself that the intimacy and closeness that inspired such confidence were hard earned, built over time and proven in trial by fire. She doubted that in the brief time Reyn would be in town to care for Lila, they'd have the chance to reach that level of openness and trust. And her ill-fated relationship with Billy Russell had proven that you never really knew a person until you reached that soul-deep level of communication and sharing.

Blinded by Billy's handsome face, she hadn't seen his lack of character until too late. He'd cheated on her, trashed her reputation with lewd lies, and cast the blame on her when things soured between them. She'd wasted months of her life on a guy whose moral fiber wasn't worth the time of day. But never again.

Yet despite her caution, a gut-level instinct told her she could help Reyn. If she could earn his confidence, maybe she could help him resolve that elusive *something* that had kept him away from Clairmont so long. Having Reyn back would mean so much to Lila.

She just had to be careful. With Reyn, she had to lead with her head instead of her heart.

Reyn slowed his truck and parked in front of the old farmhouse he'd thought he'd never see again. Gram's house was much as he remembered except for the obvious wear of time and weather. The wood siding of the Depression-era home needed a new coat of white paint. One of the dark green shutters hung at an angle, and the steps to the front porch sagged.

Reyn made a mental note to shore up the steps along with the other cosmetic fix-ups the house needed before he left town. He cut the engine and stared at the old home for a minute.

"Bring back memories?" Olivia asked softly.

"Yeah." He studied the two-story farmhouse and its carefully tended flower beds, but he felt Olivia's gaze.

His senses had been in overdrive the whole morning around her. Somehow having her in his truck, his domain, made him all the more aware. Every movement she made on the drive to Gram's house stoked his hyper-alert nerve endings, every shift in her seat called his attention back to her sleek legs.

"Good memories?"

He turned to her now, keeping his expression impassive. "Some are good."

"Concentrate on those."

Before he could respond, she opened the passenger's door and slid out of the truck. He followed her to the front porch, and she dug in her purse. When she used a key on her ring to open Gram's door, he gave her a querying look.

"I've had it for a couple years. Seemed like a good idea, and her fall the other day proves I was right." She stepped inside and flipped on the front hall light as if she lived there, then tossed her purse on the old-fashioned washstand by the stairs. "I come by every day to check on her, to see if she needs anything, to talk to her, to fix her hair, to bring her prescriptions from the pharmacy, that sort of thing."

The house smelled musty with a hint of mothballs and recent baking. The same framed, cross-stitched prayer still graced the wall by the light switch as when he had been ten. The same scatter rug lay at the foot of the stairs. The same school-age pictures of himself and his mother hung in stair-steps along the wall to the second floor. While he stood in the foyer and turned slowly, taking in the familiar details, Olivia walked over to the thermostat and clicked on the air conditioning, then disappeared into the kitchen.

"Want a cookie?" she called from the back room, drawing him out of his perusal of the foyer.

The polished hardwood floor creaked as he made his way back to the room that had always been the heart of Gram's home. He'd done his homework on the large pine table, shared meals here with Gram and his mother most evenings, and spent hours watching Gram bake or wash dishes while they chattered about whatever was on his mind.

Olivia held out the porcelain cookie jar to him with one hand while she crunched down on a fat cookie with the other. "I promise I didn't make them. Lila's specialty...chocolate chip."

He reached in the jar and took a couple cookies. "Her

specialty used to be peanut butter."

"Mmm...maybe for you," she said around a mouthful. "I gotta have chocolate or it's not worth the calories."

Reyn pulled out one of the ladder-backed chairs at the table and swept his gaze around the kitchen. The appliances were new, the ones he'd paid to have installed a few Christmases ago. He'd known the thirty-year-old appliances Gram had been using were a fire hazard, and he'd ordered the switch long distance.

"So here's what we have so far. I plan to search my attic and see if there's more, but I haven't had the chance yet between work and school and Lila's surgery." Olivia scooped a few files from the counter and laid them in front of him. Pulling out the chair next to him with a scrape, she dropped onto it.

The sweet fragrance of her perfume wafted to him, and a fist of lust tightened his gut. The simple floral scent was far sexier than the heavy designer perfumes most women he knew wore.

He tried to refocus his thoughts on the files she'd given him rather than the smooth thighs he'd glimpsed as she'd climbed in his truck. He didn't need a distraction while he was in town. A meaningless affair with him, one destined to end badly, was not the legacy he wanted to leave any woman, and especially not his grandmother's friend.

His break-up with Liz had taught him to be wary of casual sex. His ex-girlfriend had expected more than he could offer once they'd become lovers, and he'd hurt a good woman when he ended the relationship. He pushed aside that painful memory only to take on another. The fire that killed his mom.

He cleared his throat and flicked a quick glance at Olivia. "I was there, you know. I saw the fire. I watched the house burn, watched the men fight the flames. The house was a total loss."

He bit down on a cookie, which should have been sweet, but flavored with his dark memories, it tasted like cardboard.

"How old were you?" she asked, scooting her chair closer.

"Ten."

"So young. Oh God, Reyn. What a horrible thing to witness. Were you in the house when it started?" Sympathy tinged her voice, and he cringed inwardly. He didn't deserve her sympathy.

Reyn stared at the wall across from him, seeing the smoke that poured through the windows of his childhood home again, remembering in vivid detail the taunting flames and soul-deep terror that had seized him. He struggled for a breath so he could respond. "No. I was hiding in the woods when it started."

"Hiding?"

He nodded stiffly. Guilt flooded him, drowning him, choking the air from his lungs. "I'd run into the woods to hide from my mom. I'd gotten in trouble at school that day—again—and Principal Horton had stopped by to tell her about my latest screw up. I knew I was going to get a whippin', so I stayed in the woods until nearly dark. I smelled the smoke, saw it from a distance and went back to investigate. The closer I got, the more scared I got, 'cause I knew it was our house burning."

Olivia laid a cool hand on his forearm, and he glanced down at her slim, graceful fingers, the freckles dotting her ivory skin. He stared numbly as she stroked his arm. Though he registered her soothing gesture at some level, his thoughts remained focused on the horror of the day twenty years before.

"Go on," she coaxed.

He released a deep breath in a puff. He didn't want to go on. He'd kept his guilt and shame bottled up for so long he couldn't talk about it now.

Even when he'd been ordered to spend several afternoons

in counseling with the fire department psychologist three years ago, he'd kept it inside. After convincing the shrink that his risk-taking was due to job stress, he'd received a warning about taking unnecessary chances and several days off to decompress. But at the fire in question, he'd gotten a little boy out of an almost fully involved house, and that was what mattered to him.

Now, with his heart thundering, memories crashed down on him, and he shoved back his chair. Restless, he stalked over to the window in the back door to stare outside. He shoved his hands into his pockets and tried to slow his breathing to a normal pace.

"Reyn? What is it?" Olivia came up behind him and put a hand at the small of his back. "Please tell me."

"Nothing. It was just a horrible day, and Gram doesn't need those bad memories stirred up."

"But—"

"No."

"You haven't even looked at the files yet. Don't make up your mind until you see what my dad had found out. Things you and your grandmother were apparently never told."

He whirled to face her and jabbed a finger toward her face. "Damn it, *I* don't want to know any more! I already know what the smoke smelled like, how it choked me and made me want to throw up. I felt the flames' searing heat from a hundred feet away. I lived every horrible minute of it, and I love my grandmother enough to spare her the details."

Olivia's eyes misted, and their amber depths glittered as she stared back at him. "You became a firefighter because of that day. Didn't you?"

His breath hung in his lungs. For several seconds he said nothing, only able to stare back into her insightful gaze. Finally, with a shudder, he murmured, "Yes."

Her expression softened with concern, and he turned away. "Don't go jumping to any conclusions about me or over-analyzing it. I've always been fascinated by fire, always had a notion I'd be a fireman. That day just sealed the deal."

"Why do I think there's more you're not telling me?"

He crossed the kitchen, to get distance from her knowing gaze and to buy himself time to think. And because having her close toyed with his senses. "The fire started in my bedroom. A candle I'd apparently left burning caught the curtains on fire. Case closed."

"No. There's more. My father was on to something before he died. It's in his files. Read it for yourself."

As he turned to face her again, the calendar on the opposite wall caught his attention. The firemen's calendar he'd posed for. Open to his picture. *Geez.*

"My dad had suspicions about the fire being set on purpose. He apparently had evidence that there was foul play at work," he heard Olivia say as he walked over to the calendar. "But if you have something to confess, perhaps you owe it to Lila."

He glared at the image of himself, wishing he'd never agreed to pose for the damn picture. The proceeds might have helped a worthy cause, but the picture projected an impression he despised. He took the calendar off the wall with a huff. "I didn't set the fire if that's what you're implying."

"I wasn't implying anything."

"Plenty of other people accused me at the time. They knew my reputation with matches and assumed the worst."

Olivia's gold eyes watched him closely. Too closely. He sensed that those keen eyes saw far more than he wanted the red-haired spitfire to see. The vibrant light shining in her gaze seemed to cut through the walls he'd built, straight into his soul. The idea unnerved him.

He turned the calendar to face her. "Is this who you think I am, Olivia? Is this who Gram thinks I am?"

"What are you talking about? That is you."

"It's me in the picture, but it's not real."

Olivia crossed the kitchen, frowning. "I've lost you."

Growling his frustration, he waved the calendar at her. "This picture. What it says is a lie."

She knit her russet brows and wrinkled her freckled nose. "What do you think the picture says?"

He shifted his weight and looked down at the image. His stomach pitched. "It creates this idea that I'm some kind of hot-shot stud or hero. The big, bad fireman straight out of some Hollywood version of life. It's a fantasy image created to sell calendars." He grimaced and tossed the calendar aside with a grunt. "What a crock."

"Then why'd you do it? Why'd you pose?" she asked, picking up the picture and studying it closer.

"When the Firefighters Association asked me to do it, they made it sound like I'd be doing them this big favor. I knew the money was helping a good cause...the proceeds from the sales went to help burn victims...so I agreed."

"Sounds like a good reason to me. So what's the problem?" Her lips tugged into the sexy, lopsided smile she used so often. And like every other time he'd seen that grin today, the urge to kiss her tempting mouth kicked him in the solar plexus.

He had his work cut out for him, keeping her at bay when what he wanted was to hold her close, kiss her senseless. For her own good, he couldn't allow her any closer, couldn't let her expect things he couldn't live up to. He refused to let her get hurt, no matter how tempting the thought of tangling with her in the sheets.

He gritted his teeth. "There's no problem as long as you and Gram don't believe that this—" he poked the picture with his finger, nearly knocking it from her hands, "—is who I really am, what I stand for. When people see this, they form expectations about me that I can't live up to. I'm not perfect or fearless or some fantasy. And I'm for damn sure no hero."

Olivia's smile disappeared, replaced with a scowl. She crossed her arms over her chest and glared back at him. "You're a hero to the people you rescue, to the people whose homes or pets you save."

"I'm just doing my job." He knew he was yelling but didn't care. His body shook with frustration and the injustice of what the calendar portrayed. "I'm doing what I'm paid to do, what I'm duty-bound to do. That doesn't make me a hero."

"It does to me," she said, her voice soft but firm.

"Then you're in for a disappointment." With effort, he matched her calm tone then stalked away. He stopped at the back door again and braced his arms on the frame. His muscles trembled, and his gut swirled with pent-up emotion, the acid bite of once-buried demons rising to haunt him again. "Ask around town if you don't believe me. They'll tell you what a screw-up I was as a kid. Maybe I didn't set the fire, but I caused it. My carelessness caused it."

"Maybe. Maybe not. What if the info my father had proves someone else is involved? If someone else set the fire, don't you want to know who and why?"

"And what if it doesn't? What if his findings prove I was responsible? How do you think that will make Gram feel?"

Olivia stepped up beside him and laid a gentle hand on his

shoulder. "Is that what's kept you away from Clairmont all these years? Guilt?"

A shudder raced through him. How had they gotten this close to the truth? Why had he let his guard slip around her?

He stalked away from her and glared at the files on the table. "I can't explain why your father had questions about what happened," he said, purposely avoiding her question. "It all seems pretty cut and dried to me."

With a deep sigh and a nod, she glanced away. "Okay. You may be right."

The tension stretching his nerves eased a bit, and he drew a breath in relief.

Too soon.

"But we'll never know for sure if we don't look into it." She clicked a fingernail against her teeth, her expression contemplative. "I think I know where we can start."

He scowled at her. "*We* aren't."

"Oh, don't be a mule." She sauntered across the kitchen to him and patted his chest. "If you'd be honest with yourself, you'd admit that you want answers as badly as Lila does. You need closure. You might even be exonerated."

"What are you planning to do?" he asked, his tone rife with suspicion.

She flashed him her flirtatious smile again and drew circles around his shirt buttons with her fingernail. The light scrape of her finger on his chest sent a crackling awareness over his skin. Like heat lightning, dancing from one cloud to another on a summer evening, his every nerve ending came alive as desire streaked through him.

"Leave the details to me. Just read through my dad's file tonight and meet me at Burdeaux's Diner for breakfast tomorrow morning at seven."

"I'm not up at seven," he countered, even though he knew he'd meet her at four a.m. in the bayou if she asked him.

"Suit yourself," she returned and flounced by him. "I'll do this alone then."

"Like hell you will."

As she left the kitchen, she gave him a satisfied smile that said she knew she'd gotten her way. He followed her to the front door, where she paused to sling her purse strap over her shoulder. Rising on her toes, she startled him with a peck on the cheek. "It's been a pleasure meeting you, Reyn. I'll see you tomorrow at seven."

"Don't you want a ride back to your car?"

"Naw, I just live through the woods about a half mile. I'll walk home." Olivia bounced down the front steps and strolled out into the midday sun. The bright beams set her hair ablaze, and heat flared in Reyn's blood.

She turned and shielded her eyes to look up at him on the porch. "I'll ride with Hank to the diner and get my car after breakfast. The church is about a block from Burdeaux's."

Hank? Something sharp-edged twisted inside him, something he refused to call jealousy. Hank could easily be a brother, an elderly neighbor, even the school bus driver. And he wouldn't voice his questions and let her know he'd cared enough to wonder.

"Bye," she called cheerfully as she jogged off toward the woods at the side of Gram's property.

A rare summer breeze stirred the humid air, carrying her light floral scent up to him like a parting gift. He sucked in a deep whiff, filling his lungs with the intoxicating aroma and savoring it. By doing so, he held onto her essence, her vibrancy for another moment after she disappeared into the line of trees.

She'd been a pleasant surprise for him today. Perhaps his time in town, while arranging for Gram's care, wouldn't be as bad as he'd imagined. At least, it wouldn't be if he could dissuade Gram and Olivia from pursuing their mission to dig up the past. His memories of his mother and the fire were hard enough to deal with without parading them out for public scrutiny. Gram's request for answers was a tailor-made nightmare.

When nothing was left outside but the glaring sun and stifling heat, he walked back inside Gram's house. The dimly lit rooms seemed lonely without Olivia there. And quiet. Too quiet.

Sitting at the table, he opened one of the files and scanned the first page. The handwritten note on top read, "Coroner's report on Claire Erikson lists smoke inhalation as cause of death. No explanation of other findings. Look into inconsistencies."

Reyn slapped the folder closed again and fought a wave of nausea. He couldn't do it. Damn it, he couldn't stand to relive the nightmare he worked so hard to put behind him.

A voice from his past, the gloating cackle of his personal demon called from the dark corner of his soul where he'd locked it away years ago. *Coward. You let your mother die. You can't run from the truth.*

He snapped on the radio on Gram's kitchen counter to drown out the taunting voice in his head. His thoughts returned to Olivia's mysterious plan to learn more about the twenty-year-old fire, and his stomach bunched. He dreaded learning what her scheming mind had concocted to unearth information about the fire. Yet he couldn't deny that part of him couldn't wait to see her again.

She'd been eager to see Reyn again. Olivia admitted as much to herself when she arrived at Burdeaux's twenty minutes earlier than they'd arranged. And when she found him already there, waiting for her, she experienced a rush of pleasure that tingled from her head to her toes. Who needed caffeine with Reyn around to get your blood racing?

Easy, girl. Don't forget what happened last time you let a handsome face dazzle you.

Right. Trusting Billy Russell, giving him her love before he'd shown her who he really was deep inside had been a colossal mistake. She wouldn't be so gullible this time.

She was eager to get beyond the calendar-created fantasy that Reyn was. But even if she did learn what made him tick, Reyn wasn't sticking around. He had a life back in Atlanta, and he'd demonstrated over the years that his job and his life in Georgia took precedence over his family. How could she even consider involvement with a man who didn't put his family first?

With a deep breath, she headed toward the back booth where he sat drinking coffee. Reyn's gaze found hers but quickly shifted to the man who entered the restaurant behind her. Reyn's eyebrows lowered, and he frowned.

She glanced over her shoulder at her stepfather, Hank Harrison, and wondered why the man seemed to upset Reyn.

As she crossed the diner, she returned the half dozen greetings called to her. Behind the counter, Mabel Smith held up a pot of coffee, and Olivia nodded. "And don't try to slip me any of that decaffeinated junk either."

Reyn stood as she reached the booth and gave her a terse nod in greeting. "So, you're a caffeine junkie? And here I thought you were naturally chipper and energetic."

"And I thought you wouldn't be up at seven."

She slid into the booth and gave him a saucy smirk.

"Actually, I was up at five-thirty. My body still thinks I'm on Eastern time." He took another swig of coffee then pinched the bridge of his nose.

His face looked freshly shaved, his hair was still a tad damp, and the black T-shirt he wore made his eyes look more blue than gray. The clean scent of soap clung to him and mingled with the aroma of fresh coffee and sizzling sausage filling the restaurant. His gaze roamed over her in a lazy appraisal, and she shifted in her seat self-consciously. She'd taken a little more time with her makeup that morning and chosen her sleeveless, denim blouse and hip-hugging shorts with him in mind.

"So why did you drag me out at this hour of the morning? What kind of scheme are you hatching?" he asked.

Olivia flattened her hands on the sticky Formica tabletop and leaned toward Reyn. "Well, I figured if we want answers about a fire that happened twenty years ago, the best place to start is with the people who would have been there, the men who'd have been at the scene."

She hitched her head toward the table across the diner where her stepfather had joined two other men for breakfast. "Those men, and a couple others who aren't here yet, are all members of the Clairmont Volunteer Fire Department. Most of them have been volunteer firemen since before I was born. They would have been the men who came to your house when it burned."

Reyn furrowed his brow, shot a glance to Hank's table, and then shifted a hard gaze back at her. "Bad idea. I don't want anyone else knowing what we're doing."

"Why?"

He huffed impatiently. "For starters, it'd raise questions,

start people talking. And if someone else is involved, do you really want them tipped off that we're looking into the fire again? There are other ways of getting information. Microfilm of old newspapers at the library. Official records at the parish courthouse and coroner's office." He paused when Mabel brought her coffee and left the pot on the table. "Do me a favor. If we have to do this at all, let's keep it quiet, okay?"

"But eyewitnesses, the people who were actually there, would have a unique perspective. They can give us details you just can't get from some old document." She glanced at the table of firemen then back at Reyn. "The guy I came in with is my stepfather, Hank. Sitting next to Hank, the one with the glasses, that's Lou Farris. He's the pharmacist at the store where I work. He's got a mind like a steel trap. He can tell you everything about anything that's happened in this town in the last thirty years, and what the weather was like the day it happened. I know he'll be able to give us something to go on. Now come on, or I'll go alone."

She stood and took Reyn's hand, urging him to follow.

He grumbled something under his breath about her blowing his low profile, and she headed for the table of volunteer firemen.

"Morning, Olivia. What brings you out so early on a Monday morning?" Lou sent her a friendly smile and adjusted his glasses as he glanced at Reyn. "Who's your friend?"

She introduced Reyn to Lou, Hank and the third man at the table, Charlie Smith, the town barber. Charlie stood and shook Reyn's hand then offered Olivia his seat.

"No, I'm fine, thanks. We just have a few questions to ask about a fire that happened about twenty years ago. It was Reyn's house, and his mother died in the fire and—"

"Olivia, what's going on? What're you up to?" Hank

interrupted.

"Just trying to get some information straight about the Erikson's house fire. I knew you men were a good place to start."

"That fire was a long time ago, Liv." Hank cast a wary glance to her hand still in Reyn's.

Her hand still in Reyn's. He hadn't pulled away. A sweet sensation flowed through her veins, and she savored the feel of his warm fingers wrapped around hers.

"You might not get far," Hank said. "People tend to forget things—"

"I remember that fire," Lou said, stabbing a bite of ham and shaking his head. "Terrible fire. Destroyed the place completely. By the time we arrived, the house was fully involved, and we had no choice but to fight it defensively."

Good ol' Lou. She knew he would remember.

"You fought it defensively...meaning from outside the house. Right?" she asked for confirmation. She'd heard Hank use the term but wanted to make sure she had her facts straight.

"Exactly," Lou said and nodded.

"I knew that much already and told you so yesterday," Reyn murmured close to her ear, his breath a warm tickle against her skin. She shushed him, and he frowned.

"What else were you looking for?" Lou asked.

"Anything you can tell me. We—"

"What the hell is he doing here?"

Olivia and Reyn turned in unison in response to the hostile male voice. Reyn muttered a scorching curse, jerked his hand away and ran his palm across his cheek. Olivia's stomach reeled when she met the two grim stares behind her.

The last two members of the Monday Morning Breakfast Group had arrived. George Russell and Vance Horton.

Chapter Three

Every muscle in Reyn's body tensed at the sight of his old nemeses. He'd always believed Principal Horton had it in for him. He'd swear the man had watched him like a hawk, just waiting for him to slip up so he could slam another punishment down Reyn's throat. The circumstances didn't matter. If Reyn was involved in an infraction at school, no matter who else was involved, Reyn bore the burden of blame.

And George Russell had made it clear yesterday he still bore a grudge for the loss of his barn. Not that Reyn could blame him. His carelessness had hurt the farmer's livelihood.

As the men crossed the diner toward them, Horton's flinty eyes narrowed on him with the same suspicion they'd held when Reyn was ten. "Reyn Erikson. I knew this town hadn't seen the last of you."

Reyn met the man's gaze evenly, and he offered his hand. "How are you, Mr. Horton? It's been a long time."

"Not long enough." The man sat, ignoring Reyn's proffered hand.

Tamping down the flash of fury at the man's cold dismissal, Reyn squared his shoulders and tried to ignore the look of gall on Olivia's face. Better she saw now the Reyn Erikson other people saw, the reputation he had earned.

George Russell crossed his arms over his thick chest and

propped a hip on the back of the booth bench. "Did I hear you mention something you were looking for?"

Olivia raised her chin. "Yes. Information."

"What kinda information?" Russell's thick country drawl grated on Reyn's raw nerves.

"About a fire you would have responded to several years ago." Olivia divided her gaze between the two new arrivals.

Reyn watched Russell and Horton exchange glances.

"Guess we don't have to ask which one, now do we?" Horton pinned a hard look on Reyn. "The investigation into the fire at your house has been closed for years. A simple case of carelessness. A candle left burning too close to the curtains, and—" He waved his hand, letting the rest of what happened go unspoken, as if the death of Reyn's mother and the loss of his home were too mundane to mention.

Anger and resentment twisted inside Reyn. His mother had been treated poorly by the town when she was alive, but he'd be damned if he'd let this man or anyone else dismiss her life, her death as irrelevant.

"And," he said tightly, "my mother died in that fire. She was only twenty-eight."

"What's your point?" Russell asked.

Reyn bristled, balling his fists, and Olivia put a hand on his arm. When he glanced at her, he saw fire burning in her gold eyes as she stared at Russell. She'd had the same intensity about her when she'd argued the need to look into his mom's death, when she'd challenged him on his reasons for staying away from Clairmont.

"The point is," Olivia said, "an innocent woman, a mother, a daughter, someone loved and cherished died. Her life was worth something, and we owe it to her and her family to find out why." She turned to Horton as she continued. "And we're not convinced we do know everything there is to know about how the fire started. My father was still investigating it when he died. I found some of his old files the other day, and he had questions about the coroner's findings, the possibility of arson. We intend to pick up where my dad left off."

"Isn't that a job for the sheriff, Olivia?" Hank asked.

"I'm looking for something concrete enough to take to the sheriff. That's why I need your help. Anything you remember that could shed new light on things." When no one said anything, she looked at the man sitting by her stepfather. "Lou?"

The pharmacist shrugged and glanced at the other men. To Reyn, he seemed suddenly nervous. "Sorry, Olivia. I don't know what else I can tell you."

"You're wasting your time. It was an obvious case of negligence, a candle that got out of control." Horton poked a finger toward Olivia. "End of discussion."

Reyn knocked the man's hand away from Olivia and placed himself between her and the principal. "If that's all there is to it, then you shouldn't mind if we took a look at the coroner's report or the fire marshal's write-up of the fire."

He hadn't wanted to dig up the past, but the resistance from these men warned him something wasn't right. Combined with the suspicions Olivia's father had outlined in his notes, Reyn began to believe there *could* be a basis for re-opening the case.

Charlie Smith put a hand on Horton's shoulder. "Take it easy, Vance. If the kids want to waste their time reading some dusty old reports, let 'em." He turned to Olivia. "But like we've said, I can't see where you'll learn anything we haven't told you already."

"And coroner reports are hardly proper reading material for a respectable lady." Russell's tone oozed sarcasm. "But then my boy Billy tells me you ain't respectable."

Pain flashed in Olivia's eyes, and Reyn remembered her reaction to a similar comment from Russell yesterday. He itched to wipe the smug, condescending look from the man's face. But pummeling a man old enough to be his father was exactly the kind of trouble the town expected from him, the kind of ruckus that would haunt Gram even after he left town. For Gram's sake, he swallowed the knot of fury and shook the tension from his hands.

"You two head on outta here now." Hank rose to his feet and gave his stepdaughter a warning look. "No need to stir up problems."

"It's the boy, Hank." Horton shifted his gaze to Reyn and shook his head. "Trouble is his middle name. Always was."

"Frankly, that fire was the best thing to happen in this town for years," Smith said with righteous condemnation in his tone. "We got rid of the town slut, and then her trouble-making son got shipped off to another state."

Reyn had heard enough. He launched himself at the barber, planting his hands in the man's chest with a shove. "Shut your mouth. Don't talk about my mother like that, you sonofa—"

Hank grabbed Reyn's arm and pulled him back. "Easy, son."

Smith's expression was smug. "I rest my case. Fact is, I always wondered if our resident arsonist didn't have something to do with startin' that fire. You want some answers, boy, maybe you should start by lookin' in the mirror."

Reyn seethed, his body tightly strung and ready to snap. He'd expected Clairmont to open old wounds, had known he had enemies here, had expected the insults and innuendo. But that didn't make it any easier to hear, any less painful to endure.

"There a problem over there, gentlemen?" Mabel called from the counter. "Do I need to call Sheriff Anders?"

Hank raised a hand. "Everything's fine. Reyn and Olivia were just leaving."

Olivia's stepfather shot her a look that said she should suit his words to action. "Please, Liv."

She huffed and shook her head. "All right. We're going." She started to leave then turned back. "Will you be home in time for dinner tonight, Hank? I'm making spaghetti."

"I'll be there. Wouldn't think of missing one of your home-cooked meals." He winked at her and gave her arm a loving squeeze.

"Good, see you then." Olivia gave her stepfather a chaste hug, and then tossing her mane of red hair over her shoulder, she directed a pointed gaze on the men. "Don't think this subject is closed. My father had questions about what happened, and I, for one, intend to find answers. You men can stonewall all you want, but I will find out what I want to know."

She spun on her heel and marched back over to their table with her chin high and her shoulders back. Reyn watched her walk away, proud of the way she'd held her own with the contemptuous and uncooperative men. He experienced another irritating punch of lust as he drank in her long legs and swaying hips.

Reyn averted his gaze from Olivia's tempting backside and passed a hard look over each of the men before he too walked away. The grim faces left no doubt what he and Olivia would be up against if they pursued their investigation.

The challenge that stared back at him in the eyes of his

opponents was unmistakable. His intentions of lying low and avoiding trouble while in town shattered at his feet. He wouldn't, couldn't back down from a challenge.

If these men wanted a fight, he'd give them one.

"Looks like we have a fight on our hands," Olivia said, sliding into their booth.

"Looks like." Reyn rolled the tension from his shoulders and glanced to the back of the diner. He needed a moment to decompress before he discussed the reaction of the volunteer firemen with Olivia. He jerked his head toward the men's room as he left her at the table. "I'll be right back."

In the bathroom, he stepped over to the sink to splash cold water on his face. When he glanced into the cracked mirror in front of him, graffiti on the wall by the sink caught his eye, and he read the scribbled words.

It was about Olivia, a crude report on her ability to perform a sexual favor, illegal in some states.

Reyn gritted his teeth and stormed out of the bathroom, disgust burning in his gut. He stalked past their table and to the galley area where the waitress was refilling her coffee pot.

"Would you give the manager a message for me?" he asked tightly. "The men's bathroom could use a new coat of paint." He didn't try to hide the fury in his tone.

Their waitress shook her head. "We just painted the whole diner last summer."

Reyn stepped closer and nailed a hard look on the woman. "The men's room needs to be painted again."

She gave him a patronizing look. "Reyn, is it? I'm not sure I understand what your..."

"There's graffiti on the wall." Reyn braced his arms on the

counter.

The waitress frowned and sighed. "If we repainted every time some kid scribbled on the wall, we wouldn't have money for—"

Reyn cursed loudly and dug in his pocket. He slapped a twenty-dollar bill on the counter. "There. That should cover a gallon of paint and a brush. Now have someone paint the damn bathroom."

"Reyn?"

Olivia put one hand on his back and tugged on his arm with the other. "Come sit down. Whatever's wrong, I'm sure they'll take of it. Calm down."

He closed his eyes and drew a deep breath. "I'm sorry, ma'am. I shouldn't have lost my cool like that."

Shoving away from the counter, he shrugged off Olivia's hand and headed for the door.

As he stalked to the passenger's side of his truck, Reyn wore a hard, determined expression. Olivia scurried to catch up with him.

"What was that about?" Olivia studied the tense lines bracketing the angry slash of Reyn's mouth. The muscle in his jaw was jumping again, and his eyes were dark and stormy.

"You heard it all." He crossed his muscled arms over his chest and huffed, clearly still fighting to calm his temper.

"This...graffiti. What did it say?"

"Drop it."

"It was about me, wasn't it?"

He jerked his head around to look at her. He didn't say anything, but the look in his eyes answered her question. A rock settled in her belly, but she gave him the best smile she could. "Defending my honor could be a full-time job in this town. I'm a popular target thanks to Billy Russell and his friends. I appreciate your concern, but it's not worth getting riled up about."

He dragged a hand through his hair and blew a slow breath through pursed lips. He didn't respond at first. When he did, his gaze drifted away, focused on something in the distance.

"I spent a lot of time in the principal's office as a kid. For fighting mostly, though there was other stuff too." He flicked a quick glance to her. "Kids used to talk about my mom...repeat things they'd heard at home." A deep furrow pocked his forehead. "Truth is, I don't know who my father is. I guess...I guess it's possible she earned her reputation. But no kid wants to hear his mother called a slut...or worse."

"Of course not."

She laid a comforting hand on his arm, but he pulled away and braced his arms against the truck's hood. She searched for something else to say but could tell he didn't want placating words. So she remained silent, gave him time to deal with his memories.

"Whatever else she was—or wasn't—she was a good mom."

Olivia blinked back tears. She knew all about missing lost parents.

Finally, he opened the truck door and placed a hand under her elbow to help her up to the high seat. His warm touch and gentlemanly gesture soothed the rough edges of her frayed composure.

Billy tells me you ain't respectable. George Russell's taunt slithered through her mind, and she shivered. Heaven only knew what lies Billy had fed his father about her that had turned the man so vehemently against her. At least Billy's mother, Hannah, treated her with a measure of civility.

Reyn's fingers tightened around her arm. "You all right? You're shaking."

She turned to him with a quick smile. "Yeah. Too much caffeine, I guess."

He held her gaze, his stormy eyes searching hers, and she knew he didn't buy her lie.

If she'd done anything to earn the bad reputation she had, it would be different. She shouldn't care what the bitter man thought of her, but his scathing taunts still hurt. Billy had been worse, spreading tales about a kinky sex life they hadn't had. Sighing, she pushed thoughts of George Russell and his son's vindictiveness aside. She'd moved on, hadn't she? And she knew better than to jump in without looking next time, right? Right.

For now she would focus on what mattered. Family. Lila. The investigation.

"I have a little time before I have to go to work. I thought I'd go see Lila. Wanna go with me?"

He nodded. "That's where I was headed. I need to talk with her doctor."

"We can update Lila on the interesting roadblock we've hit in our investigation, before we've even really begun."

Reyn looked away, shoved his hands in his jeans pockets and drew a slow breath. She watched his expression carefully.

Over the years, she'd learned to be a student of people. She read their body language, interpreted the emotion in their eyes and looked at the whole picture.

Right now, Reyn's eyes were clouded with conflicting emotions, though he schooled his expression to give nothing away.

"Reyn? What are you thinking?"

He cut his gaze toward her. "There's a lot of history between me and Horton. Russell too, for that matter. But I can't think of any reason why Charlie Smith would be so bitter."

Olivia shrugged. "Some people don't need a reason to act ugly. Hank says he's always complaining about something. Don't sweat it."

"I honestly don't care what they think of me. I'm used to their abuse. But even their distrusting me, disliking me doesn't explain the reaction we got when we mentioned the fire."

She fingered the ladybug pendant at her throat. "Yeah. I smell a rat."

"I read your dad's files last night. I can't explain his suspicions, but if there is something more to the fire that killed my mother..." He paused, watching her stroke the ladybug charm before turning his gaze to the sleepy town street. "I want to know what it is."

Hope blossomed inside her. "Then you're in?"

"Yeah, I'm in," he said with a grudging tone, his expression grim. He closed her door, and as he walked around to the driver's side, satisfaction swelled in her chest, warm and fulfilling. His cooperation would make finding answers for Lila easier. And infinitely more intriguing.

She welcomed the opportunity to spend more time with Lila's sexy grandson, to get to know the man behind the erotic calendar pose. But while getting to know Reyn appealed to her, her practical side warned her not to get too attached to him.

Something had kept him away from Clairmont for twenty years, and although Lila's emergency had brought him back this time, he had those unknown ghosts to deal with.

She simply couldn't risk her heart with a man who didn't share her values and priorities. That commitment to her principles and voice of caution should have been reassuring. So why did it leave her feeling restless and uneasy?

Reyn climbed in the driver's seat and cranked the engine, his chiseled features bathed in sunlight, and she knew. Priorities or not, she *wanted* Reyn. She'd never been prone to crushes on movie stars like her friends in high school. Yet Reyn's sexy picture had stirred a deep visceral reaction in her, a desire that burned hot and left her achy with need. What's more, believing all the wonderful stories Lila told about his heroics on the job and his caring nature gave her physical longings another dimension, a personal level.

She sat on her hands, squelching the impulse to touch the places where the sunlight kissed his square jaw and sandy hair. Oh, yes, she wanted Reyn to be everything she'd imagined he was. But wanting didn't make him so. She still had to break down his walls before she could justify deeper involvement with him. Perhaps their search for the truth would even quiet the ghosts that haunted him and kept him away from Clairmont. That thought fired a spark of optimism in her. She swore to give it her best effort. For Lila's sake as well as Reyn's.

While she waged her internal debate, she studied his hands, draped casually on the steering wheel as he drove. Light brown hair dusted his wrists, and neatly trimmed nails tipped long fingers. As powerful looking as those hands were, she remembered how gently they'd held Lila's frailer grasp yesterday. She had no doubt those fingers could be equally gentle when he made love. She indulged briefly in the image of his hands stroking down her bare skin, and goose bumps rose on her arm. Swallowing a moan, she rubbed her elbows.

"Too cold?" Reyn asked, glancing at her. He flipped the switch on the dash to turn down his air conditioner.

Too hot is more like it.

"No, I'm fine. Just thinking about—" *You. Your touch.*

Liquid fire pooled in her belly.

"Yeah? About?" he prompted.

"Everything. Just wondering what we should do next."

"I have a few ideas." He didn't elaborate, and since they'd reached the hospital, she didn't ask. She filed her questions away for later and focused on cheering Lila.

Lila greeted them with her usual warmth. Like the day before, Reyn's mood lightened as well, as if the affection he shared with Lila obliterated the worries of the world. She understood that kind of bond, having shared it with her parents.

She greeted Lila with a kiss on the cheek and listened as Reyn questioned his grandmother about her level of pain, her ability to sleep and her satisfaction with the care she was receiving.

"I brought you something," Reyn said, presenting Lila with a small brown bag he'd brought up from his truck.

"How sweet of you." Lila's eyes sparkled like a child's at Christmas as she unrolled the top of the sack and peeked inside. "Lemon drops! Oh, Reyn, you remembered."

He tugged up the corner of his mouth, obviously pleased by his grandmother's response, and a dimple dented his cheek.

Olivia's heart missed a beat. A dimple. Proof positive that one could improve upon perfection.

"Lemon drops have always been my favorite indulgence."

Olivia realized Lila was talking to her and had caught her staring at Reyn.

"He used to bring them to me on special occasions like Mother's Day or my birthday, before..." Lila sighed, and the light in her eyes dimmed. "Before his mother died, and he went to live with my sister."

Reyn took his grandmother's hand in his. Olivia saw the shadow that crept into his eyes and knew before he spoke he was ready to tackle the topic of the fire.

"I'm working on getting the answers you want, Gram. But..." He hesitated, and a muscle in his square jaw twitched. "We've already met hostility from folks when we mention what we're doing. They made it clear they don't want us investigating."

Lila clutched the bag of lemon drops to her chest and frowned. "Which people?"

Olivia scooted her chair closer to the side of Lila's bed. "The firemen who responded to the call. I thought they'd be a good place to start, but even Hank discouraged us from opening the case again."

Lila sighed, and her disappointment was palpable. "Does that mean you can't get the answers we want?"

Olivia mourned the joyful mood that fled with the change of subject. She hated seeing the concern that filled Lila's eyes.

Reyn shook his head. "Not at all. I'm not quitting because a group of stodgy old men don't like what I'm doing."

"Hank's not stodgy." Olivia echoed her protest with a scowl.

Meeting her gaze, Reyn quirked an eyebrow. "Regardless, he's not happy about our investigation. My question is, why."

She shook her head. "I don't know. He tends to worry about me. Understandable since he's family. Since my mother died and he took over raising Katy, he's suffered a lot of hardship. It makes him protective. Frankly, I admire him for it."

Reyn raised a hand, conceding her point. "That doesn't explain the reaction we got from the rest of them."

She nodded. "Okay, so we forget about the firemen. For now. My dad's main interest seemed to be the coroner's report.

Let's find a copy and see what his concerns were."

"I agree. Gram, did you—" He paused and ran a hand along his jaw, clearly looking for a delicate way to broach the painful subject with his grandmother.

Olivia's heart went out to both of them. She was no stranger to pain and loss, and she sympathized with the awkwardness Reyn clearly felt discussing tough issues with his grandmother. But she knew Lila was stronger than he gave her credit for being.

"Lila, did you get a copy of the report back when it was issued?" she said gently when Reyn continued to hedge.

"I...I don't recall." Lila pressed her fingers to her lips, her brow scrunched in deep thought. "I know they told me the cause of death was smoke inhalation. That was expected. But I... Oh, I don't remember!"

The old woman's frustration speared through Olivia.

Reyn, too, seemed disturbed by Lila's upset. "It's okay, Gram." He patted her hand and shook his head. "It doesn't matter. We'll get a copy another way."

"I was in such shock over Claire's death and worried about you and...it's a blur to me now. I just..."

"Gram." Reyn leaned forward, clasping Lila's hand more tightly. His own face reflected a deep regret. "It's okay. I don't want you to worry about this."

He ducked his head and raked his fingers through his short hair, leaving it slightly ruffled. Like she imagined it might look first thing in the morning. Or right after sex.

A delicious thrill spun through her, but Olivia tucked that thought away, saving it for another time. Right now, she needed to concentrate on the matter at hand. "We can check my attic for more papers. I haven't had a chance before now to go back up and look, but I'll make the time later today."

"I'll help you. And we can always get a copy of the coroner's report from the state. Surely as her family we have the right to request a look at the report." Reyn faced his grandmother, focusing on her. "But the important thing is that you rest. Let us handle this. I don't want you worrying. Okay?"

Lila raised a frail finger and shook it. "It's a grandmother's job to worry." She gave him a small smile and stroked his cheek. "But I'll let you take care of this as long as you promise to be careful."

"Deal." He gave his grandmother a tender smile.

Olivia absorbed the warmth of his smile and stored the memory with everything else she was learning about Reyn. His affection for Lila was endearing. Still, it just didn't make sense that a man who cared deeply for his grandmother could have refused to return home to visit her for so many years. That incongruity glared like a warning light. Until she got past the layers of mystery surrounding Reyn, she had to be cautious.

Glancing at her watch, Olivia winced. "I hate to say it, but I've gotta get to work. Would you mind dropping me by the church, Reyn? My car's still there."

"Go on, darling, and take Olivia to her car. I'm feeling rather tired." Lila patted Reyn's hand, and he gave her a worried frown.

"You'll be all right?"

"Of course. I just need a nap. You'll be back later?"

He kissed her cheek. "Save me some lemon drops."

"Maybe," Lila chirped.

Olivia laughed and hugged her friend before following Reyn out to the hall. His body radiated tension, and she slipped her fingers around his fist while they waited for the elevator. "I know this is hard for you."

He gave her a startled glance. "I'm all right."

She sandwiched his hand between hers and squeezed. "If you ever want to talk—"

The elevator opened with a ding, and he jerked his hand away. "I said I'm fine."

He stepped into the elevator and jabbed the button with more force than necessary. Crossing his arms over his chest, he stared at the lit numbers marking their descent. His body language was clear. He was shutting her out.

Disappointment settled in her chest like the morning fog. It scared her how much she wanted to earn his trust, have his respect, form a friendship. None of which he seemed ready to give her. A tiny voice deep in her soul told her Reyn was worth a little patience, a little extra effort. But could she trust that voice until she'd seen for herself what kind of man Reyn was deep inside?

For now, she would settle for helping him uncover the truth about his mother's death. Perhaps by working together on the investigation, he'd grow more comfortable with her, learn to trust her, know she was there to help when he was ready to talk.

Once in his truck, she filled the silence between them by chatting about her job as Lou's assistant at the pharmacy, her classes twice a week and the upcoming Founders Day festival and fireworks. "Would you like to go with me to the festival?"

His sharp glance said she'd surprised him with her request.

She cocked her head, inviting his reply. "I figured you didn't have a date yet, since you just got into town."

He kept his gaze on the road now. "Doubt I'll go. That sort of thing's not my style."

"What is your style? A movie? A home-cooked meal?" She dropped her voice an octave. "Moonlight walks? Breakfast in bed?"

That got his attention. He gave her a long, penetrating stare, arched one light brown eyebrow, and then turned back toward the windshield. "Strip clubs. Hard liquor. Kinky one night stands. They're more my style."

She narrowed a suspicious glare on him, twisting her lips as she watched his face. Sure enough, when he flicked a sideways glance at her, the corner of his mouth twitched.

She slugged him in the arm and laughed. "You're full of it, Erikson."

"Think so?" His expression held a challenge.

"I'm sure of it." She flashed him a smug expression as he parked next to her jalopy in the church lot. Unbuckling her seatbelt, she turned on the seat to face him. "I have an hour at lunch. If you want to pick me up, we can—"

She stopped abruptly when she noticed the addition to her car. A large rock sat on her windshield, pinning a piece of paper. "What the...? Damn! They broke the glass."

Yanking open the passenger's door, she hurried around the front bumper of Reyn's truck. She snatched the rock away to examine the new cracks in her windshield with disgust and anger roiling in her stomach.

Reyn climbed out and moved up behind her. He reached around her and plucked the paper from her hand.

Raking the hair back from her face with her fingers, Olivia groaned. She couldn't afford to fix the cracked windshield now. Not with fall tuition due at the end of the month and a set of new tires to finish paying off.

With a sigh, she turned toward Reyn, watched his face

darken as he studied the paper in his hand. He swore under his breath and raised an iron stare to her.

"What is it?" she asked.

His eyes were the color of a storm cloud, and she braced for the lightning strike.

"It's a death threat."

Chapter Four

Reyn studied the hand-written letters while fingers of dread crawled up his spine. He gave Olivia a grim stare, and she trembled, the color draining from her face.

"Tell me you're kidding," she whispered.

"Wish I were."

She snatched the paper back from him and read aloud the short message written in red, "Curiosity killed the cat."

With a grunt, she balled the note up and tossed it at his chest. "Give me a break. It's just a prank, an idle threat at worst."

Reyn bent and picked up the wad, careful not to touch it more than he had to. "You shouldn't have done that. They might be able to get prints off it."

"Prints?"

He set the wad on the front seat of his truck. "Yeah, fingerprints. Whoever left this might also have left his fingerprints."

She scoffed. "You're not taking that ridiculous cliché seriously, are you? Someone's just trying to scare us. I'm more ticked that they broke my window."

He pinned her with a hard look. "It might be an unoriginal warning, but I think the message behind it is sincere. We'd be crazy to blow it off. Just in case."

"Are you saying you're going to give up looking for answers about the fire because of this?" Olivia's tone was incredulous, her gold eyes wide with disbelief.

"Hell, no. But you are."

She snorted contemptuously. "No way. I'm not letting some crackpot scare me off. This is important to Lila, and I owe it to her to find the answers she wants."

He shook his head. "You don't owe her anything. This is my fight. My investigation. You're officially out as of now."

"You can't do that!"

"I just did."

She huffed angrily and crossed her arms over her chest. "I don't need your permission to do this. I'll work by myself if I have to. Besides, you need me for my access to my dad's old files."

Frustration torqued his muscles tighter. "Damn it, Olivia. This isn't a game. Someone is issuing threats. There's serious foul play at work here, and I want you out of harm's way."

"What about you? You're at risk too."

"It's my job to take risks. I face life and death danger on a regular basis."

"But not like this." She stepped closer, wrapping her cool fingers around his wrist. He wished like hell she wouldn't touch him all the time. Her sometimes casual, sometimes comforting touches made it extremely difficult not to put his hands on her in return.

"At a fire," she said, "you know the dangers and can go in prepared. Assuming the threat is real, we don't know where this danger is coming from, who we can trust, who has something to hide."

"I'll give you five guesses who's involved."

She blinked. "Pardon?"

"Who knows that we are looking into the fire? Five people." He counted off his fingers as he listed the names. "Horton, Russell, Charlie Smith, your pharmacist friend Lou, and Hank."

She gave him a harsh laugh. "Don't be crazy. Lou wouldn't hurt a flea. And you can't tell me my own stepfather would threaten to kill me!"

"Willing to stake your life on it?"

"Yes. He's family. I know Hank. He didn't do this." She huffed her frustration and waved her hand at her broken windshield. "This isn't happening. This is Clairmont, for crying out loud, not New Orleans or Atlanta."

When her shoulders drooped, he fought the urge to wrap her in his arms and comfort her. If he ever had her in his arms, comforting would not be where it stopped.

"So what do we do now?" She raised worried amber eyes to his, and his heart slammed against his chest. He didn't want her needing him, looking to him for answers, expecting him to be the rock she could cling to through this escalating mess.

He shrugged and turned away, avoiding her gaze. "We call the sheriff, report this. Then you go to work and watch your back. Don't talk about this incident or the investigation to anyone."

She acquiesced with a weary nod.

He dug his cell out of his pocket and flipped it open. No signal. "Damn it."

"Yeah. Cell phones are just about worthless around here. Reception is pitiful. Maybe we can use the church's land line." She glanced toward the church door then back at him. "Meantime, why don't you plan to meet me at lunch? I can show you where I found the files in my attic, and you can look for more files while I'm at work."

Reyn rubbed his hands over his face. The threat against them changed everything. He'd wanted to avoid getting more involved with Olivia, hoped to keep her at arm's length until he made arrangements for Gram's extended care and could get out of town. But now he felt a responsibility for her safety. He had to make sure nothing happened to her because of the trouble they'd stirred up. And she wasn't going to give up, no matter how much he insisted. That much was clear. He blew out a harsh breath. "Yeah. Okay."

"And I want to go when you look into the coroner's report."

"Would you listen if I said no?"

"Nope." She flashed him a saucy grin.

Even this early in the morning, the Louisiana sun and humidity raised a sheen of perspiration on his skin. He swiped away a trickle of sweat from his cheek with his shoulder.

"That's what I thought."

The truth of the matter was, until he was certain she would be safe, he'd have to keep close tabs on Olivia. He'd never forgive himself if something happened to her because of this can of worms they'd opened. Anger twisted a knot in his gut. Who the hell could have left that note and what were they hiding?

"Reyn?"

Her voice quivered, and with dread squeezing his chest, he faced her. Her eyes were wide with trepidation, her face pale.

"When Lila first suggested the fire at your house wasn't an accident, I didn't really take her seriously. But I'm starting to wonder if—just maybe—someone could have *set* the fire that killed your mom? Do *you* think she was...murdered?"

A shudder raced through him, and his stomach pitched. "I don't know what to think. But...it's a possibility we have to consider."

"If so, then...what's to stop this person from killing again to keep us from finding him out?"

He saw her tremble, watched her pull her bottom lip between her teeth, and before he could fight his instincts, he drew her into his arms.

Holding her tightly, he absorbed her quivers and nestled her head in the curve of his throat. With her face buried against him, she fit perfectly under his chin. The press of her soft curves along his body stirred an elemental longing inside him, a male response to the sensual woman he held.

She felt good in his arms. So good. It had been a long time since he held a woman. Even longer since he'd allowed himself to offer his arms for comfort. He filled his lungs with the light floral scent of her shampoo and reveled in the silky feel of her hair against his cheek. He admitted his own nerves had been jumpy and holding her soothed his edginess, gave him a chance to center himself.

Her arms circled his waist, and she grew still, clinging to him, firing a protectiveness inside him that clawed his soul. He said a silent prayer that this time he wouldn't fail, that he wouldn't let this woman down. Too much was at stake.

The crunch of gravel broke the spell of the moment and drew his attention to the sedan that pulled into the parking lot and stopped under the shade of a nearby tree. Olivia tensed and raised her head to see who'd driven up. When she spotted the tall, lean man stepping out of the sedan, her body relaxed. He seemed familiar to Reyn, and he searched his memory to place the middle-aged man.

"Olivia? Is everything all right, dear?" The man closed his

car door and approached them.

Olivia gave Reyn's chest a pat as she backed out of his hold. She gave the man a polite smile, not the beguiling one she'd used on Reyn so often. "Reverend, have you met Lila's grandson? Reyn, this is our minister, Reverend Halmon."

The men shook hands and exchanged greetings before the minister aimed a concerned look toward Olivia. "Is everything all right here? You seem upset."

"Actually, we..." She glanced up at Reyn, her face dark. "We need to use the phone in the office to call the sheriff."

The man blinked his surprise. "The sheriff? What's happened?"

"Someone left a—"

"Someone vandalized her car," Reyn interrupted, knowing they'd better not give anyone, even the minister, any more information than necessary. Not until they could begin to sort out what was going on, and who might be involved. "We just need to report it."

Olivia gave him a questioning look, then nodded her understanding.

"Gracious. Well, by all means. Follow me. I just stopped by to pick up a book I left here. I was beginning work on my sermon for Sunday..." The minister's voice faded as he headed to the door of the church with Olivia behind him. Reyn took a moment to lock the incriminating note inside his truck before following them inside the church.

When he stepped inside the back door, he glanced down the short, dim hallway and saw light spilling from a room near the far end. He heard Olivia's voice drift from the same room. Passing a bulletin board with colorful flyers tacked to it with pushpins, a stack of metal folding chairs and a narrow table with an open Bible, he made his way toward the end of the hall.

"That's right. I'd left it parked in the church lot overnight, since the end of services really," he heard Olivia say.

Across from the office, he noticed a men's room and decided to use the facilities before they left. The hinges squeaked when he pushed the door open and he flipped on the light. The room was eerily silent, like the pall in a funeral home, and the pungent scent of pine disinfectant assailed him. As he stepped in and let the door close, a flash of memory flickered in his mind.

As a boy, overwhelmed by guilt and grief, he'd fled his mother's funeral and hidden in this very room, crouched in a corner with tears streaming down his face. Pain sliced through him, filled his chest with a leaden ache. He hadn't allowed himself to think about his mother, his loss for years.

Do you think she was...murdered?

Time didn't heal all wounds, it seemed. With sheer will, he shoved the memory aside, but the pain resounded inside him like remnants of a nightmare.

Olivia dropped her purse under the counter at the pharmacy, and Lou looked up from the computer where he hunted and pecked to enter a prescription order. "You're late."

"Sorry. I—" She stopped, remembering what Reyn had said. Five people knew they were investigating the fire. Reyn had insisted they not tell Sheriff Anders what they were doing until they had something solid to give him.

"I had...car trouble." She watched Lou's face carefully, holding her breath.

He began counting out pills, his nose scrunched as he concentrated. When he finished, he glanced at her, his eyes twinkling with mischief. "When you gonna get rid of that old rattletrap anyway? Only thing holding it together is the rust."

"When you give me a raise."

He barked a laugh and shook his head. "I walked into that one, didn't I?" He snapped a lid on the prescription bottle and handed it to Olivia. "Mrs. Thibideaux called. She wants a refill of her allergy pills, but I haven't had a chance to enter it in the computer yet."

He poked his glasses back up the bridge of his nose and studied the next order form on the counter. He'd hardly blinked when she mentioned her car. She released a sigh of relief and greeted the customer who approached the register. Like she'd told Reyn, Lou was no killer.

A steady stream of business kept Olivia mercifully busy, her hands and mind occupied for most of the morning. Equally busy, Lou didn't mention the confrontation that morning at the diner, for which she was extremely grateful. In light of the threatening note left on her windshield, she wasn't sure how to proceed, what she could or should say if Lou did mention their investigation. She needed to talk about a strategy with Reyn.

But the steady business didn't stop the occasional thought of Reyn from popping into her head. Once, a little boy came into the pharmacy with his mother, and she imagined Reyn as a child, sitting in the principal's office for fighting, for defending his mother's honor. Another time, when the air-conditioning kicked on, blowing on her neck and giving her a chill, she remembered the warmth and security of Reyn's embrace that morning. His comforting gesture had been just what she needed at the time and fit the image of him forming in her mind. A man of honor and decency, a kind and gentle soul behind his hard exterior. Her dream man wrapped in a dreamy body.

When she thought of his tortured expression when he'd told her about his mother, a frisson of sympathy spun through her. Maybe learning the truth about his mother's death would help heal the old wounds. And maybe she could help him work past the grief and pain that held him prisoner. But first he'd have to trust her enough to bridge the distance he kept between them.

Olivia sighed. Somehow she'd draw Reyn out. Somehow.

At noon, the bell over the front door tinkled, and she glanced up to greet the new customer as she had many times that morning. But her voice stuck in her throat.

Reyn stood in the doorway, his tall frame and broad shoulders filling the entry. It seemed the atmosphere in the pharmacy changed with his presence, charged and crackling with energy like the air preceding a storm. He stopped long enough to cast his gaze around the store before spotting her. With his gaze locked on her, he strode toward the register. The way he looked at her, predatory, possessive, made her toes curl. The look held a note of promise, hinted at things to come.

"Hey, handsome. Gimme one second, and I'll be ready to go."

"No rush." He slid his hands in his jeans pockets.

She gathered her pocketbook and draped the strap over her shoulder. "So what did you do to keep busy this morning?"

Reyn shifted his gaze to Lou, who watched the two of them with interest. Taking her hand, he tugged her out from behind the counter and started for the door. "We'll talk in the truck."

His grip on her hand echoed the possessiveness of his gaze, and she savored the warm, encompassing grasp of his large hand. His touch gave her a delicious shiver, and when he sent her a quizzical look, she just smiled.

Once safely ensconced in his Sierra, he cast her a sideways glance as he cranked the engine. "Any problems this morning with Lou? How'd he act?"

"He acted like Lou. Sweet, lovable Lou. I even mentioned that I'd had car trouble, and he didn't bat an eyelash, except to tell me I needed to ditch the jalopy, like he always says."

Reyn grunted an acknowledgment as he backed out of his parking place and headed down Main Street.

"So what's up with you? Any leads on getting a copy of the coroner's report?"

"I made some calls this morning, and it looks like the autopsy records we need are kept in Baton Rouge. Since we can't make it there and back during your lunch hour, I figure I'll go alone after we grab a bite to eat."

"Can you wait till tomorrow? I have Tuesday and Thursday afternoons off so I can get to my classes in Monroe on time."

"Thanks, but I don't need you to go with me."

Olivia sighed patiently. "Reyn, I want to go with you. I want to help with this. Not just because of what Lila means to me, but because of that note. I won't sit back and let someone make veiled threats against me without doing something to find out who did it and why."

He was silent for several moments, scowling. Fine. He didn't have to like it. But she would convince him somehow to take her with him. Reading an autopsy report on your mother had to be tough. She wanted to be there for him.

"Okay," he said finally. "We'll go tomorrow. I'm just ready to get started. The sooner we get the information we need, the sooner we can put this mess behind us."

"Good. I'll ask our babysitter Gloria to stay late with Katy, and I'll be all yours."

He gave her a goose-bump-raising look, and she realized what she'd said. Winking at him, she let the double meaning stand.

He drummed his fingers on the steering wheel restlessly. "I want to take a look in your attic, see if there's anything else your dad left that would steer us in the right direction."

"Sure. Anytime. The evening would be best, though. It's sweltering up there during the day."

"Mmm. Tonight maybe?"

"All right. You're on."

He fell silent for a moment, watching the other traffic with more concentration than needed. The seriousness in his face told her his thoughts had drifted elsewhere. "I've been thinking..."

"Yeah?" she prompted when he hesitated.

"If my mom was...murdered, there'd have to be a motive. I can't think of any reason for someone to kill her, but then I was just a kid."

"So where do you start looking for a motive? Her will? Did she keep a diary? Maybe insurance papers?"

"Any of those are possibilities. I'll just have to sort through her personal papers and see what I come up with. I hate to ask Gram about where those papers would be, but I—"

"Check the shoe box under her sewing machine. That's where Lila keeps her will and deed to the house and stuff."

Reyn turned toward her with wide-eyed disbelief. "She keeps that stuff in a shoe box?"

She wrinkled her nose and nodded. "'Fraid so. When she showed it to me a couple years ago, I tried to convince her to get a lockbox at the bank. She said she wanted her things close by, knew her lawyer had copies if anything happened to hers."

A frown creased his brow. "Why'd she show *you* where she kept her will?"

"She wanted me to know where they were...just in case

something happened to her. So I could show you."

Reyn pulled into the drive-thru of the only fast food restaurant in town, still frowning. "Burgers okay with you?"

"Sure."

He said nothing as he studied the menu that was, no doubt, virtually the same worldwide, but obviously provided him an excuse to avoid her gaze.

"She trusts me, Reyn."

His grip tightened on the steering wheel.

"And you can too."

Now he faced her, his gaze searching hers as if seeking the assurance that he could, in fact, trust her. His piercing gray gaze probed hers, and she read emotions in their silvery depths that gave her a glimpse of the soul he worked so hard to protect. Loneliness. Longing. Lust. She felt his stare all the way to her bones, felt his need chipping away her own defenses. He didn't look away until the tinny voice over the speaker box asked for their order.

"I've been thinking too," she said as he pulled up to the window to pay.

"I'm not surprised." He waved away the money she tried to give him and pulled out his wallet.

"Obviously confronting the firefighters as a team was a mistake. Maybe we should talk to them each individually then compare their answers."

He shook his head. "One of them has already threatened us, and none of them had anything to say before. What do you think we'll accomplish by taking them on one-on-one?"

"Maybe they'd feel freer to talk if the others weren't around. Maybe they saw someone hanging around the area after the fire, found something in the house that struck them as strange, any kind of detail we could follow up on."

"Maybe, but until we know who left that threat, I don't want you approaching any of those men by yourself."

"So go with me. Considering how defensive they were, I have to wonder what they're hiding." She aimed a finger at him to punctuate her point. "Someone knows something. We just have to get them to talk."

Reyn grunted. "They won't talk to me. Most of the people who remember me don't like and don't trust me. I gave them plenty of reasons not to like me when I was a kid."

She wanted to explore that topic with him more, but she saved her questions about his youth for later.

He rolled his shoulders and frowned. "I still think it's a bad idea until we know who left that threatening note."

"We can start with someone safe. Like Hank. He's family, and I know I can get him to talk to us. Maybe over dinner tonight? As long as you're going to be looking through my attic this evening, you might as well stay and eat."

"Real food, huh? That's a mighty tempting offer."

She laughed and aimed a finger at him. "See. I knew you were the home-cooked meals type. Strip clubs, my eye."

He narrowed a serious gaze on her. "This isn't a date."

Shrugging, she tucked her hair behind her ear. "Maybe, maybe not. Guess that depends on what we do after dinner, hmm?" She sent him a mischievous grin and waggled her eyebrows.

His eyes heated, and her smile faltered. The desire in his gaze stirred a fluttering sensation in her stomach, made her skin tingle with anticipation. She'd only been teasing him, but there was nothing playful about the hunger in his eyes.

Chapter Five

When the doorbell rang at six o'clock, Olivia added punctuality to the list of Reyn's attributes.

By the time Olivia had turned down the spaghetti sauce, taken off her apron and stopped long enough to check her hair in the hall mirror, Katy was leading Reyn into the living room by the hand.

Olivia hung back, her protective instincts on full alert, and watched the interplay between her undersized half-sister and the towering firefighter. Because of Katy's handicap and because she'd taken over raising the little girl when their mother died years ago, Olivia tended to be wary of how people reacted to Katy. Her sister picked up on strangers' awkwardness around her because of her leg braces and took it personally.

But Katy babbled while she showed Reyn a picture she'd just finished coloring for him. "That's you. My dad's fire truck is red, but I had to make your fire truck orange 'cause I can't find my red marker."

Reyn sat on the edge of the sofa and studied the picture Katy handed him. "No problem. I think orange is a good color for a fire truck. Some fire engines are even bright yellow. Know why?"

Olivia stepped in from the entry hall, remembering Reyn's

ready smile for Katy at church yesterday. His ease around her sister did her heart good. Ever since she'd told Katy that Reyn would be coming for supper, the five-year-old had been giddy with excitement. She would have been crushed if Reyn hadn't responded to her with genuine warmth.

Katy shrugged in answer to Reyn's question. "Because it's the color of fire?"

He grinned broadly and tugged her ponytail. "Good guess, but no. Bright yellow trucks are easier to see, so people can get out of the firemen's way when they're going to a fire."

Katy's face lit up. "I have yellow. I'll make a yellow truck for you!"

"After dinner, Katy," Olivia said from the door. "Go wash your hands so you can set the table."

Katy groaned but obeyed. Once her sister had trooped down the hall, Olivia turned back to Reyn with a smile. "Hey."

"Hi. Something smells good."

"Don't be too impressed. I just opened a jar." She crossed the room to sit beside him. "Did you find anything in your mom's papers that would give someone a motive?"

He shook his head and reached in the back pocket of his jeans. "But I found this and thought it was interesting."

She took the folded sheet from him and opened it. "Your mother's death certificate," she said when she read the heading on the photocopied page.

"Cause of death is listed as smoke inhalation. We already knew that. But look who signed it."

She scanned down the sheet to the signature at the bottom. "Lou? He never told me he'd served as Justice of the Peace!"

"That's an elected position here, right?" Reyn took the sheet back from her and refolded it.

"Yeah. So?"

"So that'd explain why a pharmacist is the Justice of the Peace."

She crossed her arms over her chest and shook her head. "Hmm. Lou was Justice of the Peace once. I had no idea."

"Goes to show ..."

"What?"

"You might not know your boss as well as you think."

The back door slammed, and Hank's voice boomed through the house. "I'm home. Hey, something's burning in here."

"The sauce!" Olivia jumped up and ran for the kitchen.

"Daddy!" Katy squealed as she clomped into the kitchen to throw herself into Hank's waiting arms.

"Hey, baby girl." Hank squeezed Katy and kissed the top of her head. "Were you a good girl for Miss Gloria today?"

"Uh-huh. Gloria and me played with dolls and rode bikes."

"Gloria and I," Olivia corrected. "And you get to play with Gloria even longer tomorrow."

Hank arched an eyebrow. "Why is that?"

"I've got somewhere to go. Gloria says she doesn't mind and the extra money comes in handy."

Hank didn't appear satisfied with her answer, but before he could quiz her any further about her plans, Katy grabbed his attention.

"Daddy, Daddy, Reyn's eatin' with us." Katy tugged on Hank's shirt, her face glowing with excitement.

Hank frowned. "Reyn?"

"Run and get him, pipsqueak. I think everything's ready." Olivia faced Hank once Katy lumbered out. "I invited him. We want to talk with you about the fire that killed his mom."

Sighing, Hank pulled out a chair at the table and sat. "You'd be wasting your breath, Jelly Bean. I don't remember much about it. That was a long time ago."

Jelly Bean. Olivia cherished his use of the pet name he'd given her years ago, the affection in his tone when he spoke it.

"...and my Barbie's name is Crystal 'cause you can put sparkly stuff in her hair." Katy led Reyn into the kitchen by the hand, chattering away. "You can sit by me, Reyn."

"I'd be honored." He pulled out the chair by Katy then reached across the table to shake Hank's hand. "Evening, sir."

"Sweet tea all right with you, Reyn?" Olivia set the pot of sauce on the table then started taking glasses from the shelf.

"Sure."

"Just water for me, Liv." Hank eyed Reyn as their guest took his seat. "So you're a dragonslayer in Atlanta, huh?"

Katy's eyes rounded. "They have dragons in Atlanta?"

With a chuckle, Hank served himself some spaghetti noodles. "No, baby girl. That's just something we firefighters call ourselves."

"Fires are the dragons we slay," Reyn told Katy and helped himself to the salad. "Starting my tenth year this fall."

Olivia set Reyn's glass by his plate and took the seat across from him. Hank blessed the meal, and Katy piped up again as soon as he finished praying.

"I'm going to be a vet when I grow up."

Reyn turned to her sister. "Are you? Well, all right! I bet you'll be a good one, too."

Katy giggled. "I already help 'Livia with her dogs."

Hank grunted. "You may have noticed the assortment of mutts in the yard when you arrived. Most people collect stamps or coins." He cast Olivia a teasing grin. "Olivia collects dogs."

"I only keep the ones I can't find homes for," she amended.

Katy tugged on Reyn's sleeve. "And we saved a baby bird once that had fallen from his nest."

"Sounds like you're getting lots of practice for being a vet," Reyn said with a smile. A subtle quirk of Hank's eyebrow told Olivia he noticed the rapport Reyn had with Katy.

The conversation turned to further discussion of Katy's day with Gloria, Reyn's visit that afternoon with Lila, and the local farmers' desperate situation due to the current drought.

Anxious to get to the questions she had for Hank, Olivia had no appetite. Impatience started nervous flutters in her stomach, and memories of the threatening note on her windshield, tied her gut in knots. But they had to wait for Katy to finish eating and leave the room before she and Reyn could talk to Hank.

"I'm ready for dessert," Katy announced, slurping in her last noodle.

Hank shook his head. "Not until everyone's finished."

Olivia sighed quietly, watching Hank help himself to seconds, then sat on her hands to keep from fidgeting.

Reyn leaned toward Katy and whispered in her ear, loud enough for everyone to hear, "Why don't you ask if you can work on that yellow fire truck for me until time for dessert?"

Katy raised bright, eager eyes to her sister. "Can I?"

Olivia smiled her relief. "Sure."

"I don't think—" Hank started, but Katy had already bolted from the kitchen with an awkward gait. Hank frowned at Olivia. "You know I don't like her leaving the table till everyone's finished. You're teaching her bad manners."

"I don't want her hearing what we have to discuss." Olivia pushed her plate out of the way and leveled a steady look on her stepfather. "I received a death threat today."

Hank's fork stopped halfway to his mouth. He raised his eyebrows and cocked his head. "Come again?"

"You heard me. Someone either has a sick sense of humor, or they don't want us looking into the death of Reyn's mother."

Hank put his fork down. "All the more reason to drop this asinine goose chase. I want you to forget this whole business, understand me? It's ancient history."

Olivia shook her head. "I can't do that. I won't do that."

With a huff, Hank glared at her, the worry in his eyes softening his scowl. "Even with someone threatening you? What if this person is serious and tries to kill you?"

Hank's concern was no less than she'd have expected. Though touched by his worry, she couldn't give up so easily. "I'll be careful. But I won't let this person intimidate me."

Hank turned a dark glower on Reyn. "Do you see what you started? Why would you drag her into something like this? What do you think you're going to prove with all this anyway?"

"He didn't start this. I did." Her stepfather turned back to her when she spoke. "I found some of my dad's old files in the attic when I was sorting through things for the church bazaar last week. He'd apparently begun an unofficial investigation into some inconsistencies he'd found regarding Claire Erikson's death. I brought them to Lila's attention and then to Reyn's when he arrived in town yesterday."

"That case has been closed for years. You don't need to go stirring up trouble." Hank threw his napkin down on his plate.

"Why has our interest in the fire and my mother's death made so many people nervous?" Reyn asked in an even tone.

"I don't know. I'm not a mind reader," Hank said, his own voice reflecting his frustration and irritation.

"Fair enough. Forget everyone else." Reyn leaned forward, narrowing his gaze on Hank. "What has *you* so nervous?"

Reyn's shift to a more direct and combative mode startled Olivia. Hank wasn't the enemy. She sent Reyn a quelling look, but his attention was fixed on her stepfather.

Hank met Reyn's challenge with a steady gaze. "Maybe I'm just looking out for my family. You heard Olivia. Someone left her a note with a death threat. Wouldn't you call that a reason to be worried? I don't want her getting hurt."

"Neither do I." Reyn held the older man's gaze.

She cleared her throat. "Hello? Gentlemen? I'm still here. And I'm a big girl. I can look out for my own safety." She divided a grin between them, hoping to diffuse the tension. "But thanks for your concern."

Katy picked that moment to clomp back into the room and thrust her new drawing at Reyn. "Look, Reyn. I even put a siren light on top."

Hank scooted back from the table and took his plate to the sink, his movements jerky, tense.

"I made a pie for dessert, Hank," she called to him as he marched out of the kitchen.

"Maybe later."

"I want pie." Katy plopped down in her chair, and her eyes sparkled with enthusiasm.

Olivia smiled at her sister, working to hide her disappointment that they hadn't learned any more from Hank. But then what had she really expected? Why should she think Hank knew more than he'd already said?

Glancing at Reyn, she studied the thoughtful look he wore. "Peach pie, Reyn?"

He lifted his gaze. "Sounds good. Thanks."

When Olivia would have turned away to get the pie, she balked. Reyn's eyes held hers in a serious, unreadable stare. The hard edge to his gaze negated the thrill she usually received from having his gray eyes probe hers so intimately. She furrowed her brow and mouthed, "What?"

His gaze flicked to Katy then back. "Later."

Olivia's curiosity kicked into high gear. What had Reyn so upset? Once again she found herself waiting for Katy to finish eating so she could talk to Reyn alone.

Reyn waited outside in the purple cloak of dusk for a chance to speak to Olivia alone. He watched the light in a bedroom window go out and imagined Olivia kissing her sister goodnight. The chirp of tree frogs and sweet fragrance of gardenia filled the evening air. The inviting glow of the porch light and quiet comfort of the country home stirred a longing in him he dared not name. His chest squeezed with bittersweet nostalgia as an unbidden memory of his mother tucking him in for the night spun through his mind.

He'd forfeited his right to such domestic bliss when he'd let his mother die. He'd lost his family and his home and had only himself to blame. He quickly shoved the thought and the accompanying sense of loss down, pushing it back into the tiny box where he'd kept his pain for years. It was the only way to manage the grief or it would consume him.

But since he'd returned to Clairmont, the memories popped up more easily, demanding his attention. The sooner he finished with his business here and got back to Atlanta, the better.

He shoved his hands in his jeans pockets and leaned back against an ancient oak tree with a weary sigh. The rough bark prickled his skin through his shirt, abrading him the way his conscience chafed his mind.

When he heard the screened door squeak, he glanced up. Olivia stepped out on the porch and immediately several scruffy dogs that had been sleeping in the yard scampered to her feet. She stopped long enough to scratch each one behind the ear and speak to the mutt in a soft voice. Then, her feet bare, she picked her way across the yard.

Backlit by the porch light, her expression was difficult to read, but he savored the sight of her lithe form moving through the shadows toward him. He battled the urge to pull her body against his. Or tried to, at least.

Olivia had a potent effect on him. His nerve endings zinged with an awareness of her every movement. He heard the seductive sough of her breath as she deeply inhaled the night air, and he filled his own lungs with the scent of floral perfume and peach pie that clung to her. She was a fascinating blend of sensuality and domesticity. She was everything he could never have, couldn't let himself want.

"I think I've read *The Cat in the Hat* ten thousand times. I've memorized it, because she wants the same book every night." Olivia stood close enough now for him to see the flash of her white teeth. "Thanks for waiting."

"No problem."

She stepped over to the tire swing tied to a low branch of the massive oak. The rope creaked as she climbed on, draping her shapely legs over the top of the tire and resting her cheek against the rope. "You wanted to talk?"

"Yeah." The doubts and suspicions that had plagued him at dinner resurfaced and kicked up his pulse. "I want you to watch yourself around Hank."

Her only response was a hiccup-like laugh.

"I mean it." He pushed away from the tree trunk and

caught the rope of the swing. The edge of the tire bumped his hip. "Promise me, Olivia."

"First my boss, the kindest, gentlest man on the planet, is a suspect, then my own family. I think you can scratch Hank off your list. What reason would he have for hurting your mother...or threatening me?" She slapped at a mosquito that buzzed at her ear.

"You didn't tell him the death threat was in a note, but he said as much when he was warning us away. Lucky guess, or did he already know about the note?"

She raised her cheek from the rope and wrinkled her brow. "Are you sure I didn't say—"

"I'm sure." He stepped between her knees to meet her querying look straight on. "And after his slip I started thinking about some other things. The note was written in red, and Katy said her red marker was missing."

A nervous smile tugged at her lips, and she shook her head. "A stupid coincidence. You can't think Hank wrote that note. Hank's my family. He'd never hurt me."

"I hope you're right. I guess we'll find out when the sheriff finishes checking the note for fingerprints."

Olivia stared at him for a moment then swung her legs off the tire. Placing a hand on either side of her slim waist, he helped her down. She wavered unsteadily and leaned against him until she'd found her balance. Even the brief contact of her soft body against his played with his control.

When she turned to face him, she stood close enough for him to feel the caress of her breath when she sighed. Close enough to kiss her if he wanted. And, damn, but he wanted.

"As much as I appreciate your concern, I really feel our efforts would be better spent focusing on the other men." She flattened a hand against his chest, and her warm touch burned through him. "Assuming anyone in the fire department is truly involved...which I'm having a hard time believing."

He caught her shoulders and drilled his gaze into hers. "I understand that it's hard to believe something like this of the people you've grown up with. But for God's sake, don't assume anything. Don't let your guard down, or you could get killed."

He felt the shudder that raced through her and regretted having to use scare tactics to get through to her. But if a little caution on her part kept her alive, it would be worth it. He'd do whatever it took to prevent another person he cared about from needlessly dying.

Another person he cared about. He took a sharp breath as that thought echoed in his head. Yeah, he cared about her, he admitted, then released the air in his lungs slowly. Because of the way she'd cared for Gram. Because of her sexy smile and unfailing optimism. Because he cared about anyone he thought could be in danger. It was his job to care and to protect. That was all.

Just the same, he released her and took a step back. Before he did something foolish like kiss her or wrap her in his arms the way he had that morning.

Distance. He needed to keep his distance.

"So who is next?" she asked. "Should I talk to Lou about all this tomorrow?"

"Not alone, you don't. It's bad enough you have to be alone with him while you work, but I want to be there when we ask him about the fire again."

"If you're going to see Lila in the morning, we could ride into town together. Then you could ask Lou whatever you wanted."

"Good idea. But we'll take my truck."

"Okay. Ready to tackle the attic?" She tipped her head toward the front door and started back to the porch.

He nodded and followed her silently inside and up the narrow ladder to the attic. A bare light bulb at the center of the low ceiling provided the only illumination, and Reyn had to stoop over to avoid hitting his head on the exposed support beams. Trapped heat from the summer day made the tight space stuffy, and the smell of mildew and mothballs pervaded the room.

"I know it's crowded, but I can't bring myself to get rid of some of this stuff. Most of it belonged to my mom or my dad." Olivia climbed over a dusty trunk and knelt in front of a long box.

Reyn looked around at the accumulated piles of boxes and old clothes and noticed one wall where Broadway-style posters were propped or stacked, all framed neatly, some autographed. "*Rigoletto...La Boheme*," he read. "Those are operas, right?"

Olivia stopped rifling through the box of papers and looked up at him. "Mmm-hmm, my mom was a big fan. She sang too. Beautifully. She could have sung professionally, if she'd wanted to, but—" She ducked her head, leaving her statement hanging.

"But what?" He stepped over the same dusty trunk and squatted beside her.

Olivia went back to shuffling through the box of papers as she explained. "She won the chance to audition at the Met. Her life's dream. But...a week before she was supposed to go and sing in New York, she found out she was pregnant. With me. My mom and dad had wanted to start a family and had just settled in this house and..." She paused, sitting back on her heels, and glanced over at him. "Well, to make a long story short, she didn't go to the Met. She chose to stay home. It was more important to her to be here, with my dad, with her pregnancy, starting her family."

He scratched his chin and regarded Olivia's solemn face. "Do you think she had any regrets? Later, I mean...for giving up her big opportunity?"

"She said she didn't. She said her family was worth it. She always put us first, and she thrived on being a good wife and mother. She fulfilled her love of music by directing the church choir and singing at local events."

A face flashed in Reyn's mind. "Was she a tall lady? Long blonde hair?"

Olivia lifted a startled glance. "Yeah. How did you—?"

"I remember her. From church. I think she sang at my mom's funeral."

Olivia gave him a heartbreaking smile. "She probably did."

The memory, the shared connection to the past, set an intimate mood that unsettled him. The dim light from the single bulb cast Olivia's face in shadows, but the glimmer of tears in her eyes was unmistakable.

He understood her melancholy and ached to brush the dampness from her eyes. But he didn't dare. He knew her skin would be as silky smooth as it looked, knew touching her face would make it harder to resist kissing her. He knew forming bonds with her, commiserating over shared losses was the last thing he needed if he wanted to protect her from future hurt. He needed to be able to walk away from her with a clear conscience when the time came.

No strings. No emotional ties. No risk of breaking her heart.

But, damn, her mouth was tempting. Her full, ripe lips curved slightly in a bittersweet smile. Desire pumped through him like water from a hydrant, knocking his breath from him with the force of spray from a fire hose.

He cleared his throat and pulled his attention back to the box in front of her. "Is this where you found your dad's files?"

She blinked as if he'd pulled her out of deep thought as well. "Yeah. This area around here is all his stuff." She indicated the floor around them with a sweep of her hand. "When he died, my mom just stuck his things up here without sorting anything. She couldn't handle it. She was in shock, you know?"

He didn't want to ask, but the question formed on his lips anyway. "How did he die?"

"Hunting accident. They said his gun misfired or went off when he dropped it or something. I was too young to be clear on the specifics, and Mom wouldn't talk about it. Not even later when I was older. I just knew I didn't have my daddy anymore."

Reyn cursed under his breath. He knew how unbearably it had hurt to lose his mom. But Olivia had lost both her parents. He began forming a picture of the woman across from him, drawn from the bits of information he'd gleaned in the past couple days. In light of her losses, her mother's choice of her family over her dream of singing opera, and her half-sister's special needs, he understood Olivia's fierce defense of her family, of Hank. He just hoped her family loyalty didn't get her killed.

He saw her strong bond with Gram in a new light as well. Perhaps Olivia needed Gram as much as Gram needed the attentiveness of her thoughtful and caring neighbor.

Olivia thrived on family, just as her mother had. One more reason why he had to keep his distance from her. Family, commitment, a future were things he couldn't give her. His track record spoke for itself, and he couldn't stand the thought of hurting Olivia the way he'd hurt his last girlfriend, Liz. The way he'd failed Gram and his mother.

They spent the next hour sifting through family pictures, news clippings and old case files. Nothing seemed to relate to his mother's death, however, and Reyn's frustration grew.

"Oh, well. Looks like the file I found is all there was. I'm ready to call it a night." Olivia stood and stretched her arms behind her. As she did, her blouse pulled tight, calling attention to the swell of her breasts.

Arousal fired in his veins, and his skin, already sticky with sweat from the stuffy attic, prickled with the heat of his desire. It would be so easy to lay her across one of the beds of old clothes, unbutton her blouse and fill his hands with her creamy flesh. Just imagining his mouth on her skin, sucking a nipple between his teeth sent a rush of blood to his groin.

Slowly he raised his gaze from her breasts to her face and met her eyes. She seemed to realize the direction of his thoughts and self-consciously eased her arms down.

But the fire in her gold eyes told him she'd fulfill his imagined scene and anything else he wanted. He had no doubt she'd make love to him if he initiated it.

But he was just as certain she was the type of woman who gave her heart when she shared her body. He couldn't let her involve her heart, her emotions, when he knew he had nothing to offer in return. Sex, plain sex with no promises attached, was one thing. But what were the chances Olivia would settle for sex for sex's sake? Slim to none.

"Yeah, let's call it a night." When he stood as far as the low ceiling allowed, Reyn's muscles protested having been cramped in the same position for the last hour. He made his way back to the ladder and waited for Olivia to turn off the light.

He took her hand as she found her footing on the ladder, and even that casual contact stirred crazy longings inside him. Her hand belonged in his. It fit. With stubborn determination he fought down the surge of possessiveness, the flare of protectiveness. He had no claim on her and couldn't afford to forget that basic fact.

Olivia peeked in Katy's room as they passed the little girl's room, and the maternal gesture caused a strange ache in Reyn's chest. Another reminder of what he had lost years ago, what he could never have again.

When they reached the front porch, he stared out at the dark lawn. Lightning bugs blinked, and the humid air hummed with all forms of gnats, mosquitoes and moths. A plethora of bugs was part of life in Louisiana.

Reyn fingered the coins in his pocket, restless energy vibrating through him. Frustration over their failure to find anything helpful in Olivia's attic and sexual tension strung him tight. He sensed more than heard her move up behind him. He turned to her, and she stepped close.

"Good night, Reyn." Olivia slid a hand over his cheek, letting her fingers linger on his chin. His already jangling nerves overloaded when she touched him.

Swallowing a moan, he moved out of her reach. "Thanks for dinner."

"Any time." She smiled and backed toward the door.

"Olivia."

She stopped, tilting her head so that the porch light made her hair shine with a fiery sheen.

"Be careful."

She nodded. "You too. See you in the morning."

He waited until she turned out the porch light before making his way toward the edge of the woods. Even with a bright moon out, the woods were dark and shadowed. Like his thoughts. If Olivia's father was right, Clairmont harbored a murderer. Someone who'd threatened to kill again to protect his secret. Reyn cut through the murky woods toward Gram's house and swore to himself to find that someone before he had the chance to strike.

Chapter Six

As agreed, Reyn stopped by the house to drive Olivia to work, and while she washed the last of the breakfast dishes, Katy chattered to him, obviously excited about seeing her new friend again so soon. She asked a myriad of questions about Reyn's job and the fire engines the department used. He answered Katy's questions patiently, with good humor and, more importantly in Olivia's opinion, he didn't talk down to her sister.

"Do you slide down a big pole?" Katy asked, her eyes bright with enthusiasm for the real fireman. Olivia considered reminding her sister that Hank served as a volunteer fireman for the local department in addition to his regular job as a car mechanic, but she kept quiet. Katy's hero-worship amused her.

Reyn gave Katy a crooked smile that made Olivia wonder if part of Katy's fascination wasn't simply a crush. Lord knows Reyn made her own pulse race.

"Well, the station where I work only has one floor, so we don't need a pole." He glanced at Katy and winked. "Sometimes I wish we had a pole, though. That'd be fun, don't you think?"

Katy bobbed her head, her eyes bright.

Olivia smiled to herself, and warm satisfaction filled her chest, seeing the two get along so well.

Although she'd made sacrifices, such as delaying some of

her classes in order to live at home with Katy, she never regretted the choices she'd made regarding her half-sister. Commuting to class was small potatoes compared with what her mother had willingly sacrificed for her family. Olivia would do no less. After cancer claimed their mother when Katy was a baby, Olivia had assumed the role of caregiver and never looked back.

When she finally pried Reyn away from her sister, they got on the road, headed toward the town. She gazed out the window at the central Louisiana countryside and sipped the mug of coffee she'd brought with her. Above the line of loblolly pine trees, Olivia noticed a small cloud of black smoke billowing into the air. She frowned.

"Dang it," she grumbled quietly. "There's a burning ban on. Why do people insist on burning their trash during a drought?"

"Come again?"

She pointed out the dark smoke. "Looks like someone's burning leaves *despite* the parish-wide ban."

Reyn ducked his head and leaned toward her to see the smoke out her side window. The crisp scent of soap and his freshly laundered shirt wafted to her, making her stomach do a little happy dance.

"That's too much smoke to be someone burning trash. Something big's on fire."

Olivia sent him a querying look. "Like what?"

"That's what I intend to find out." He punched the accelerator, and the truck rocketed forward.

She grabbed the armrest and held on as they bumped along the cracked pavement and bounced over the narrow bridge crossing Clairmont Creek. The closer they came to the source of the smoke, the more a chilling suspicion took shape in her mind.

"Reyn," she said quietly, almost afraid to voice her concern, not wanting to believe it could be true. "The smoke's coming from the Russells' farm."

He didn't answer, but his expression darkened. He inched their speed up another notch.

When they rounded the last turn, passing a copse of trees that had blocked their view, their fears were confirmed. Black smoke poured from the kitchen window of the Russells' house. Hannah Russell, a cordless phone in her hand, ran down the driveway toward Reyn's truck. The woman's face reflected horror and panic.

Olivia opened her door and hopped out, even before Reyn had brought the truck to a full stop.

"I can't find Sara!" Hannah sobbed, grabbing Olivia by the arms. "I thought she'd gotten out when the fire started, but now I can't find her!"

"Have you reported the fire?" Reyn asked as he darted around the front of the truck to join them.

Hannah nodded, and her body shuddered. "I think she went back inside. I can't find her anywhere!"

Reyn's head snapped around, his gaze hard. "Who went back in?"

"My baby!" Hannah screeched, near hysterics.

Olivia pulled the woman into her arms. "Her name's Sara, Reyn. She's seven."

"Which window is her bedroom?" Reyn's tone was sharp and urgent.

Hannah pointed a shaky finger. "Second floor at the end. Oh God. Get her out!"

Jerking open the passenger's door of his truck, Reyn dug under the front seat and pulled out a duffel bag. He unzipped the duffel and grabbed a small towel from what was presumably his gym bag, leaving the other contents spilled on the seat in his haste. Next he took a tire iron from the toolbox behind the cab.

"Wet this down." He tossed the towel at Olivia and sprinted toward the house.

"You're going in there?" Olivia asked, aghast. "But she's called the fire department. They'll have the right gear and—"

"And in the few minutes it takes them to get here the girl could die," he barked over his shoulder, not slowing his pace. "I can't wait for them."

Her nerves jumping and adrenaline churning inside her, Olivia scanned the side of the house for a spigot. After soaking the towel, she hurried to find Reyn again and give it to him. Heat poured from the house, and smoke choked her. She could hardly imagine how bad it would be inside for Reyn. The sound of shattering glass greeted her as she came around to the front of the house in time to see Reyn swing the tire iron at the living room window.

"What are you doing?"

"Ventilating the house." He swung again then moved to the next window, shattering it as well. "This will help clear out the smoke faster."

Dropping the tire iron, he snatched the wet towel from her and pushed her back as he jogged toward the front door. "Get back to the truck. And make sure an ambulance is on the way."

She stood rooted to the spot, a wave of terror washing through her. She watched him take the porch steps in one leap then feel the front door with the back of his hand. Stepping back, he kicked the door in, leaping out of the way as soon as it flew open. Thick, dark clouds billowed out, and Reyn dropped to his hands and knees. Holding the wet towel over his mouth and nose, he crawled inside. In seconds, he disappeared in the smoke and shimmering waves of heat.

Staggering back from the blast of fumes and hot air, Olivia could do nothing now but wait. And pray.

Reyn prayed his assessment of the fire was accurate. He judged that only the kitchen and living room were involved at that point, leaving the foyer and stairs toward the bedrooms clear. But by the time he found the girl and needed to get back out that could change. Probably would change. Already flames licked at the entrance to the living room a few feet away.

The heat was intense. Blistering. Hot enough to singe the hair on the back of his hand. The bite of burns stung his ears as he edged past the dancing flames. He squeezed his eyes closed, avoiding the irritating fumes from the smoke, and for just an instant he was ten years old again.

Come in if you dare, the demon fire crackled. He hesitated, remembering the numbing fear that had paralyzed him as a boy. The fear that had cost his mother her life.

Coward.

He pressed the damp towel over his mouth and nose. Groping along the wall to find his way, he blindly crept up the steps with only one hand free. When he opened his eyes a crack to check his progress, all he saw was black. Smoke made the interior of the house as dim as night, as black as tar. As dark as fear.

The flames taunted and jeered at him, writhing in a macabre dance that hypnotized him. Just like before.

Twenty years kaleidoscoped until the past and present blurred. He'd let his mother down. She'd needed him, and he wasn't around. He'd been hiding in the woods. She'd needed him, and he'd been too scared to go inside the burning house to save her. She'd needed him, and he'd let her die.

Coward, the demon mocked again.

"No!" *Never again.* He'd never walk away, never let someone get hurt or die because of his cowardice again.

Adrenaline shot through him, firing his determination not to fail. *Never again.*

Despite the towel, smoke filled his lungs, choking him. The heat pounded him with wave after scorching wave. Still he inched his way to the top of the stairs then down the hall, listening, fumbling through the darkness. When he reached the last door, he heard a peep like a kitten mewing. He scrambled into the room, energized by hope.

"Sara!" The effort to talk reduced him to a fit of coughing. He crawled quickly to the outside wall and found the bedroom window. Standing long enough to open the window, Reyn poked his head out and gasped for a deep breath. The smoke filling the room rolled out the opening and cleared the air inside somewhat. No much, but every little bit counted.

Then he heard the whimper again and groped in front of him until he reached a bed. Lifting the edge of the dust ruffle, he peeked through the thick smoke under the bed.

Sure enough, a small girl lay curled in the fetal position, hugging a stuffed animal.

"I'm gonna get you out, Sara. You're gonna be okay," he said hoarsely and coughed again.

The girl didn't respond.

Grabbing her ankle, he dragged the child's limp body from under the bed. Reyn knew how quickly the deadly gases from a house fire could kill an adult. And Sara was half the size of an adult. He had to get her out quickly. Get himself out.

Draping the girl over his back, he crawled back toward the bedroom door. Impeded by the weight of the girl and the thickening smoke, he struggled down the hall. His lungs ached for air. His towel had lost most of its effectiveness as a filter, but he didn't dare drop the only protection he had from the deadly smoke.

Reaching the top of the stairs, he gazed down to the first floor. His gut twisted. Just as he'd feared, fire blocked his escape through the front door.

They were trapped upstairs.

The distant wail of a siren seeped through Olivia's concentrated attention on the front door of the Russells' house. Reyn had been inside a long time. At least it seemed like a long time. It seemed an eternity.

Worry clawed at her, and she could hear the pounding of her heartbeat in her ears.

When the fire engine pulled in the long drive to the farmhouse, George Russell was the first to scramble off. He ran to Hannah who told him through her tears that their daughter was in the house.

As Hank ran past Olivia with the long hose from the pumper truck, Olivia jumped up and followed him. "Hank, Reyn's in there! He went in the front to find Sara."

Hank spun to face her.

"Reyn and Sara are in *that*?" His tone told her how serious he judged the situation.

Olivia swallowed the knot in her throat and nodded.

Hank bit out a vile curse and continued toward the house.

Once in place with his hose, he sprayed inside the front door. After a minute or two, he dropped his hose and rushed forward. "Holy cow!"

Then Olivia saw him, and her breath stilled. Stepping out of the clouds of smoke. Emerging from the front door with Sara's limp body in his arms. Walking out of the burning house like a Phoenix rising from the ashes. A conquering hero returning from battle.

Relief raced through her, so sweet it brought tears to her eyes. Hank took Sara from Reyn and ran with the girl toward the two ambulances just now bumping up the driveway.

Reyn took a few more steps, stumbled and fell to his knees. A paroxysm of coughing seized him, and he clutched his chest. Olivia flew to him, anxiety squeezing her own lungs. "Reyn!"

He raised his head to look at her. His eyes were red and tearing—from the smoke, she knew, though her own eyes watered for a completely different reason. Sweat rolled off him in streams, leaving tracks in the soot that smudged his face and blackened his clothes.

She'd never seen a handsomer man in her life.

"You did it." She dropped to her knees in front of him, swiped at the sweat on his brow with her fingers. "You got her out."

His gaze shifted to the activity behind her, where the paramedics were tending to Sara. Closing his eyes, he took a couple deep breaths then coughed again.

Frank Johnson, one of the paramedics, pushed her aside. "Come on, man. Let's get you some oxygen."

Frank helped Reyn to his feet, and Reyn stumbled toward the end of the second ambulance where an oxygen tank waited for him.

"Out of the way, Olivia," Charlie Smith shouted.

She sidestepped as more hoses were brought out to douse

the fire.

What if Reyn and Sara hadn't made it out of the house? What if— She shuddered and didn't finish the thought.

The ambulance bearing the Russells' little girl bumped down the dirt driveway, headed for the hospital, and Hannah stumbled numbly toward the house. Olivia squeezed her eyes shut for a moment. *Please, let Sara be all right.*

She met Hannah halfway and pulled the sobbing woman into her arms. "Let me drive you to the hospital. You're too upset to be behind the wheel, and I'm just in the way here."

Hannah nodded. "Please."

Glancing to the end of the second ambulance, Olivia spotted Reyn, wearing an oxygen mask, while Frank dabbed some type of ointment on Reyn's ears. She took a deep breath and shivered in the aftermath of the nerve-splitting tension. Waiting for Reyn to come out of the burning house had wrung her out. But he'd done what he set out to do. He'd saved Sara's life.

As she ushered Hannah to Reyn's truck, she recalled his agitation over seeing his calendar picture at Lila's. *I'm just doing my job...that doesn't make me a hero.*

Olivia climbed onto the front seat, and a smile ghosted across her lips. "It sure makes you a hero in my book."

With a weight in his chest that had nothing to do with smoke inhalation, Reyn stared at the smoldering house. The team of volunteer firefighters nearly had the fire under control, and according to recent word relayed to the paramedics from the hospital, the little girl would be all right after a couple days. Still, an uneasy feeling deep in his gut wouldn't allow him any peace. The fire brought back too many memories.

"You sure you won't let me take you in to be checked out?" The EMT with "Frank" on his breast pocket propped a clipboard on his hip.

Still sitting on the back end of the ambulance, Reyn nodded and removed the oxygen mask in order to speak. "I'm okay. Just give me a couple more drags on the good stuff before you take it away, huh?"

"Sure, take your time. I need you to sign here, saying you refused to go to the hospital with us."

Reyn took the clipboard and pen from Frank.

Surprised at how his hand shook when he tried to write, Reyn signed the form and handed the papers back.

"Put another dab of ointment on those burns this afternoon and tonight, and I think you'll be good to go tomorrow." Frank took a small tube from his pocket and held it out to Reyn.

"Thanks."

Behind Frank, he spotted Olivia, stepping out of his truck. She'd left about twenty minutes earlier with the little girl's mother, but now she trotted across the lawn to him, her expression a combination of worry, relief and admiration.

When she reached the ambulance, she simply stared at him for several seconds. Taking his chin in her hand, she turned his head to examine the burns on his ears then scanned the length of his body as if satisfying herself he was in one piece.

Distress darkened her eyes to the color of good bourbon. Her concern flowed through him like the burn of whiskey as it washed down, spreading warm fingers through his blood. Despite the intoxicating effect of her penetrating gaze, his gut still rebelled. Her worry was a barometer of her growing attraction and attachment to him. The hell of it was the feeling was mutual.

Yet nothing about his situation had changed. He still couldn't get involved with her, still couldn't live up to the hopes and expectations he saw lighting her eyes. He still feared he'd hurt her if she got too close. His track record spoke for itself.

Olivia took a step closer, moving into the V of his splayed legs and grabbing the front of his shirt with her fingers. "You scared the hell out of me."

He held her watery gaze and nodded. "Sorry." Through the oxygen mask, the word sounded muffled.

Shaking her head, she gave him a short laugh. "I'm not. You saved Sara's life."

Uncomfortable with the direction of the conversation, he averted his gaze.

Olivia worked her fingers through his hair to grasp the elastic strings that held the mask in place then carefully slipped it from his head.

Curious about her intent, he raised his head again with a querying look. Her gold gaze collided with his, shooting off sparks. She glided in smoothly and pressed her lips to his, the soft warmth of her mouth rocking him to his core. He couldn't have pulled away to save his life. After battling the demon, after reliving the moment he'd spent his adult life running from, he needed this, needed the balm her kiss gave his soul.

Sinking his fingers into her silky hair, he anchored her head, ensuring that she didn't escape before he'd had his fill of her sweetness. Her blazing tresses gently abraded the singed backs of his hands, but the discomfort was of minor concern compared to the velvet crush of her mouth against his. With the tip of his tongue, he traced her lips, and with a sigh, she opened to receive him. She held his cheeks and deepened the kiss, drawing as eagerly on his lips as he did hers. The honeyed taste of her mouth fed the hunger inside him, stoked the desire that flashed through his blood.

He could have gone on kissing her forever and never tired, never had enough. But his lungs seized, and he pulled away abruptly when another bout of coughing racked his body. When the cough quieted, she placed the mask over his mouth and nose again. He met her eyes as he sucked in deep breaths of the pure air.

Her lips curled into her tempting, lopsided grin, and her eyes glowed with a new warmth. "Wow. Not every day a girl gets to kiss a real live hero."

His gut wrenched. Denials sprang to his lips. But when tried to speak, his throat closed, and he started coughing again.

"Are you okay?" She rubbed his back as he fought the spasms in his lungs and caught his breath.

Lifting his arm, he twisted away from her touch and shook his head. "Don't call me that," he rasped.

"What?" She tried again to touch him, and he caught her wrist.

To be sure she heard him, he pulled the oxygen mask down again. "I'm no hero."

Her wry laugh expressed her disbelief and disagreement. "Are you kidding? You saved that girl's life. I'd say that makes you hero material."

He drew slow, deep breaths into lungs made tighter by the frustration and doubts that plagued him. "I'm a fireman. I was just doing my job."

"You're not a fireman in Clairmont. What you did went beyond the call of duty."

He shook his head and drilled a hard gaze into her. "That's not how it works. My responsibility doesn't have geographic boundaries. It was my duty to at least try to get the kid out of there."

She raised her hands in surrender. "All right, whatever your reasons or the responsibility you felt, the fact is, you did it. You risked your life to save that little girl. That makes you a hero to Sara, to her mother. And to me."

He sighed and hung his head, suddenly exhausted from coughing, from the adrenaline crash, from battling the knot of emotions he couldn't put into words. "Is that what the kiss was about? Some kind of misplaced hero worship?"

She scoffed and braced her hands on her hips. "I kissed you because I wanted to. Because I've wanted to since you got into town." She paused, tipping her head. "Why did you kiss me back?"

His gaze clashed with hers, and he prayed she couldn't see the truth in his eyes. He'd kissed her because he'd needed the solace she offered him, the sweet reprieve from the torment inside him. Because he wanted her more than he had any right. Because her sexy lips proved a greater temptation than he'd had the strength to fight. "Because I wasn't thinking straight. It didn't mean anything."

He'd wounded her. He saw the pain flicker in her eyes, and his own heart twisted. But it was better to put her false ideas about him to rest before she got in deeper, before he had a chance to hurt her worse.

She lifted her chin and said nothing for a long moment while her gaze searched his. "Liar," she said finally. "You kissed me because you feel the same thing happening between us that I feel. You know there's something kinetic between us, a chemistry you want to explore as much as I do."

"Maybe. Just don't mistake lust for something nobler." Turning from her incisive scrutiny, he put the oxygen mask back over his nose and inhaled slowly.

Before she could answer, Vance Horton and George Russell walked past, stripping off their turnout gear.

"I think the answer is obvious," Horton told Russell and cast a meaningful glance toward Reyn. "I don't think it's any coincidence this happened right after *he* showed up in town."

Russell turned a dark glare toward Reyn as well.

Reyn bristled. "I had nothing to do with this."

"We'll see about that," Russell returned.

Olivia faced the men with her arms crossed over her chest. "Have you lost your minds? How dare you suggest Reyn set this fire! He saved your daughter's life."

"Maybe he's the one who put her at risk to start with," Horton returned. "Certainly wouldn't be the first time he started a fire like this. Before you go defending the boy, ask around about his history in this town. The truth might surprise you."

Before Olivia could respond, the two men stalked to the pumper rig at the end of the driveway. Reyn tossed the oxygen mask aside and stood, tension coiled tightly inside him. "I asked you not to do that."

"What did I do?" Her brow knit in confusion.

"You were defending me. I fight my own battles, thank you." His movements stiff, he marched toward his truck and heard the thud of her footsteps as she jogged after him.

"Reyn? Reyn, wait."

But he didn't wait. He needed time alone. Time to think. Time to get the taste of Olivia's kiss out of his mind so he could focus on the investigation into his mother's death.

And then get the hell out of this town.

Chapter Seven

Olivia knew they weren't going to Baton Rouge to get the coroner's report as planned. Reyn needed time to recover from the smoke he'd inhaled at the fire that morning. Anticipating the need to take time off later in the week for the trip, she worked that afternoon until almost time to head to Monroe for her classes.

When she did leave work, though, she headed first toward the hospital to see Lila and Sara. From there, she planned to swing by Lila's house to check on Reyn before heading out of town.

The new crack in her windshield created a lonely whistling sound as she drove through town, adding to the sense of disquiet that had plagued her since the fire. She knew the source of her unrest. Reyn.

All day she'd thought of his kiss, the dark flavor of smoke and need she'd tasted when he claimed her lips. He could deny all he wanted that it had meant something, but she knew better. Something more profound than simple lust had been behind the fervor of his kiss. He wanted her, but he also needed something elemental from her, something that he seemed to find in her kiss. Something he wasn't ready to admit he needed or was afraid to acknowledge.

And what about her own reaction? Remembering the avid

crush of Reyn's mouth, a hot, tingling sensation crept over her skin. The simple fact that she couldn't stop thinking about kissing Reyn bothered her. Being attracted to him, even acting on that attraction, was one thing. Falling in love with him was another matter all together. Falling in love? Was that what she was doing?

Her fingers tightened on the steering wheel. The idea nettled her. Kissing him had been an emotional response to the fear she'd felt while waiting for him to emerge from the burning house. She knew where acting on her emotions would lead her. She'd been down that thorny path before. And based on Reyn's prickly response to her kiss, she couldn't ignore the fact her emotions were unwanted. She had to rein in her heart before it got away from her and ended up getting trampled. She had no use for another broken heart.

Olivia pulled into the hospital parking lot and scanned the area for an empty space. After cutting her ignition, she sat and stared out her cracked windshield for a moment, lost in thought.

Naturally, she wanted to fall in love, then get married and raise a family some day. *Some day.* But she had time to wait for the right man. Someone she could build a future with, share her heart with. After her disastrous relationship with Billy Russell, she set high standards for the man to whom she'd give her heart. She sensed his eagerness to leave Clairmont as soon as he could.

Heaving a deep sigh, satisfied for the moment that the issue was settled, she climbed out of the car and headed inside.

Clairmont has never been my home...even when I lived here.

Reyn's comment, made the first time they'd come to the hospital together, reverberated in her head with new clarity. At the time, she'd believed his comment held a note of wistful longing. Now, as she rode the elevator to the pediatric floor, she considered his words and the yearning she sensed in his kiss in a different light.

Could the *something* he longed for be the home and family he denied himself because of whatever ghosts still haunted him about his mother's death? Was it possible that by breaking through the defensive walls he'd erected, by helping him put the ghosts of his past to rest, she'd find a man who wanted to build a home and raise a family like she did?

The questions shook her to the core, and she was still reeling from the possibility, when a familiar male voice wafted into the hall from Sara Russell's room.

She paused outside the door and listened.

"Well, I'm glad to see you're doing better. I know you're looking forward to getting outta here so you can go swimming again."

Reyn.

Her stomach did a little flip flop hearing his voice, still gritty from the smoke.

Olivia knocked then opened the door a few inches. "Hello?"

She peered around the corner and spotted Reyn at Sara's bedside. The mere sight of him, ruffling Sara's hair, caused a riot of emotions inside her. Witnessing this caring, thoughtful side of the man who'd risked his life this morning filled her chest with a tender ache.

Oh, yes, he was definitely a hero in her book. The best kind. The kind that cared.

Hannah hovered close behind Reyn, and she waved Olivia into the room. "Look, darling, Miss Olivia came to see you too."

Sara and Reyn both glanced toward her. Sara, her face pale and a nasal cannula running to her nose, lifted a bright smile.

But Reyn's expression darkened. His gaze focused on Olivia's lips, and something bright and hot flickered in his eyes before he met her gaze. He scorched her with the penetrating intensity of his stare, and she knew he was remembering their kiss. Like she had been all day.

With effort, she shook herself from his spell and smiled at Hannah. "I...I just wanted to check on Sara before I headed to class."

"She's doing much better. Doc Humphry says she can go home tomorrow." Hannah frowned. "Though for the time being, home is the Motel 6."

"Let me know if I can do anything to help." Olivia stepped farther in the room then faced Sara. "Katy can't wait for you to come and play Barbie with her one day soon."

Reyn cleared his throat. "Well, it looks like you're in good hands. I'm going to slip out. I promised Gram I'd play cards with her."

She wanted a moment alone with Reyn but knew it would have to wait. Hannah hugged him as he walked out, and he gave Sara a little wave. He didn't look at Olivia before making a quick retreat. His avoidance raised new questions in her mind. Was he regretting their kiss?

She found him again in Lila's room a few minutes later, and he treated Olivia to the same silent treatment.

Olivia exchanged pleasantries with Lila and saw worry flicker in the older woman's eyes each time Reyn coughed.

"Are you catching a cold, darling?"

He hesitated, shot Olivia a silent warning not to say anything, and nodded. "I guess so. I'll be all right."

"Maybe you should go home and get some rest," Olivia said.

He turned his attention to Olivia, and the heat returned to

his eyes. He stared for a moment then abruptly turned away, his jaw clenched tight. Yes, he wanted her. But something kept him from acting on his desire.

A new thought occurred to Olivia. Perhaps pursuing the chemistry between them, starting an affair with Reyn, was the way to lower his defenses. Perhaps getting close to him physically would help knock down some of the walls he kept between them. Lord knows she wanted to try. But what if it didn't work? Could she give her body to Reyn without losing her heart?

"I think Olivia is right, dear. You look tired."

"Gee thanks, Gram. You sure know how to flatter a guy." He twitched his lips wryly at Lila and glanced back at Olivia again. He obviously didn't want Gram to know what he'd done, how he'd saved Sara. But why? Because he didn't want to upset her? Or because he didn't consider his deed worthy of the praise Lila would give him? Maybe both.

"Actually, I need to scoot too. I'm going to be late for my chemistry lab if I don't hustle."

"No speeding, Liv," Gram warned.

"Are you kidding? My bucket of bolts is lucky to reach fifty-five without falling apart." She kissed Lila's cheek, as did Reyn, and they headed out of the hospital together.

Reyn was quiet, avoiding eye contact with her.

Olivia broke the silence as they stepped off the elevator into the lobby. "You know she'll hear about it—the fire and your saving Sara—through the grapevine."

He shot her a sharp look. "Probably."

"Definitely. This is Clairmont. Clairmont is an old Indian word meaning, 'there are no secrets in this town'."

He gave her a nod of agreement. "Thanks just the same.

For not telling her. She doesn't need anything else to worry about."

"You can't protect her from the news forever. And I know she'd rather hear it from you than a gossip."

Frowning, he rubbed a hand along his stubbled jaw and remained silent until they reached her car. He looked at the crack in her windshield and then at her. "Drive carefully."

Without another word, he stalked across the lot toward his truck.

Reyn picked Olivia up at the pharmacy mid-morning on Thursday to make their postponed trip to Baton Rouge. He didn't want to think about what the autopsy report might reveal and tried to keep a personal detachment from the task. Thinking of the information in the coroner's report in light of his mother's death simply hurt too much. He was just on a business errand, taking care of an unpleasant detail.

Blinking away the blur of fatigue, he struggled to focus on the road and not the floral scent of Olivia's perfume. He'd already wasted too much time thinking about her. He couldn't have her and had no right wanting her when he had nothing to give her but heartache.

He sighed and pinched his eyes. Plagued by thoughts of Olivia's kiss and the Russells' house fire, he'd spent a restless night pacing Gram's guest room. Already accusations were being bandied about regarding his involvement in starting the Russells' fire, despite Hannah's admission of leaving a pan of grease on the stove while she hung out the laundry. By two a.m., he'd finally given up hope of sleep and put his time to good use, shoring up the steps of Gram's front porch.

Lack of sleep and lingering effects of the smoke left his eyes feeling gritty. He could draw a deep breath without coughing now, but his throat was still a bit raw. Not that he cared. Sara Russell was alive, and that was all that mattered.

"Have you heard anything yet from the sheriff about the fingerprint tests on the note?" he asked Olivia, who, judging from the dark circles under her eyes, hadn't slept much either.

"No. Nothing. He said it could take a little while, since they sent the prints to Shreveport to run through the national database, and since it wasn't as high a priority as a murder or rape case. Maybe later today though."

The wrinkle of her brow told him she wasn't eager to learn which trusted member of the community had betrayed her faith. He could have told her that Clairmont harbored all kinds of ill will and deceit, but he still hated to see her illusions shattered. Her optimism and love for her home were a refreshing change from the cynicism and doubt he most often encountered. Even from himself. Especially from himself.

"I know this is difficult for you," she said as if reading his thoughts.

"I'm all right," he lied.

"If you want me to look at the report first, to spare you the details of—"

"Can we talk about something else?" He realized from the sympathetic knit in her brow that his gruffness said everything he'd just denied. He huffed and pinched the bridge of his nose.

"Okay. How about you tell me what happened when you were a kid? How did you get such a bad reputation?" she asked.

"I earned it."

"How?"

He gritted his teeth. Next to his mother's death, his youthful mistakes were his second least favorite topic.

"I have a better idea. Let's not talk at all." He snapped on the radio to emphasize his request.

"Why does it bother you to talk about your childhood? It's over and done. You're not that kid anymore. Everyone does things that they aren't proud of," she persisted over the wail of Bon Jovi's guitars.

"But the things I did hurt people. I let people down." He cursed. He hadn't meant to say even that much. Why was it she could draw him out this way?

He squeezed the steering wheel tighter and turned to watch a crow peck a dead animal on the side of the road as they drove past. He knew how that animal felt. Talking about his childhood was like having his heart and soul slowly pecked away, drawn from him one painful bit at a time.

"Tell me about the fire that burned the Russells' barn. What really happened?"

"I ruined a man's livelihood and destroyed a large portion of his property. I don't blame George Russell for hating me. It was a stupid and careless mistake that hurt his income and his family." Bitterness colored his tone.

"But it was an accident."

Leave it to Olivia to try to twist the truth and look for the escape hatch for him. But he couldn't evade his responsibility for what had happened.

"It was reckless. I can't brush it off as simply a mistake." He thought back to the feeling of horror and guilt that had slammed down on him when he realized the small flame he'd been experimenting with had gotten away from him.

"But if you didn't mean to set the fire, then it wasn't arson. It was an accident."

Damn, she could be persistent.

Billy Russell, who'd been with him when the fire started,

had never claimed any part of the blame. Not that he should. He, not Billy, had brought the matches out to the barn. He, not Billy, had knocked the coffee can over when he burned his finger. He'd struck the match, lit the candle, disobeyed his mother's warning about playing with fire.

His curiosity and fascination with fire were to blame.

His carelessness. His irresponsibility. His disobedience.

Guilt and self-reproach as fresh and painful as that day when he was nine sliced through Reyn.

"Call it what you want. I did it, and I'm not looking to shirk my responsibility for it. Besides, I set other fires on purpose. They had reason to think the barn fire was intentional."

"What other fires?"

"Can we drop this?"

"I'll ask Lila if you don't tell me."

He sent her a sharp, warning glance. "You leave Lila out of this. It's none of your business what happened."

"It's my business if it will help find the person who left a death threat on my windshield."

"You should have never opened this whole can of worms to start with." Accusation hardened the tone of his voice, and he cringed inwardly. He didn't mean to take his frustration out on her. Why did he keep doing it?

"I should have ignored what I found in my father's files? Just ignore the fact that your mother could have been murdered and her murderer is still walking around a free man?"

His gut twisted, and he growled an earthy obscenity. "No. Hell, I don't know. This is all such a mess. I hate this."

"I know. But I'm in this with you for better or worse. I want to help. I want to make this easier for you. Talk to me, Reyn.

125

You need to talk about what happened. Keeping it inside is eating you up."

He dared to look over at her, despite the voice in his head cautioning against it. The tender expression in her eyes wound around his heart like a hug. He wanted to talk to her, wanted to unburden his soul. He wanted the peace that he'd found for too brief a time when he'd kissed her. He wanted to believe that telling her everything that haunted him would give him that peace. But he also knew the risk of doing so was far too high. For her. For himself.

He couldn't become emotionally attached to her, intimately involved, spiritually connected. The people he cared about were the people he hurt the most. Those were the relationships that hurt him most. He couldn't risk the pain. For either of them.

With a sigh he turned away. "I can't talk about it."

"No, you *won't* talk about it. There's a difference." Despite the chastisement in her words, her tone remained gentle. Thankfully she dropped the subject after that, and within a few minutes, they reached the outskirts of Baton Rouge.

Discussion shifted to the business at hand and finding the parish coroner's office. After locating the right room, filling out the proper forms, and showing his birth certificate to prove his relationship to the deceased, Reyn finally got a copy of the report on his mother's autopsy.

He began scanning the pages of the report as they walked back out to his truck. He skimmed over the opening lines with his mother's name, last known address and place of death then started reading about the coroner's external observations of her body, the degree and percentage of her body that was burned.

"Mama, where are you?" He looked for her in the living room, but all he saw was black. Smoke. So much smoke. Mama had to be in there somewhere. But the fire was so hot. "Mama!"

An unexpected wave of nausea washed through him, made his knees buckle. He stopped walking and braced a hand on the corridor wall, sucking in a restorative breath.

"Reyn?" Concern filled Olivia's voice, and she put a cool hand on his arm. He wanted to lose himself in her comforting touch. If only...

"I'm okay." He heard a strange ruffling sound and realized it was the papers he held. His hand shook hard enough to rattle the pages. *Oh God, I don't want to do this.*

Olivia pried the report from his fingers, and he didn't protest.

"Do you want to sit down somewhere to read this?"

He cleared his throat and forced his legs to work. He shoved his trembling hands in his pockets and headed for the door. "No, let's just go to the truck."

When he opened the driver's door of his Sierra, the built-up heat rolled out in a shimmering wave, slamming into him with brute force. He dropped onto the seat and cranked the engine, waiting for the air conditioning to move the stifling air in the cab.

Olivia sat beside him reading. She tucked sweat-dampened wisps of her fiery hair behind her ear as she bent over the report. Despite his earlier arguments against it, he was glad she'd come with him. Without her there, he might have reached total meltdown. No wonder Gram was so taken by her. Olivia had a strength and composure about her that she generously gave to others. He admired her grace under fire, her willingness to put others' needs before her own. If he wasn't careful, she was just the type of woman who could get under his skin.

Olivia winced and shook her head, and Reyn tensed.

"What does it say?" he asked woodenly.

"It talks about the walls of her lungs being singed. The evidence of smoke inhalation."

He nodded and tried not to think about his mother's last breaths. But other images came instead.

He had to find Mama. Had to get her out. But it was so hot. The fire crept closer, licking at him with its forked tongue. "I dare you, Reyn. Come in if you dare." He felt his skin blister. He couldn't breathe. Couldn't call for her anymore. Mama! Panic and fear clawed at him. He couldn't go any farther. He had to get out. "Coward," the demon-fire cackled.

Sweat beaded on his upper lip, and he fought to calm his ragged breathing. A fist of agony and regret squeezed his chest, and his eyes stung as they had that day twenty years before.

"I'll spare you the details of her stomach contents and the condition of her other organs. Nothing odd there that I see."

He'd forgotten Olivia was there until she spoke. He jerked his gaze toward her, swiping at his eyes.

"You don't see anything unusual?" His voice sounded hoarse, and he coughed, hoping she'd believe his rasp was a remnant of smoke he'd breathed Tuesday. "Don't you see anything that would have raised your father's suspicions?"

"Not yet, but I haven't finished reading." She wet her lips and tipped her head. "Are you okay?"

She reached for his cheek, and he batted her hand away, scowling.

"Just read." He turned toward the side window and pushed his memories back in the far corners of his mind.

Damn it, he would never forgive himself for turning around and running from that house. He'd left his mother to die. When she needed him most, he'd turned coward. He'd failed her in the worst possible way. The last disappointment in his history of letting her down. She'd been the best mother a boy could ask for, and she'd deserved a better son.

"Wait a minute."

He cast a glance to Olivia whose brows furrowed as she read the autopsy report. Reyn's pulse kicked up. "What?"

Her eyes darted up to meet his. "I think I found what my dad was suspicious of."

"Yeah, well?" He waved a hand hurrying her. "What is it?"

"She had a hair-line fracture on her skull. A mild concussion. Not enough to kill her, but when it happened she was probably knocked unconscious." She lowered the papers to her lap and leaned her head back, biting her lip.

His stomach swirled as he mulled what the skull fracture could mean.

"She could have been trying to get out of the house and tripped, hit her head," Olivia suggested, but her expression said she didn't buy that explanation.

"No. She was found in her bed. The assumption was she was napping and died in her sleep from smoke inhalation."

"She was in her bed?" Olivia considered this information, fingering the same ladybug pendant she seemed to wear every day. "So she hit her head and went to bed with a headache, not knowing she had a concussion."

"Maybe."

They were both silent for long moments, watching the cars on the street outside the coroner's office.

Olivia scoffed and faced him. "Who are we kidding? You're thinking it, I'm thinking it, my dad obviously was thinking it. Someone hit her. Maybe they thought she was dead, maybe not. But they panicked and set the fire to cover their tracks. Either way, I'd bet my life your mother was murdered."

Reyn was numb. He should feel something, he knew. Satisfaction that their suspicions had been confirmed. Anger for the injustice of his mother's death. Relief that suspicion for starting the fire shifted off him. Something. Yet he was numb. Shock, he supposed. He took a slow breath. "So now we have the evidence that made your father suspicious enough to continue looking into my mother's death. If he suspected someone murdered her, the next question we need to solve is—who would want to kill my mother? And why?"

Chapter Eight

Reyn said little on the return home. His haggard expression told Olivia how difficult the trip had been for him, and she respected his need to think and reflect, to be alone with his memories of his mother. When they got back to Clairmont, she'd worry about distracting him and redirecting his energy in a positive direction. Maybe she'd invite herself to Lila's to cook him dinner. Better yet, she decided, gazing up at the scalding July sun, she'd entice him to go down to the bayou for a swim. Anything to get his mind off the troublesome autopsy report. Just for a while.

She flipped through the papers in her lap again, re-reading the portion of the report that detailed the skull fracture. She frowned. Why had this information been kept from Lila? Just one of many unanswered questions.

Unfolding a sheet from the bottom of the autopsy papers, she scanned the page curiously. Reyn's birth certificate. When she'd wrested the autopsy report from Reyn in the hall of the coroner's office, he'd given her the birth certificate as well, his proof of his relationship to the deceased.

She made note of his birthday, January 11, and recalled helping Lila shop the after-Christmas sales for a shirt to send him for his birthday last year. Then her eyes stopped on the space where his father's name should have been listed. The line read "unknown". Chewing her bottom lip, she glanced over at Reyn and studied his profile with new insight. He'd grown up never knowing who his father was.

She took for granted the love she'd known from her father, even though he'd been snatched prematurely from her life. She wrapped her hand around the ladybug on her necklace and squeezed. The cool metal pendant, a reminder of all her parents had instilled in her, filled her with a sense of warmth and reassurance. Her mother and father had created a safe and stable home for her as a child, grounding her in the importance of family, of roots, of putting loved ones first in her life.

But what kind of home life had Reyn grown up with? He loved his mother. Of that she was certain. But what had it meant to a young boy, growing up with no male role model?

"Did you miss not having a father?" She blurted the question that rose to mind before she could catch herself.

He turned a startled glance her way, then noticed the certificate in her hand. Frowning, he returned his gaze to the road. He took so long to answer, she'd almost decided he wasn't going to when he mumbled, "Can't miss something you've never known."

"But there had to be days when you wished you had someone to throw a ball with you, or take you fishing. Do guy stuff with."

He shrugged. "My mom threw a ball with me. I went fishing with my friends."

She hummed her acknowledgment.

His piercing gray gaze shifted back to her. "I wanted a dad sometimes for Mom's sake though. She seemed so lonely some days. Kinda sad."

She held his gaze for a moment, and she saw in his chiseled face the same isolation and melancholy. She reached for him, aching to break through the walls he used to keep himself set apart, distant. She smoothed her fingers over his hair, kneaded the tight muscles in his neck. Though he didn't pull away, neither did he show any reaction to her touch. He held himself stiff and apart, his expression closed. Except for the pain that swirled in his eyes like the morning fog.

He needed the same love and companionship he'd wished for his mother, yet he denied himself that very intimacy. She sensed that he'd shut that part of himself away in self-defense. But what was he protecting himself from?

She aimed to find out. Because she cared about him, because he'd cared enough to save Sara Russell, because someone who risked his life for others deserved to be happy. Whatever it took, she would save Reyn from his self-imposed prison.

When he dropped her off at her house, she handed him the autopsy report and birth certificate then caught his wrist before he pulled away. He raised his head with a querying look.

"Meet me by the bayou at the boat dock in ten minutes."

He arched an eyebrow. "Why?"

"I want to show you something."

Eyeing her suspiciously, he nodded. "Ten minutes."

Nine minutes later, her feet thudded down the worn wooden planks of the boat dock. The quiet inlet of the bayou was nestled half a mile through the woods between her house and Lila's. Reyn was already there, and the hollow clump of her footsteps drew his attention from the murky water. For as long as she could remember, the dock had been a private escape, a secluded spot where she could think or relax or sunbathe topless if she felt like it. Who would see her except the dragonflies and minnows?

"Hey." She sat beside him, drawing her legs to her chest.

"So what'd you want to show me?"

"Just this. All of this." She motioned with her hand to the lush pines, the knobby cypresses wading in the still, green-brown water, the hazy summer sky. "My private retreat. I figured you might need a peaceful place like this to do some thinking while you're here."

A corner of his mouth curled up, and he angled his face toward her. "Darlin', I knew about this place before you were even born. Who do you think built this dock?"

Blinking her surprise, Olivia laughed. "You're kidding."

"Nope. Technically this is Gram's property. I built this dock with my grandpa the summer before he died. I came here as a kid to feel close to him. And to fish." His expression turned sly. "And to spy."

She chewed slowly on the piece of cinnamon gum she'd gotten at the house and cocked her head. "Spy?"

He aimed a finger across the water to the far shore. "You see that house?"

"Yeah? That's the Hortons'." She didn't need to look to know the white house he meant, so far away it looked like a miniature dollhouse.

"Well..." Reyn's gaze dropped to her mouth where she blew a bubble with her gum and bit down to pop it. "I discovered as a kid that with a pair of binoculars, I could watch Principal Horton and his wife when they were in their backyard or if they stood in front of the glass sliding door to their family room."

She gaped at him slack-jawed. "You little fink."

He shrugged. "I told you I earned my bad reputation. I didn't watch often, though. Mostly all he and his wife did was fight. I did catch their daughter making out with her boyfriend once. That made quite a show."

She almost swallowed her gum. Instead she swatted at his arm. "Did Lila know what you were up to down here?"

"Doubt it. That was the point. It was my special private place."

"And then it became mine. Funny, huh?"

He met her eyes and something electric crackled in the air between them, something beyond a shared hideout.

When his gaze dropped to her chest and he reached toward her, a tingle of anticipation spun through her. His warm fingers grazed her skin as he lifted the ladybug from the hollow of her throat. She could feel her pulse beating wildly, like hummingbird wings, while he studied the pendant. The back of his hand skimmed her sensitive skin, and she longed to feel his hands all over her bare skin, stroking her.

"Is there a story here?" He nodded toward the pendant.

"My father gave it to me. He used to call me ladybug. Because of my red hair and spots."

"Spots?"

"That's what he called my freckles. Thank God most of them have faded."

He studied her nose and cheeks with a heavy-lidded gaze. "I kinda like your spots. They're sexy."

Her breath hitched. Slowly she tugged her lips up in appreciation. "Thanks."

His attention went to her mouth. The message in his smoky eyes was obvious. He wanted to kiss her. God, she'd do about anything for another one of his mind-blowing kisses. She returned his scrutiny, remembering how his lips had seared hers, branding her as his own.

He swallowed hard as he looked away, his body tense, and she watched the movement of muscles in his strong throat. He propped his arms on his knees as he stared out across the water, pulling the fabric of his shirt taut across his wide back and shoulders.

When he swiped at a bug buzzing by his long legs, she savored the athletic tone and the crinkly dark hairs on his calves. Kicking off her sandals, she crossed her own legs and ran a toe over the curve of his taut leg muscle, enjoying the tickle of the dark hair near his ankle. "Wanna show me what Horton's daughter was doing with her boyfriend?"

His gaze collided with hers, and his eyes grew dark with desire. "I could."

Her heart hammered an apprehensive rhythm, and her nerve endings hummed with expectation.

He blew out a harsh breath. "But I won't."

The jangle of welling excitement fizzled, but not her hope. She knew Reyn wanted her as much as she wanted him. And if she could melt his resistance, she'd have crossed an important hurtle toward breaking through his defenses, earning his trust and his confidence. She wanted an emotional connection as much as, maybe more than, she wanted the physical intimacy. Knowing who he was deep inside was what mattered to her, what she'd lacked with Billy, what she owed her heart before she could let herself fall in love. But that was what Reyn seemed so determined to withhold. Himself, his heart, his soul. *One step at a time.*

One day at a time. He'd convinced himself he could resist the tempting beauty if he took each day as it came. If he mustered the willpower it took to resist her as he encountered each temptation to indulge, he'd be all right. Now he wondered if one minute, one second at a time weren't more apt.

He knew what she was up to. She wanted to seduce him,

despite his warnings of what she would be risking. The woman was persistent. She was wearing him down, and he felt ready to snap with all the sexual tension stringing him tight.

"Geez, I'm melting." Olivia raked her fingers through her hair and caught the thick waves into a ponytail. She held the hair off her neck and fanned herself with her other hand.

He watched a drop of sweat trickle down the slim column of her neck to her back. Her skin glistened, and he knew if he gave in to the urge to nibble the curve of her throat, he'd taste her salty perspiration mixed with the honeyed sweetness of her skin. He'd been craving, and denying himself, a sample of her skin for days now. The enticing view of her neck, of her pulse fluttering in the dip near her chin, tested his willpower.

"We could always go up to the house." The sun and humidity sapped his energy. And watching her perspire heated him from the inside, reminded him of ways to get sweaty that didn't involve scorching sun and oppressive humidity.

"Maybe." She let her hair fall back into place and climbed to her feet. "What I'd really like to do is go for a swim."

She rolled her red chewing gum between her teeth as she eyed the water speculatively.

He considered the idea and shrugged. "I'm game. Get your swimsuit and meet me back here in a few minutes."

Pushing himself up from the dock, he dusted off the seat of his shorts. He stooped to pick up his tennis shoes and straightened in time to see Olivia whip her T-shirt over her head. His breath caught in his lungs.

"What are you doing?"

She began unfastening her shorts. "Who needs a swimming suit? I usually just swim in my skivvies."

Today, her panties were pale pink and matched the lacy

bra hugging her breasts. The sunlight kissed the ripe curves of her womanly body, and her ivory skin glowed in the bright yellow beams. His response came instantly, his body humming with a carnal hunger.

"Are you with me?" She flashed him a devilish grin and stepped out of her shorts. "Come on, hot stuff. I dare you."

He arched an eyebrow, and adrenaline shot through him. "You *dare* me?"

He looked toward the line of trees, muttering a curse. How did she know just the right buttons to push? He'd never walked away from a dare in his life, even when he knew caution was the better choice. His private battle with the demon drove him to push the envelope, to test his limits and never again let cowardice or doubts keep him from acting. *Never again.*

She stepped to the edge of the dock and gracefully dove in. When she emerged, she whooped. "Oh, man, it feels great. Get the lead out, fireman. I thought you guys knew how to hustle."

He yanked off his shirt, battling down the stream of reasons why this wasn't a good idea. He was tempting fate, risking a scandal that could hurt Gram if they were discovered, testing his own ability to keep his hands off her. Olivia swam over to the wood plank ladder nailed to the end of the dock and climbed out. The wet fabric of her bra and panties left little to his imagination. The thick ridge at his fly left little to her imagination concerning how she affected him.

She stepped close and grasped the button of his shorts. "Need some help?"

He cleared his throat and put a hand on each of her arms to push her away. "This is a bad idea, Olivia. I'm trying to be a gentleman around you, but you're making it very hard."

Her eyes sparkled with mischief, and she stroked a hand over his erection. "So I see."

His breath hissed through his teeth, and he struggled to maintain a steely control over his body. "Don't do that."

"Why not? It's obvious you want me, and I want you. So what's the problem?"

"I don't want you to get hurt." He removed her hands from his shorts and stepped away.

She scowled at him, bracing her hands on her hips while water dripped off her in thin rivulets. "I'm a big girl, Reyn. I can take care of myself."

The dusky pink tips of her breasts and the dark patch at the top of her thighs showed through her wet bra and panties.

He averted his gaze, forcing himself to rein in his lust. "I can't give you any promises beyond right now. I'm not in this for anything long term."

"Did I ask for anything long term?"

"I just don't want to let you down...have you expecting something from me I can't give," he said, as much to remind himself as for her benefit.

"As much as I appreciate your candor and integrity, I don't need you to protect me. Just come swim with me. Okay?" She took his hand and tugged him toward the end of the dock.

"You know swimming's not all we'll do."

"Well, I can hope." She flashed him a wicked grin, wiggled her eyebrows then dove smoothly into the water again.

Reyn groaned. If he hadn't been hot before, he sure was now. Before his conscience could rear its head again, he dropped his shorts and kicked them over by his shoes. Turning toward the murky lake, he thought briefly of the danger of diving into unknown water. He brushed aside the concern, telling himself the water wasn't unknown to Olivia. Following her lead, he dove shallowly for the same spot where she'd entered the lake.

The cool water hitting his heated skin shocked his system and sent an energizing jolt through him. He surfaced and swiped water from his face. Spotting Olivia close by, beaming at him, he swam toward her.

You know swimming's not all we'll do.

Well, I can hope.

As he had when diving into the murky lake, he pushed his doubts to the back of his mind. Olivia knew the risks of tangling with him and hadn't balked. If sex with him was what she wanted, he would follow her lead. He'd warned her it would only be sex.

He stopped in front of her, close enough to see her dark brown eyelashes, spiked by the moisture clinging to them and framing golden eyes that sparkled with a joy for life.

Olivia looped her arms around his neck, and her legs brushed his as she treaded water along with him. "Nice dive. Good form." Her lips tugged to one side. "Nice skivvies, too. I like blue."

She ran her toes over his calf, and sparks of desire shot through him. He pulled her closer, so that her body aligned with his, her breasts grazing his chest. As he treaded water, he stared into her eyes, absorbing like a dry sponge the happiness she radiated. Her spirited nature reached an empty place inside him and filled the cold places in his soul with sunshine. Her optimism and vibrancy were intoxicating, addicting. Something he needed, especially today, especially after reading the autopsy report. God, he needed what Olivia offered. Escape. Solace. A temporary reprieve.

He ran a hand over her back, and the slick silkiness of her skin in the water conjured erotic images in his mind.

"Now isn't this better than staying cooped up inside in the

air conditioning?" She tweaked his earlobe then pulled away to swim the sidestroke toward the dock.

"You know, this bayou is full of snakes and leeches and other slimy creatures."

Olivia laughed. "If you're trying to frighten me, Reyn, it won't work. The snakes don't bother me, and in all the years I've been swimming here, I've never gotten a leech on me." She reached the ladder and turned to face him while she held the top rung. "As far as other slimy creatures go, Billy Russell stayed in Baton Rouge after graduating LSU, so I don't figure he's lurking around here."

Her cattish comment caught him off guard, and he had to laugh as he swam toward her.

"Oh my gosh." Her worried expression caused a flare of panic in his gut.

"What?" He checked behind him to make certain there wasn't a cottonmouth bearing down on him.

"You laughed. You actually laughed."

He caught one of the wood planks of the homemade ladder and pulled up beside her. "Yeah. So?"

She stroked his cheek, her brow knit with concern. "Aren't you afraid of cracking that stony face. Even a smile could do serious damage to your scowling countenance."

He sobered. "My what?"

She dragged a fingernail over his chin. "You heard me."

"Is that what you think? Have I been that bad?" He wrapped his hand around hers and rubbed his thumb along her wrist.

"Worse."

He winced. "Ouch. Well, we have been dealing with some pretty serious stuff. And I'm worried about Gram. But a stony face? That sounds bad. What do you recommend?"

"I think we should give you something to smile about." The husky, suggestive tone of her voice was enough to earn a half smile from him. Plucking her gum out of her mouth, she tossed it in the water with a little *splunk.*

He slid an arm around her waist and hauled her closer. Steadying himself on the ladder with one foot on the bottom rung and an arm looped through the top rung, he cupped a hand on her bottom and pulled her hips against his. Dipping his head, he caught her lips. In return, she anchored his head between her hands to deepen the kiss. He traced his tongue over the seam of her lips, and she invited him inside, meeting his plundering tongue with her own. The satiny surfaces of her mouth proved a feast for his senses. He tasted her cinnamon gum and her eagerness. She tasted sweet, feminine. Forbidden. He lost himself in the heady rush of sensation, indulged in the pleasure of her welcoming lips moving under his.

Sighing, she sank against him, and the crush of her breasts against his chest caused a shudder to race through him. Olivia wrapped her legs around his hips, and even in the cool water, he felt her heat when she rubbed herself along his erection. A groan rumbled from his throat, and his body ached for more. Despite her eagerness, he fought to keep things slow and savor what she offered him.

Gliding his hand over her back, he found the clasp of her bra and worked to unhook it with one hand. After a moment, she reached behind her and finished the task for him. With his heart thundering, he peeled the wet fabric away and tossed the scrap of pink lace on the dock.

With her legs still hooked around his hips, she held his arms and arched her back, offering herself to his view. To his touch. He brushed a finger over the rosy tips of her breasts and watched her nipples bead in response. The sight landed a sucker punch of lust to his gut. He covered one breast with his free hand and squeezed the soft swell then swooped down on the other with his mouth. He sucked her swollen nipple between his teeth and flicked it with his tongue.

She cried out, clutching his arms until her fingernails bit into his skin. Her legs tightened around him, and fire flashed through him. Drawing greedily on her taut nipple, he soon grew impatient with their awkward position and growled his frustration and hunger for her. He pulled her upright slowly, working his lips, his tongue from her breast to her chin. He trailed his fingers over her skin lightly like a lazy dragonfly buzzing over the surface of the water.

"I have to have you. Now," he rumbled in her ear.

"Please," she whispered hoarsely.

Needing no further enticement, he grabbed her under her arms and hoisted her out of the water and onto the dock. She scooted back and stretched out on the sun-baked boards as he climbed up the ladder. Dripping water onto her, he crawled closer until he hovered over her, his knees imprisoning her thighs and his hands on either side of her head. Her eyes met his and burned with a desire that matched the need flaming inside him. She reached for the waistband of his briefs and dragged the wet fabric down his hips. Then she touched him, wrapping her fingers around his heat, and he nearly exploded.

He caught her mouth with his and ravaged her with his kiss. Time and space ceased to exist. All that mattered was Olivia, the feel of her body arching and writhing beneath him, the pounding need to fill her and have her body wrap him in her warmth. He skimmed his hands over her body, hooked her panties with his fingers and pulled them down her legs in one long, swift motion. Olivia's hand roamed over his back and buttocks, testing and squeezing and driving him out of his mind. When their clothes had been discarded, she opened her legs for him, and he nestled against her, groaning in sweet agony.

He stroked her tender skin and found her slick and ready for him. Desire coiled tighter in him, ready to burst, and he sealed her mouth with another deep kiss.

"Please, Reyn. Now." She raised her hips, echoing her words with her body.

He raised his head and peered into her eyes, seeking confirmation, permission—and receiving both. Holding her gaze, he positioned himself and slowly guided the tip of his erection into her. She stretched to accommodate him, her body tight as he tried to slide deeper. And met resistance.

His body screamed for release, and it took all his strength not to drive himself deep and hard. Gently he tried again, and Olivia winced.

Dear God, he was hurting her. As if she were a—

He froze, icy horror splashing him when the truth penetrated his haze of lust. With tense, jerky movements, he pulled away from her and clambered to his feet. Plowing his hands through his hair, he sucked in a steadying breath.

"You're a virgin." His voice was filled with anger and accusation, and she flinched.

"Y-yes."

He sucked in a deep breath, trying to control the tension wringing his body. Damn it, he still wanted her, even knowing what it would cost him. And cost her.

"Why didn't you say something?" he growled.

"I... Why does it matter? What difference does it make to you?" She crossed her arms over her breasts, hugging herself, and drew her legs up close to her body. He saw her shiver, despite the scalding sun, and pain squeezed his chest.

"It matters. It just does." He snatched up his wet underwear, gritting his teeth. His body still throbbed with unfulfilled need, and knowing he could do nothing about it made him madder.

"I don't understand. If I'm willing to—"

"But *I'm* not willing." He continued dressing while Olivia stared at him with wounded eyes. Sucking in a deep breath, he turned to her, trying to organize his thoughts despite the riot of emotions and yearning still battling inside him. "I don't want to be your first. I don't want you to have any emotional connection to me." He sighed and met her querying look with a hard gaze. "A woman's first time is...special. Something she never forgets. I don't want to be special to you. It has to be only sex."

She stared at him silently, her eyes glittering with tears.

He shoved his feet in his shoes and turned toward the woods. The rustle of clothes told him she was finally dressing. He screwed up the nerve to face her again. "Olivia, I'm sorry. This is just how it has to be."

He waited for her to glance up before continuing. He wanted to make sure she understood what he had to say next. "Don't fall in love with me. I'm not what you want or need in your life, and I don't want to hurt you."

She shook her head. A deep V creased her brow over sad eyes. "Why won't you let me in? What are you afraid of?"

His heart slammed against his ribs, and he tensed. "I'm not afraid. But you should be."

Olivia watched Reyn retreat into the woods, her wet clothes chafing her sensitized skin. She quivered with frustration, disappointment and unfulfilled longing. The irony of her situation bubbled from her in a harsh laugh. She finally wanted to give herself to a man, had found a man whom she respected and trusted enough to give her virginity to. And that same honor and nobility stopped him from finishing the act.

Despite her dissatisfaction, she respected Reyn all the more because of his convictions and restraint. She should probably thank him for having more control than she could muster. He was right that she'd attach certain significance to her first sexual experience and hold her first lover in a special regard. Knowing that Reyn would be leaving for Atlanta eventually spun their involvement in a new light. Realizing they'd likely never share the same priority of home and family made it easier to accept his abrupt break in their lovemaking.

But, damn it, her body still craved his touch. She closed her eyes and remembered the sensual feel of his hands and mouth on her skin, her breasts. Her stomach performed a long, slow roll, and shivers of exhilaration spread through her body again. The anticipation of their joining had been sweeter and more urgent than anything she'd ever experienced. If only she could break through his defenses, help him resolve whatever made him feel he would let her down. If only they could...

Disgusted with her pointless wishing, she slapped her hand on the hot wood of the dock and shoved to her feet. She padded down the rough planking toward the shore then gingerly picked her way through the prickly pine straw and grass toward the woods.

She needed to clean up and get ready for class. She needed to stop lusting over Reyn and realize a fling with her favorite fantasy man would be a mistake. He was unlikely to change his mind, and she didn't need to fall for someone who couldn't—wouldn't—commit to her. A few moments of ecstasy was not worth the heartache she was bound to feel when he left. And he would leave. Of that, she was certain.

Following the well-worn path toward her house, she tried to focus on her classes, on the investigation, on anything except the sense of incompleteness for their aborted lovemaking.

The coroner's mention of a skull fracture definitely made Claire's death suspicious. So why hadn't—

The snap of a twig behind her yanked her from her musings.

But before she could turn to see who followed her, a gloved hand clamped over her mouth, another snaking around her waist.

Olivia tried to scream, but the hand smothered her breath. Her captor jerked her backward, and she stumbled. When she fell, the hand slipped off her mouth, and she released a shattering scream. As she was hauled to her feet, she glimpsed a man in hunting camouflage and wearing a black ski mask.

"Shut up," he growled. Again he clamped a hand over her mouth. She wiggled and twisted, trying desperately to free herself. But his unrelenting hold squeezed tighter. Her lungs burned with the need for air. Her vision dimmed, and panic swelled in her chest.

Oh God, I don't want to die!

Chapter Nine

Reyn sat on Gram's front porch steps and raked his fingers through his damp hair. Giving in to Olivia's tempting offer of sex had been foolish and costly. Now he knew what he was missing. Now he knew the satiny feel of her skin and the dizzying sensation of her legs wrapped around him. He knew how her soft moans of pleasure inflamed him and—

A scream rang from the woods and startled a mourning dove from its roost on Gram's clothesline. Alarm prickled the back of his neck.

Curiosity killed the cat.

"Olivia!" He sprang from the porch and sprinted toward the woods. Low-hanging limbs slapped his face and chest. He stumbled twice, tripped by the vines and roots in the path. But he didn't slow his pace. He couldn't.

Instinct told him Olivia's scream didn't mean she'd seen a snake. When he reached the bayou, he staggered to a stop and scanned the surface of the water. He saw nothing, not a ripple, not a flash of color indicating where she might be. Over the thundering of his heart, he heard leaves rustle in the woods.

"Olivia!" He darted into the trees, following the path to her house. "Olivia, answer me!" He squinted in the bright sun that peeked between the branches, occasionally blinding him. Shielding his eyes, he spotted a commotion ahead of him.

His gut pitched. Someone had Olivia.

Horror washed through him, chilled him to the marrow. He poured on every ounce of speed he had, leaping over a fallen tree. "Let her go!"

The masked man jerked his head toward Reyn when he shouted.

Releasing her, the man fled to a nearby four-wheeler.

Olivia crumpled to the ground.

Reyn rushed to her and dropped to his knees at her side. "Olivia, are you...all right?"

He panted for breath while raking his gaze over her, looking for evidence of injury. She, too, gasped for breath. The bastard had been smothering or choking her. She raised a shaky finger and pointed toward the man, escaping on his four-wheeler.

"Stop him," she rasped.

He glanced over his shoulder at the man who was getting away, and anger boiled inside him. With the other man's lead on the four-wheeler, Reyn couldn't catch the attacker now. And he wouldn't leave Olivia until he was certain she was all right.

Smoothing her hair back from her face, he met her wild, frightened eyes, and his chest tightened. "Are you hurt?"

Tears hovered on her lashes, but she blinked them back. "He would have killed me if you hadn't—"

He drew her into his arms and held her close. "Did you recognize him?"

"No," she mumbled into his chest. "His face was covered. I was so scared that I didn't think about—" Her voice broke.

"Shh. It's okay." He hugged her closer, and a tremor shook him. After a moment, he gently pushed her away, scanning her body again for bruises or cuts. "Can you stand? Do you need a doctor?"

"Yes and no. I'll be fine...in another minute. I just need to...catch my breath...and quit shaking."

He heaved a ragged sigh then clenched his teeth. "That settles it. You're out of this investigation."

Fire flared in her eyes. "Not a chance! I want to help catch that jerk."

"Are you out of your mind? He just tried to kill you. What makes you think he won't try again?"

Olivia jutted out her chin, though he saw shadows of trepidation in her eyes. "I won't let him intimidate me. We have to find this guy and make him pay for what he's done. To me and to your mother."

For all her foolish stubbornness, he admired her guts, her loyalty. He balled his hand in a fist to stop himself from drawing her chin up to kiss her pouting, defiant mouth.

"No arguments. You're out. This is my fight. And we'll let the sheriff look into finding the guy who attacked you."

"Reyn," she started, her disagreement blazing from her gold eyes. He held up a hand to forestall her protest.

"And I'm not letting you out of my sight until I know that maniac is caught."

She narrowed her eyes. "Kinda hard to keep me out of the investigation and keep me in your sight at the same time."

Her expression was smug, and he grimaced. Damn it, she was right. "Okay, you win. But I am going to stick close to you. I don't want anything like this to happen again."

She didn't answer, but her gaze lowered to his lips and lingered there. Her pupils dilated like those of a cat ready to pounce. Heat swirled through him. He knew she was thinking the same thing that echoed through his mind. How the hell were they supposed to spend every minute together and keep their hands to themselves? Just looking at her, seeing the haze of desire darken her eyes to the color of whiskey, had him ready to spontaneously combust. It took every ounce of restraint he possessed not to cover her with his body and finish what they'd started at the bayou.

"I don't need a babysitter," she said, her voice husky.

"Too bad. You've got one."

Pursing her lips in an irritated frown, she dusted off her shorts. "Does that mean you're going to class with me tonight?"

"Looks like."

"Then get the lead out, hot stuff. I don't want to be late." With that, she started toward her house.

Reyn caught her arm. "We still have to report this attack to the sheriff."

Her shoulders drooped, and she sighed. "I know."

He followed her back to her house, where they called the sheriff and waited on her porch swing for an officer to arrive.

Sheriff Anders responded to their call a few minutes later. "Looks like whoever left that threatening note tried to make good on it, eh?" The sheriff slipped off his sunglasses as he stepped into the shade of the porch. "That should make things easy. We have a report back on the fingerprints from the note."

Olivia cast a quick glance to Reyn.

"And?" Reyn prompted.

"Besides your prints and hers, most of what we got was smudged. 'Cept one. Belongs to Hank Harrison."

"Hank?" Olivia gasped. "There has to be some mistake. He wouldn't—" She turned toward Reyn, her face drawn, and he knew she was remembering his deductions from a few nights before. The missing marker. Hank's knowledge that the threat was in a note.

Olivia shook her head violently, crimson staining her cheeks. "The man who grabbed me was not Hank. Wrong height, wrong voice, wrong everything. Hank didn't do this. He wouldn't—"

"He could have hired someone," the sheriff interrupted.

"No!" Her eyes flashed angrily. "There is some other explanation for his fingerprint on that note. Hank is not a threat to me. He's family."

Reyn clenched his teeth. As much as he respected, admired Olivia's dedication and love for her family, he knew firsthand that sometimes family members failed. Sometimes family loyalty wasn't enough. He prayed her blind faith in her stepfather didn't end up getting her killed. If he had anything to say about it, she'd never get the chance to test her theory.

"One way to find out. Let's talk to Hank, get your statement, take a look at the scene of the attack." The sheriff took out a pen and a notepad, and Olivia ushered him inside.

Hank pressed his mouth in a tight grimace. He swiped a hand over his face with a sigh, sinking back in the living room couch.

"Yeah. I left the note. I was trying to scare you away from this nosing around you're doing." He turned to the sheriff's deputy and aimed a finger at him. "But I had nothing to do with this attack on her. You heard Mel say I was at the auto shop. My time card will show that and so will Mrs. Skinner. She was hovering over me the whole time I was working on her car...like she knew squat about spark plugs," he grumbled.

Olivia's mind whirled. She squeezed her hands in tight fists. Hank left the note? Reyn's instincts had been right, but she'd been blinded to the truth by her stubborn pride. Hank was family. Never mind that he claimed to have done it to scare her away from the investigation of Claire's death. Never mind that in some convoluted way he thought he was protecting her. Hank had frightened her, broken her car window, toyed with her emotions. Fury burned her gut.

Hank turned to her, an apology in his eyes. "Jelly Bean, I'm sorry. It's just that after I left the diner that morning you approached us, I started thinking about the hostilities you stirred up and...and the timing of some things."

She avoided Reyn's gaze, afraid she'd see an I-told-you-so look that would only infuriate her more.

"If what you say is right," Hank continued, "your daddy died before he finished investigating the Erikson fire. I may be way off here. I mean, nobody asked questions when he died—at least not that I recall...but hell, Liv, I just got a bad feeling and I thought...maybe it wasn't an accident."

"Why not just talk to me about it? Why scare the bejeezus out of me and break my windshield?"

"I've told you a hundred times, I'll help you buy a new car. Something more reliable."

"I don't want help buying a new car. I'll do it on my own or not at all. Just answer my question. Why the threat?"

Hank pressed his mouth in a grim line and glanced at Reyn before answering. "I didn't think you'd listen to me if I just warned you away. In all your years, you've never followed my advice. Not about your car, not about going away for school, not about Billy Russell or—"

"All right, you've made your point." Slapping her hands on her legs, she rose from the couch. "Well, now that *one* mystery is solved, I'll leave you gentlemen to catch the creep who jumped me in the woods." Her tone could have frozen lava. "If you'll excuse me, I'm late for class."

"Do you think it's a good idea to go to class tonight after what happened in the woods?" Hank asked.

She spun to face him. "Yes. I think it's an excellent idea. I refuse to let you or anyone manipulate or terrorize me. I will not be bullied into submission."

No one spoke for a moment as she divided her angry glare among the three men in the living room.

"I'm going to class with her." Reyn spoke quietly, his tone calm but adamant. "In fact, I plan to stick real close to her until this guy is caught."

She gritted her teeth. She'd almost forgotten her self-appointed bodyguard. With a huff, she headed out to her car. "Fine. Come if you insist. It's your time you're wasting."

She jerked the front door open and heard the sheriff give a long, low whistle. "That's one hot little firecracker you got there, Harrison."

Olivia marched out, letting the door slam behind her without waiting to hear whether Hank made any reply. Reyn appeared at her passenger's door as she tried to crank her Chevette. If nothing else, Reyn's insistence to accompany her to class gave them time to discuss the new information they had.

He opened the door but didn't get in. "You're gonna flood the engine."

"Huh?"

"Sniff. You smell that gas?"

She sniffed. He was right, damn it. In her snit over Hank's betrayal, she'd pumped too much fuel to the engine as she tried to start the car. "Great."

"Just as well. I wasn't looking forward to chewing my knees all the way to Monroe. I'll get my truck and be back in a sec."

Leaning her head back on the seat, she sighed and watched

him head toward the woods, stooping long enough to pat the beagle that loped along beside him. Reyn's tall, muscular body moved with a controlled power and confidence. He'd employed that same cool control to rein in his passion this afternoon, to stop himself when his body was on the brink of no return. Closing her eyes, she imagined what it might be like to have him finally unleash all that raw energy and feel his body fuse with hers in fast, frantic abandon.

For months she'd studied his provocative picture in the firemen's calendar and wondered what kind of lover he would be. Today she'd had a sample of her fantasy, and just a little of the flesh and blood Reyn blew her fantasy to smithereens.

Yet she was no closer to breeching the wall he kept around his heart, getting him to open up to her with his innermost secrets and dreams. She still didn't feel she knew the real Reyn and what made him tick. Her heart told her he was a good man deep down, and she'd seen plenty of proof of that. His rapport with Katy, Sara and Lila demonstrated his kindness. He had integrity and honor. Courage and convictions. But his determination to shut her out, to fight the attraction growing between them baffled her, frustrated her.

She was falling for him without the assurances she needed to protect her heart. Just because she knew he was attracted to her didn't mean he would fall in love with her or that her love would be enough to make him want the things she wanted.

Family. Home. Commitment.

A knot of cold despair lodged in her stomach. A little voice inside her said she was asking too much of Reyn. He'd made his feelings about getting involved with her clear. His life had been very different from hers. He'd had no father. He'd lost his mother while young. He'd been separated from his home, his grandmother at a turbulent time in his life. No wonder his priorities didn't include starting a family. She couldn't force him to change. She'd already seen the strength of his iron will.

But neither could she give up without trying. She still wanted to reach him somehow, help him quiet the ghosts haunting him about his past. Maybe he'd come around. Please, God.

She only hoped she didn't lose her heart in the process.

Despite Olivia's protests, Reyn went in to the pharmacy the next morning, determined not to give whoever had grabbed her a second chance to hurt her.

"You should be at the hospital with Lila, not babysitting me." She frowned at him and sidled up to the computer to start processing orders.

"I called the hospital this morning and explained what happened. Lila agrees with me." He picked up a pamphlet on heart disease lying on the counter and gave it a cursory glance. "Besides, she starts her physical therapy today and doesn't think she'll be in the mood for visitors afterward. So I'm all yours."

"Swell," she said with fake enthusiasm. Arching one eyebrow and casting a furtive glance at Lou, Olivia gave Reyn a sultry grin. "Too bad we have an audience. I could think of lots of ways to pass the time."

Heat flashed through him, remembering the press of her naked flesh against his.

Her eyes brightened, along with her smile. "Maybe later?"

Oh, yeah! his body screamed.

Don't even think about it, his head warned.

He milled about in the store aisles to avoid engaging in her sexual banter. Such repartee only heightened his awareness of her and drew the vise of longing tighter. He was already coiled tight and ready to spring, and his cold shower that morning had done little to relieve the frustrating ache. Knowing she was a virgin, he should be running the other way. He couldn't touch her again. He'd done enough damage as it was, had her thinking they'd started something they would finish. Yesterday's interlude had been a mistake, and his body was paying the price.

He sat at the back of the store in a folding chair, reading the newspaper for a while. When business slowed, he chatted with Olivia and Lou, deciding to use the time to milk the head pharmacist for information.

"I guess by now you've heard about the attack on Olivia?" He watched Lou carefully, gauging the man's response.

Lou flicked a brief glance from the solution he was mixing. "Hmm. No, I—" His head whipped back around, and his eyes widened, as if he just realized what Reyn had said. The syrup he was pouring dribbled on the counter. "Attacked? Olivia, what—"

"I'm okay," she assured her boss, holding up a hand and scowling sideways at Reyn. "A guy grabbed me in the woods behind our house, tried to suffocate me, but Reyn heard me scream and scared the guy off when he came running."

"Land sakes, girl! Who'd want to do a thing like that to you?" Lou noticed the spill and grimaced.

"Thought maybe you could tell us that." Reyn crossed his arms over his chest.

Olivia sent Reyn another dirty look, but he ignored her. Instead, he focused on the small-framed man, who grumbled to himself as he wiped up the mess he'd made. Perhaps Lou didn't fit the physical description of the man who'd jumped Olivia, but he could know something.

"I have no idea why anyone would hurt—" Lou paused and furrowed his brows. He took off his glasses and pinned a worried look on Olivia. "Do you think this is because you're asking questions about Reyn's mama? Seems to me some folks would rather you not be diggin' around in that garden."

"Oh? Like who?" Reyn propped a hip against the register counter and crossed his legs at the ankle.

"Like Betty Smith was in here the other day, sayin' Charlie was fuming about your confronting the volunteer firemen at the diner. And like Frances Skinner mentioned she'd heard you were receiving death threats or some such." Lou faced Olivia. "Can't say *I'm* too pleased about you re-opening Claire's death either."

"Why?" Olivia tipped her head in query.

Lou took a deep breath and blew it out slowly. "Just seems that poor woman deserves to rest in peace. She suffered enough scandal while she was alive." He sent Reyn an apologetic look. "No disrespect, son, but your mama had quite a reputation."

Reyn tensed.

Lou raised a hand to forestall Reyn's protest. "Some of it was just talk, I'm sure. Petty jealousy and all. She was a real purty lady. Always was popular with the fellas from the time we were in junior high on up. Heck, even I had an eye for her."

Olivia sent Reyn an unreadable look. He didn't like the direction of Lou's reminiscences. He didn't want to hear about the reputation his mother had or that she might have earned it. Hell, he'd spent most of his childhood defending her for that very reason. A familiar restlessness skittered through him and knotted his gut.

"Your mother could have had her pick of men. I don't know a man in the parish who didn't stand a little straighter when she'd walk by." Lou's expression sobered. "Of course, she dated

George Russell steady for the last two years of high school so none of us other fellas had a chance."

"She dated George Russell?" This news stunned Reyn. His mother had never mentioned her connection to George.

"Yep. The prom queen and the basketball star. A story as old as time." Lou shook his head. "It was a real tragedy, her dying so young like she did."

Reyn's chest constricted with grief, and he struggled not to show how Lou's comment affected him.

"If you ask me, she got what she had coming."

Reyn jerked his head around to face the woman behind him who'd spoken. The sharp tone of the woman's voice, not to mention her harsh judgment, set him on edge.

"Excuse me?" he asked in a low, foreboding tone.

"Mrs. Horton." Olivia moved to the register, pushing Reyn aside with her hip. "I didn't hear you come in."

"Obviously not. Is my refill ready?"

"Let me check." Olivia sent Reyn a warning glance, then stepped over to flip through the bags waiting to be picked up.

Mrs. Horton turned to Reyn, a haughty expression on her pinched face. "My husband had the dubious honor of serving as assistant principal at the high school when your mother was there. She was as much trouble in school as you were...though in different ways. Seemed like he'd just gotten rid of one thorn in his side when you came to the elementary school where he'd transferred as principal."

"I don't see how that makes her deserving of death in a house fire." Reyn worked hard to keep his tone modulated, though what he wanted was to punch something. It seemed Mrs. Horton had the same pious attitude her husband had.

"If she had controlled you, put a stop to your pyromania

the first time Vance warned her about your trouble with matches at school, then you might not have gotten as far as burning down the Russells' barn and your own house." Helen Horton lifted her beak-like nose higher. "But she didn't do anything to stop you. That's why it's fittin' that she should die by her own mistakes."

Fury rose in Reyn's throat, and he nearly gagged on the taste of bile as he swallowed his anger. Nothing would be served by getting into it with the arrogant and scornful woman. Just let him finish his business here and leave town without causing Gram more shame. He balled his trembling hands into fists.

"Well, it's a good thing you're perfect. Right, Mrs. Horton?" Olivia's overly bright tone and smile matched her too-chipper tone. "Why, if we all got what we deserved and died by our mistakes, then you could live forever." She punched a key on the register with a vicious poke. "That'll be twenty dollars even. *Ma'am.*"

Reyn's own anger quieted a notch as he watched Olivia's barely controlled rage. Her body quivered, and her teeth clenched in a tight, grim smile.

Mrs. Horton sent Olivia suspicious glances as she scribbled out a check. "Don't be flip with me, young lady." She thrust the check toward Olivia and frowned. "Vance is right. You're just like Claire. Prancing around town in your short skirts and stirring up the menfolk. You're nothing but trouble." Mrs. Horton jabbed her pen toward Olivia, and Reyn stiffened.

Reyn leaned toward the older woman, glaring at her, and she drew back with a gasp. "You and ol' Vance deserve each other. Tell my favorite principal hi for me, won't you?"

Mrs. Horton backed away from the counter, her mouth puckered with disdain. "I'm going to have a word with the preacher about you two. The likes of you shouldn't be allowed at church. You're nothing but trouble. Devil spawn!"

Still sputtering, she backed through the pharmacy door.

"Olivia, where'd we put that disinfectant spray?" Lou asked, looking under the counter. "I'd sure hate for any of our customers to catch whatever nasty bug she's been infected with."

"Lou, with her and Vance it's more of a birth defect. A genetic trait for meanness. No wonder their daughter ran away at sixteen." She shuddered dramatically as if shaking off a residue the sour woman left behind.

"Sad thing is, Vance used to be a pretty likeable guy. He hung out with my oldest brother way back when. Helen changed him." Lou shook his head and went back to work.

Reyn tried to dismiss the woman's comments as well, but the cutting remarks reminded him too clearly of the judgmental town he'd grown up in, the accusations following the house fire, the reasons he hadn't been back in twenty years. His heart ached for his mother because of the pettiness she'd endured raising an illegitimate son, facing the rumors and innuendo every day, struggling to make ends meet. Why had she stayed in the face of such cruelty? Why not move on? Why not start over in Shreveport or Monroe or Alexandria?

And did he really want to know why? Just scratching the surface of his past, of his mother's life back then and the troubles she'd faced left him raw inside. He didn't want to dig deeper, didn't want to face the harsh truths about what his mother had endured for his sake. Already the guilt and anguish over her death were eating him alive. He drew a deep breath, but still felt as if he were suffocating.

"I'm going outside for a minute. I...I need some air." God, his voice sounded awful. Gritty and rough like sandpaper.

Olivia gave him a worried look. "Reyn? Are you all right?"

"Fine. I just—" He didn't finish. Yeah, he'd be just fine. As soon as he could get out of Clairmont and lock the past away once and for all.

"Do you have to go?" Katy whined to Reyn.

"Afraid so, fair lady." He gallantly kissed Katy's hand like the prince he'd been playing with the little girl. "I must go with Princess Olivia to ensure her safe passage to class. But I shall return this evening." He bowed with a flourish.

Katy giggled. "Okay."

Olivia grinned at her sister. "Why don't you play on the swing till Daddy finishes heating up dinner?"

Katy clomped outside, and Olivia turned to Reyn. "You really don't have to go to class with me again."

"Yes, I really do." He pulled his keys from his pocket.

Olivia sighed as she gathered her books for class. For the last few days, Reyn had stuck to her like fly paper. Not that she minded his company. He was easy on the eyes, and every minute together was a chance to get closer to him. If he'd let her. But for all his physical proximity, he'd been more distant than ever. His withdrawal had started after their aborted lovemaking on the dock. The day she'd been attacked in the woods. And he pulled farther into himself after Mrs. Horton's verbal attack at the store. Dang the bitter woman's hide.

Yet despite his somber mood and unwillingness to talk about what bothered him, Reyn had endeared himself to her in numerous ways. She admired his teasing rapport with his grandmother when they visited Lila on Olivia's lunch breaks and after church on Sunday. He'd charmed Katy with his willingness to play dolls when the little girl asked.

Sunday evening, he'd even accompanied her to choir

practice at the church. He'd sat in the back pew, staring at the stained glass with an odd expression darkening his face, and waited patiently for her to finish her rehearsal. Monday night he'd helped prepare dinner and stayed through the meal, even though Olivia swore no one could hurt her in her own home with Hank right there. After dinner, they'd retreated to her front porch. In the gathering dusk, as the mosquitoes buzzed around them, they'd talked about nothing specific yet found a comfortable camaraderie, as if they'd known each other for years. Reyn had proven an interesting and intelligent conversationalist—as long as the topic centered on the historical accuracy of recent movies and stayed off him.

They'd hit a wall in their investigation of the fire. Reyn seemed reluctant to dig further, ask more questions, unearth a motive for someone to kill his mother. The search for answers was clearly painful for him, and Olivia was ready to turn all their information over to the sheriff, if it would spare Reyn more pain. But running away from the things that haunted him wouldn't resolve anything for Reyn, and she was determined to find a way to help ease his pain.

The phone rang as they were walking out the door to drive to her class, and Olivia groaned. "Just a minute, Reyn. Let me get rid of whoever this is, and I'll be right there."

He propped his shoulder against the doorframe and watched her as she answered the call.

"Olivia, is Reyn there? I've called and called to the house, and he doesn't answer." Lila's voice sounded panicked.

"Yes, he's here. You just caught us. We were headed—"

"Please, dear. I must talk to him. It's important."

Apprehension prickled up her spine. "Sure. Here he is." She held the phone out to Reyn. "It's Lila. She sounds upset."

Concern furrowed his brow, and he snatched the phone.

"Gram? What is it?" He listened for a minute. "What's wrong?"

She watched his face and chewed a hangnail, wondering what had upset Lila.

"Of course. I...I'll be right there." Reyn disconnected the call, and his face grew pale. "I have to go to the hospital. She said something's come up, but wouldn't say what it was. I need to take care of it, whatever it is."

"Then let's go." Olivia put her books down on the coffee table and headed for the door.

Reyn caught her arm. "No. You go on to class. No point in missing. I'll talk to Gram alone, and then fill you in later."

She opened her mouth to argue, but when she saw the blaze of determination in Reyn's eyes, she swallowed her protest. "Okay."

An odd disappointment niggled in her mind that he was pushing her aside to do something else. Until she reminded herself that the *something else* was his grandmother. This was the kind of thing she wanted from Reyn, wasn't it? An obvious case of putting his family's needs first? Proof of his love and loyalty? Evidence his priorities matched hers?

Perhaps it was the worried tone of Lila's voice that had her feeling out of sorts. Maybe it was a prick of jealousy that she wouldn't have his companionship on the long, lonely drive to Monroe. With a sigh and a mental shake of her head, Olivia pushed the strange feeling aside.

Following him outside, she cast an eye to the gray clouds rolling in from the west. Reyn's countenance matched the dark sky as he cranked his truck and shot her a glance.

"Have someone walk you to your car after class, and drive carefully. Looks like a storm's blowin' in."

"I will. Give my best to Lila."

He gave her a quick nod, closed his car door and drove off in the direction of the gathering storm.

Chapter Ten

"Gram?" Reyn didn't wait for a response before hustling into his grandmother's room. "What is it? What's happened?"

Breathless from running in from the parking lot and taking the stairs three at a time, he dropped in the chair beside her bed and carefully took her frail hand in his.

"My goodness, you got here fast." She chuckled. "They teach you that speed at the firemen's academy?"

He wrinkled his brow, puzzled by her mood change. Had this been a false alarm?

"You sounded upset on the phone. Said it was important, so I rushed."

"Where's Olivia?" Gram glanced toward the door as if expecting her friend to appear.

"She has class tonight, Gram. That's where we were headed when you called."

"We? Are you two a *we* now?" Gram's eyes twinkled with affection. A pang of regret twisted inside him. Just one more way he was going to have to let his grandmother down.

"No, there's no *we*. I just meant I was going to ride with her to class. I wanted to make sure she was safe."

Gram pressed fingers, knotted with arthritis, to her lips. "Oh my. And I pulled you away from that. Didn't I? I'm sorry. I didn't mean—"

"It's all right. I don't think she really wanted me tagging along anyway." He rubbed his free hand on his khaki pants. "Gram, on the phone you sounded upset. You said it was important that you see me right away. What's wrong?"

Her grip on his other hand tightened. "Oh. Right. It's about your mother. I remembered something she said to me before she died."

"Go on," he said warily. His heart beat faster, and he held his breath, not sure he wanted to hear what Gram had to say.

Gram's eyes met his, their blue as clear and vibrant as he'd ever seen them. "I never connected it with her death before, 'cause up 'til a few weeks ago, I believed her death was just bad luck. One of life's tragedies."

The directness of her gaze caused a self-conscious prickle on his neck. Had she blamed him like the rest of the town?

"So I'd almost forgotten the conversation I had with Claire about two weeks before—" she paused to take a deep breath, "—before the fire."

"What was the conversation about?" A raspy quality darkened his voice.

"Your father."

Her answer kicked him in the chest with a force that stole his breath, knocked him back in his chair. He shook his head. "But she didn't know who my father was. She put *unknown* on my birth certificate, and—"

Gram's short burst of laughter startled him, and he frowned.

"Didn't know? Boy, did you think she was asleep when you were conceived? Of course she knew who he was."

"I just thought maybe he was a one-night stand, or one of

167

several men who—"

"You've been listening to the town gossips, haven't you?" Gram scowled. "You should know better than that. Your mother made a mistake, a youthful error in judgment. One time. That's all she'd tell me."

Reyn mulled this bit of information for a moment before leaning forward and shaking his head. "Why—" His voice cracked, so he started again. "Why did he have to be a secret?"

Gram shrugged. "You know how the gossips are. Mostly she was protecting you. I thought maybe she was protecting your father from scandal, too, until they could be together. Several boys from Clairmont went off to college 'bout that time. Maybe she didn't want to keep him from getting his education 'cause of obligation to her." Gram looked away for a minute before turning back to face him. "And maybe it was loyalty to her best friend that kept her from saying."

Gram gave him a pointed look that sent chills down his spine. His mother's best friend? Hannah Russell? He remembered Lou saying that his mother had dated George Russell in high school. Was it possible that George Russell was his father?

Gram gathered herself and sighed. "I just don't know, dear. She never would tell me, though I asked enough times. I finally learned to leave it be. All we did was fight over that subject."

"So what was it she said right before she died?" Reyn forced the question from a dry throat.

"She was ready to tell you about him. Ready to give you at least a name. She said you deserved a father, and she was tired of waiting for him to claim you."

Stunned disbelief rocked him, and he shook his head. "She never said anything to me."

"I guess she didn't get the chance. Besides, she was going

to tell him of her decision first. She wanted him to come clean to his family. I guess she was going to force his hand on the issue."

Reyn's mind raced forward. "You're saying she was going to confront my father? Do you think he could have killed her to keep his identity a secret?"

A pit of black apprehension settled in his stomach.

"It would sure answer a lot of questions. Motive for one."

He nodded numbly. Could his father have killed his mother? The idea was staggering. Chilling. Sickening.

The taste of bile rose in his throat, and he forced it back down with a deep gulp of air.

"Reyn, darling, are you all right?"

"My father," he mumbled, trying to wrap his brain around the concept. The man who'd never claimed him.

"I'm sorry, darling. I didn't mean to upset you this way, but I thought you had a right to know. I thought...that it might help find the person responsible for killing Claire."

"Yeah." He scrubbed a hand over his face. "It's more to go on than we've had. But without knowing who he is—"

"Hannah might know. If anyone will know, if Claire told anybody her secret, I think it would be Hannah. They were close right up until Claire passed."

Reyn nodded slowly. Hannah. Maybe he should have started with Hannah days ago. Then again, maybe he'd been avoiding Hannah, knowing his mother's friend might tell him truths he didn't want to hear. He'd thought he could get answers about his mother's death through cold facts in documentation. But the people who'd known his mother, loved and laughed with her, held the keys to his past. Memories that could rip his heart out.

Remembering the beautiful, vital woman who'd taught him to love and to embrace life was more than he thought he could endure. He'd let that woman down, let her die.

You and me, Reyn. We're a team. We gotta take care of each other. He saw his mother's smile as she kissed him goodnight, heard her singing "You and Me Against the World", imagined her warm hand ruffling his hair.

God, he missed her. He squeezed his eyes shut, despair knifing through him. He should have done more to save her. He should have protected her better. He shouldn't have been hiding in the woods when the fire started. *Coward.*

"Reyn?"

His hand was trembling he realized, and he jerked it away from Gram's grasp.

"What's wrong, darling? You look like you've seen a ghost." She reached for him, patted his knee.

"I have. I've been seeing ghosts all week." He sighed and stood up to pace. "Being back here, re-living everything that happened back then..." He drew a shaky breath and faced Gram.

"I understand that. After all, you lived through so much pain here. Being back is bound to stir up those memories." Her eyes glowed with a warmth that reached out to him. "It's no wonder you've been scared to come back before now."

Reyn's breath caught. He stared at Gram, uncertain what to say, what to make of her assessment. Her tone was matter-of-fact. Non-judgmental. Full of understanding.

"You...knew?"

"Of course I knew. You had every right to be afraid, considering how this town treated you, considering the bad things that happened to you here."

"But I owed you better than that. I let my bad memories get in the way of my responsibility to you. I left you alone here because I was running from my past. I was a coward." He fisted his hands in frustration and self-disgust. "I let you down."

"No." She shook her head. "I couldn't be more proud of you and all you've made of yourself. My grandson the fireman."

He scoffed. "But that's not who I am. Firefighting is my job. It's just something I do. What matters is the way I hurt the people I care about. You. Mom. Liz."

"Liz? Your old girlfriend? What does all this have to do with Liz?" Gram's gaze followed him as he paced.

"She wanted to get married. I panicked and...I ran. I dumped her. Broke her heart. Hurt her."

"Why?" His grandmother's incisive blue eyes cut into him.

He turned up his palms then let them drop. "I don't know. 'Cause I'm a coward and a jerk. 'Cause I didn't think I could make her happy long term. I knew that somehow, some way, down the line I'd fail her, despite my best intentions. Just like with mom and you."

"You were right," Gram said softly, and her bluntness startled him a bit. She motioned for him to come closer. With his shoulders back and swallowing a knot in his throat, he stepped over to the side of her bed. She curled her fingers around his hand. "We all fail the people we love at some point, Reyn. We live and learn. We make mistakes and try again. Then we kiss and make up. It's the human experience."

He pinched the bridge of his nose. "Gram, I—"

"Love is hard work, Reyn. Raising a child, making a marriage work, surviving the hard times life throws in our path. It's all scary stuff. Lord knows it scares the beans outta me!"

He gave his grandmother a wan smile.

She caught his hand and pulled him closer to meet his gaze squarely. Her eyes darkened to the color of steel. "Real courage comes from doing the things that scare us most. It takes a lot of courage to give someone your whole heart and soul. But until you let yourself love someone that deeply, you won't know real joy either. Your mother loved you that much, James Reynold. And so do I. Don't you ever think you let us down."

His breath hung in his lungs. Gram's gaze pierced the dark corners of his heart. He wanted to believe her, wanted to accept the hope and love reflected in her face.

But the demon still whispered to him. *You didn't even try to save her. You ran away. Coward.*

"Thanks, Gram. I hear what you're saying, but it's not as simple as that for me. I've done things all my life that hurt people. Things that I can't change. That's unforgivable."

Gram cocked her head on the pillow. "By whom? Seems to me you're the only one who can't forgive you."

"I haven't earned the right to forgive myself."

Before Gram could respond, a nurse bustled into the room with a tiny paper cup in her hand. "Evening, Mrs. Erikson. Are you ready for your pain medicine?"

"I think so. I'm rather tired and ready to sleep."

Reyn took the hint and backed away from Gram's bed, fumbling in his pocket for his keys.

"Do you want a sleeping pill?" the nurse asked.

"No, no, I think I'll sleep just fine tonight." Gram swallowed the pills the nurse handed her then glanced at Reyn. "Now my grandson is another matter. I think I've given him a whole lot to think about."

In other words, her look said, *don't dismiss what I've said so easily.*

Reyn nodded. "Yes, ma'am. A whole lot to think about."

He kissed Gram on the cheek and backed silently out of the room. The rain that had threatened as he drove over poured down in fat drops, and he dashed for his truck. The rain matched his mood and gave him an excuse to hole up at Gram's house and brood.

By the time Olivia's lab class dismissed, the storm had arrived in full force, remnants of a hurricane from the Gulf of Mexico with the potential for flooding. Rain came down in sheets, and the wind pushed her lightweight car all over the road as she maneuvered down the dark, rural highways toward home. Already fatigued by stress and lack of sleep, the treacherous driving conditions stretched her nerves taut.

While lightning flickered in the night sky, the worry in Lila's voice when she'd called filtered through her mind. A shiver that had nothing to do with the damp chill in the air crawled up her spine.

Olivia sighed. Had the killer tried to hurt Lila? The thought made her sick to her stomach. Should she convince Reyn to drop the investigation before someone got hurt? Katy. Lila. Reyn. She couldn't stand it if something happened to the people she cared about. But how could they walk away when they'd come this far? They couldn't let the killer get away.

Let the sheriff handle it. No. She'd never been a quitter, and she wouldn't give up now. They were so close to figuring this whole puzzle out. Her gut told her they were on the brink of making the pieces fit. For what felt like the millionth time, she rolled the facts over, wondering what she'd missed.

When she grew frustrated with her circular thoughts, she tried to distract herself by singing the hymns they'd rehearsed Sunday at church. Her windshield fogged over, and she reached for her glove box to get a leftover napkin. A cold drip plopped on her arm. Flipping on the interior light, she discovered that her cracked windshield leaked steady droplets of rain onto her passenger-side floor. With a groan of disgust, she fumbled for the napkin, then wiped her windshield, grumbling. "Broken windshield, broken de-fogger, broken radio. Might as well walk."

When singing hymns lost its effect as a distraction from brooding thoughts, Olivia focused on the lab work she'd done tonight. But, as he frequently did, Reyn invaded her mind.

She and Reyn had reached a precarious point, not only in the inquiry into his mother's death, but also in their relationship. Her intuition said they were a breath away from a breakthrough. The friendship they were forming was nice, but the attraction between them couldn't be denied much longer. She sensed his tension and hunger like a vibration between them.

But would the breaking point drive him away or into her arms? Would he leave, fleeing from her and the phantoms she seemed to stir in him? Or would he finally open up to her and give into the desires that hummed in the air when they were together? And what would she do if he never returned the affection she felt?

She'd grown deeply attached to him in the past several days, despite her intentions. But since when had her heart ever listened to her head? She was dangerously close to falling in love with a man who refused to share his innermost self with her, a man who made it clear he didn't want an emotional involvement, a man who showed no interest in commitment or family. But how could she not care when at every turn he showed her kindness and integrity and intelligence? And why couldn't he see those things in himself? His hurting soul called to her, louder every day. She knew she could help heal him if he'd give her the chance.

She passed the turnoff to the Russells' farm then crossed the bridge over Clairmont Creek. A flash of lightning showed her the creek, normally an easy meandering stream, was swollen and coursing with the runoff from the hard rain. Flash flooding was a possibility every Louisiana driver knew to be wary of in weather like this. As flat as the state's terrain was, rain accumulated quickly in the ditches and could flood the roads in a matter of minutes.

Olivia glanced in her rearview mirror and discovered another car had turned onto the road and moved up close behind her. She flipped her rearview mirror to the nighttime angle to cut the glare of the other car's headlights. Before she could return her hand to the steering wheel, the car zoomed up and rammed her back bumper.

With a startled gasp, she grabbed the wheel, fighting to steady her car, which fishtailed wildly from the impact on the wet road.

"You idiot!" she fussed, watching in her mirror the crazy driver who still tailgated her. Gritting her teeth and squeezing the steering wheel, Olivia pumped her brakes, hoping the impatient driver would pass. For a moment it appeared that he would. She watched the car pull into the lane for oncoming traffic and move up beside her. Once more she slowed to let the car go by. But rather than pass, the light-colored sedan sideswiped her, nearly forcing her off the road.

A bubble of fear swelled inside her. The maniac had intentionally hit her! Like lightning, understanding struck her with a terrifying jolt. The other driver *wanted* to run her off the road, wanted her to wreck. Wanted her dead.

Again the sedan slammed into the side of her Chevette. Her wheels lost traction, sending her car careening toward the ditch. Horror washed through her in a powerful wave. She jerked her steering wheel hard to the right and regained control of the skidding car.

Her body shook, but she concentrated on her driving. Tried to anticipate the other driver's next move. She considered stopping at the side of the road. But stopping would leave her vulnerable to the madman should he come after her on foot.

Tasting the metallic twang of blood on her tongue, she realized she'd bitten her lip when she was rammed. Swallowing hard, she fought the rise of nausea and fear in her throat and braced to defend herself from the killer.

With the next blow to the side of her car, she turned her steering wheel to the left to counteract the force of the impact. She heard the other car's tires squeal.

Just a little farther. She was almost home.

But in a snap decision, Olivia drove past the turn to her house. No way would she lead this danger back to Katy and Hank. Besides, if she stopped at the house, she'd be just as vulnerable as if she pulled over at the side of the road. She had to keep going and pray that the lunatic would give up. Or lose control of his own car with his wild driving.

She was on her own. Alone. Trying to outrun a killer.

The dark, deserted highway stretched before her. Her headlights glowed feebly in the curling fog and curtain of rain.

When the sedan pulled alongside her again, she tensed, waiting for the next blow. Her chest squeezed as they raced past the turn-off to Lila's. A short distance down that road, Reyn waited for word of her safe return.

Reyn. God, she wished he were with her now. But even if he were, what could he do? Other than die with her, if and when the maniac finally drove her off the highway and into a tree.

Wham!

She jerked as the other car crashed into her again with a crunch of metal. She blinked back tears that blurred her vision. She had to stay calm and keep her head. Her life depended on maintaining control. Ahead, she saw a turn in the road and gripped the wheel, ready to negotiate the curve and battle the lunatic for a place on the highway.

With a screech of rubber, the sedan zoomed past her, cutting her off, just as they entered the turn. Olivia cut her wheels to avoid hitting the other car, but a deep puddle on the road destroyed her traction. Her car spun out of control, skidding toward the waterlogged ditch at the side of the highway. Panicked, she stood on her brakes. But, with a lurch, her Chevette dove front-end into the ditch and came to a jarring halt. Her head banged the steering wheel, and her knees bumped the underside of the dash with a whack.

Trembling, she raised her head and watched the sedan's taillights disappear down the road. She knew with an eerie certainty that the driver would be back. To see if she was dead.

And to finish the job if she wasn't.

Throwing the Chevette in reverse, Olivia gunned the engine. Whirring and grinding, her wheels spun. But she went nowhere. The Chevette was stuck. Probably a complete loss.

She swallowed the whimper of fear that rose in her throat and struggled for a calming breath. She had to get out of there before the killer came back. Abandoning her car, her textbooks, she grabbed her purse, pried open the door and crawled out into the knee-deep quagmire in the ditch. Mud sucked at her shoes as she grappled through the marsh toward higher ground at the edge of the woods. Lila's house and Reyn were less than a mile back down the highway. But along the side of the road, she was an easy target when the killer returned.

As if summoned by that thought, she heard the rumble of a car engine. She splashed through the water, out of the ditch and scrambled for the cover of the trees.

Praying that she could find her way in the darkness, she headed through the woods toward Lila's house. Toward the safety of Reyn's arms.

Headlights sliced through the shadowy woods, and she darted behind a tree as the car on the road slowed. Her heartbeat pounded in her ears, counting the interminable seconds while the killer searched the interior of her car. *Please, don't let him come looking for me. Please let him drive away.*

A flashlight beam flickered across the trees around her. She held her breath, pressing her back against the prickly trunk of a large pine. A car door slammed, and she heard the sedan *vroom* away.

Olivia wilted as her muscles relaxed. Cold rain trickled down her face, mingled with hot tears of relief. She'd escaped. For now.

But she was sure the killer wouldn't give up. He'd come after her again. She shivered at the thought and started running through the black woods.

Next time, she might not be as lucky.

Chapter Eleven

Reyn stared out the kitchen window, watching the rain fall, seeing nothing. His conversation with Gram echoed in his mind, haunted him. *She said you deserved a father, and she was tired of waiting for him to claim you.*

His father.

His whole life he'd gone without knowing the man who'd given him life. Long ago he'd accepted the fact that he'd probably never know him. The idea that his father could be the same man who killed his mother made him burn with hatred and disgust.

He now had what was likely the last piece of information that would make everything else fit. Hannah would know who his father was. He was sure of it. His gut told him he could resolve the questions surrounding his mother's death with one name. His father's name. But here he stood.

Because he didn't want to know.

He wasn't ready to learn the truth about the man who'd turned his back on his own son. He didn't want to hear the lurid details of his mother's affair and how this man had abandoned her and her baby. He didn't want to know how his birth had complicated his mother's life and possibly ruined her chance to be with the man she loved. Pain like a dull knife in his chest slashed through him.

Coward, the demon in his head shouted.

Jamming the heels of his hands to his eyes, he tried to mute the voice of his tormenting doubt.

At first, when the soft knock sounded at the front door he thought he'd imagined it. His mind was playing more tricks on him, like the cackle of the demon's taunting laughter. *Coward.*

Then he heard the quiet rapping again and dropped his hands from his eyes.

Puzzled over who would come to see him at this late hour on such a stormy night, he headed to the foyer to answer the knock.

When he opened the door, he met a wide, golden gaze.

"Olivia? What—" He stopped short, stunned by her appearance.

Dripping wet, hugging her elbows, and visibly shaking, she stared back at him with red-rimmed eyes, eyes shadowed with fear. Her chin trembled when she tried to speak. "R-R-Reyn."

Something was wrong. Something was terribly wrong. His chest clenched.

"Dear God," he muttered, taking her by the arm and pulling her, stumbling, into his arms. "What happened?"

She nestled into his embrace with a mewling sound that clawed at his heart. He kicked the door closed and stroked a hand down her soaked back.

"Olivia, talk to me. What's wrong?"

"H-He tried to k-kill me. He r-rammed my car. Ran me off the r-road."

Ice ran through his veins. He clutched her shoulders and pushed her back to look in her eyes. "Who? Are you all right?"

Even as he asked, he scanned the length of her quivering body to assure himself she was okay. On the heels of his concern came anger. With the bastard who'd tried to hurt her. And with himself.

"Damn. I should never have let you go to class alone." He gritted his teeth and squeezed his eyes closed, cursing his lapse in judgment. He'd sworn to protect her, and he'd failed. Self-reproach coursed through him and swirled in his gut. He drew her back into his arms, wrapping himself around her shivering body. Too little, too late. He should have been there...

She shook her head as if reading his mind. "But Lila n-needed you. Family comes first."

Family. The word reverberated in a lonely, empty place inside him.

Not until Olivia curled cold fingers against his bare chest did he realize he'd never put on more than a pair of shorts after his shower. Cool water dripped off her hair and clothes and collected on the floor at their feet. As he hugged her, the puddle grew and seeped under his toes. Her rain-soaked clothes squished against him, soaking his shorts and sending icy rivulets trickling down his own body. The air conditioning vent blew frigid air on his damp skin.

But he was on fire.

His temper flamed with fury toward the man who'd dared to go after Olivia. He burned with shame for having let her down, having shirked his duty to protect. But mostly, his blood heated with the need to possess the woman in his arms. The soft press of her body, tucked perfectly in line with his, sparked all the desires he'd been fighting since the day beside the lake. His body remembered too well her silky skin, her honeyed scent, her erotic moans and cinnamon-sweet kiss. This latest attempt on her life ignited a possessiveness he'd never felt toward a woman before. And it bothered him.

"He'll try again. I know he will," Olivia whispered, her

breath a warm caress on his skin.

He knew she was right and clenched his jaw in frustration. "Did you get a look at the guy? Did you recognize him or the car?" he asked, levering her back a bit to see her face.

"No. A light-colored sedan of some kind, but...I didn't recognize it. It was too dark to...see who was driving. I didn't—" Her voice broke, and he pulled her back into his arms.

"Shh. Easy. You're okay now." He stroked her hair and rubbed his cheek across the top of her head.

She didn't know who had run her off the road. But he did. The same man who'd killed his mother. The same man who'd hidden his dirty secret from the town for years.

His father.

A shudder raced through him, and Olivia tipped her head back to look at him. "Reyn?"

He tightened his hold on her. Sinking his fingers into her thick, soft hair, he anchored her head to his chest, kissed her temple. "You, ah...you should get a hot shower to warm up. And something to drink. Coffee maybe." The delicate skin of her cheek against his chest felt like satin, and he didn't want to let her go. But she was deeply chilled and needed to get warm.

He released her, and she stepped back, chafing her arms. "I am kinda cold."

"I'll fix the coffee. You go on upstairs and get out of those wet clothes. You can use the guest room shower, and I'll find you clean towels and something dry to wear."

Her lips curved in a faint, sad smile, just enough to play havoc with his already swirling emotions. He balled his fists and took a deep breath to stop himself from grabbing her back into his arms and kissing that glimmer of a smile. But he knew if he kissed her once, he wouldn't stop until he'd done a whole lot more than kiss her.

He wanted to erase the cold fear from her eyes and watch pleasure warm her face as he made slow, sweet love to her. He wanted to drown out the voice of doubts in his head with the sound of her seductive sighs. He wanted to blot out the nightmarish events of the past several days and his dread of what lay ahead, languishing in the sensual ecstasy promised by her kiss.

"I should go home. I...I didn't go earlier, because I didn't want to lead the danger back to Katy and Hank. I—"

"Good thinking. But tonight at least, you're staying here."

Her eyes widened, and she shook her head.

"No arguments. I'll call Hank and the sheriff while you shower, but I want you where I can keep an eye on you. I have a lead on who might be behind all this, and with a little luck, I can wrap this whole thing up tomorrow."

She lifted her eyebrows in interest. "What did you learn?"

He waved her off. "We'll talk about it later. Go on and get your shower."

She hesitated only a moment, frowning at being put off, before she climbed the stairs and disappeared down the hall.

In the kitchen, Reyn started a pot of coffee brewing and found a bottle of bourbon Gram used for making bourbon balls at Christmas. He splashed a little of the liquor in Olivia's coffee and downed a shot for himself straight.

He heard the shower running upstairs and tried not to think about Olivia standing in the same shower he'd used an hour ago, her body slick with soap, water running down her pale, bare skin.

Groaning, he drank another shot of bourbon and savored the bite as it slid down his throat. He carried her coffee up to her and dug in his drawer for a clean T-shirt for her and dry shorts for himself. He walked into the steamy bathroom and found a towel in the linen closet for her and set it on the counter next to her coffee.

"Reyn? Is that you?" The shower curtain rustled, and she peeked around the edge.

"Just getting out your towel." He picked up the towel again and stepped closer to hand it to her.

"Thanks," she said, reaching for it. The curtain drooped, and he glimpsed the curve of her breast.

His mouth went dry. *Oh Lord.*

He edged toward the door, his heart thumping, his body thrumming. *Get out, Erikson. Walk away.*

"I put a shirt on the bed for you." Did she hear the rasp in his voice that he did? "Call if you need anything else."

"Mmm-hmm."

Olivia came down the stairs ten minutes later. Reyn had tried to read a magazine but found himself re-reading the same paragraph over and over again. His mind was on Olivia, her brush with the killer tonight, Gram's hypothesis about the killer's motive.

She padded, barefooted, into the living room and stopped in the middle of the floor, holding her mug of coffee. "What did you put in this?"

His T-shirt hung to her knees, the shoulders sagging to her elbows. But for all its size, the shirt's thin fabric still revealed far more than he'd imagined it would. The light from the kitchen shone through the material from behind her, silhouetting her slim waist and rounded hips. Her nipples pressed against the front of the T-shirt, and the neckline slid down, off one shoulder.

He dragged his gaze to her face, feeling a prickly heat rise on his skin. "Bourbon," he rasped.

"I don't need—"

"Drink it."

She lifted her chin at his high-handedness but tipped the mug up to her lips. When the doorbell rang, Olivia's eyes widened, and she sent him a nervous glance.

"Probably the sheriff. I called him after I called Hank." He headed for the door, and Olivia snatched one of Gram's crocheted afghans off a chair to wrap around her shoulders.

Reyn showed the dripping sheriff into the living room, and Olivia wearily relayed what little there was to tell about the latest attempt on her life. As before, the sheriff promised to do all he could. "Until we catch this guy, whoever he is, you best not go anywhere alone, ma'am."

"She won't," Reyn assured the officer, then ushered him to the door with his thanks. When he returned to the living room, Olivia had dropped the afghan onto the chair and was rubbing the muscles at the back of her neck.

"You can take my bed. I'll sleep on the couch."

She spun to face him. "No! I can go to Lila's room or something. You stay in the guest room."

"I'm not having this argument." He drilled a hard gaze on her. "Take my bed." Placing his hands on her shoulders, he turned her back toward the stairs and swatted her behind.

Mistake. The little swat was enough to remind him that she had no underwear.

"All right, already. Never let it be said I kept you from being chivalrous." She tossed her hair as she headed out of the room, and the scent of his shampoo wafted to him. Yet on her the scent became more delicate, more feminine. Decidedly more erotic. The coil of sensual tension in his gut twisted tighter.

He cleared his throat. "I just have to get a few things out of there, and then the room's all yours."

Following her up the steps, he watched the provocative sway of her hips as she glided up the stairs in front of him. The T-shirt clung to her backside, molded to her enticing curves. A little moan escaped his throat.

"What?" she asked, glancing back at him.

"Nothing."

She slipped into his bed, while he gathered a change of clothes for the morning. He heard the whisper of sheets and her tired sigh as she settled in, and felt himself get hard.

Get out, Erikson. Walk away.

He turned to tell her goodnight and found her winding the sheet in her fingers.

"Reyn, I...I'm still kinda rattled about...what happened." Her voice trembled, as if to give credence to her words. She raised her eyes to him and drew her bottom lip between her teeth. "Would you stay for a while and...hold me?"

Her request kicked him in the gut. "I can't do that. I—"

With leaden legs, he walked toward the door.

"Please," she squeaked. Her heard tears in her voice.

Perspiration beaded on his upper lip. "Olivia," he started, his voice thick with his need for her. "You know what will happen if I stay. You know why I can't..."

"Yeah, I know." Disappointment and defeat colored her tone.

He stood in the doorway, staring out at the hall, paralyzed by the battle waging inside him. *She's a virgin. You can't give her what she needs. You'll hurt her.*

The bed creaked as she resettled, and the sound chased along his nerves. Then she sniffed, a broken sob. And he looked at her. She watched him from the bed with sad eyes, her fiery hair fanned on his white pillow. Void of makeup, her face appeared more fragile and sweet, and he could better see the freckles dancing across her nose.

Don't do it.

For a moment he just stood there, lost in her gold eyes, calling himself a million kinds of fool.

Finally he took one step toward her, then another. The bed squeaked as he climbed in next to her. His hands shook as he pulled her trembling body close. His heart bumped wildly as she laid her head on his chest and whispered, "Thank you."

Then he closed his eyes and listened to the pattering rain on the window while he held her tight.

Chapter Twelve

Reyn's heart pounded a steady, life-affirming cadence in Olivia's ear. The tension inside her slowly unfurled, giving way to drowsy security and contentment. Lying curled against Reyn's broad chest, in the safe circle of his arms, felt right. Felt good. So good.

It occurred to her that Reyn might think she'd been manipulating him, using her scare that night as an excuse to seduce him into bed with her. She frowned and tipped her head back to peer up at him. "Reyn?"

"Mmm."

"I really was frightened tonight. I—"

"Shh. It's okay." He hugged her closer, kissed the crown of her head. "You're safe now."

"No," she tried again. "I mean, I didn't plan this as some big seduction scene or...well, I just don't want you to think I'm exploiting the situation to put your back to the wall or—"

"I don't."

She released a deep breath. "Good."

His fingers trailed lightly up her spine and down again in a hypnotic stroke that he repeated until her bones melted. He worked his other hand into her hair and massaged her scalp until her all of her skin tingled.

Slowly she brushed her hand over his chest, letting the scattering of crisp brown hair tickle her palm. The gentle rise and fall of his chest grew heavier, hotter. A slow swell of arousal blossomed inside her, and her own breathing grew ragged.

Smoothing her hand over the muscles of his chest and washboard abs, she thought of the calendar picture that had fueled her fantasies regarding this man. A grin touched her lips. A few weeks ago, if someone had told her she'd be here snuggled next to the sexy man in that picture, she'd have checked him for fever. But here she was.

And the thick ridge straining against his shorts told her it wouldn't take much to convince him to live out a few of the fantasies she'd imagined.

Peering up at him, she studied the firm set of his face, his tight jaw. "Reyn?"

"Yeah," he answered huskily.

"What are you thinking about?"

He didn't answer right away, instead drawing a slow, deep breath and grunting. "I'm thinking that it's time to change the oil in my truck."

Not what she'd expected.

"Really?"

"Yep. That and trying to remember the preamble to the Constitution. Anything to get my mind off the fact that your leg is draped over mine and that you're not wearing any panties."

Oh.

How could he sound so matter-of-fact? Now that he'd called those details to her attention, she could barely breathe. She tried to move her leg off his, but the slide of her freshly shaved leg against his hairy thigh caused a delicious shiver to chase through her.

"Stop movin' around, Red. You're killing' me."

"Sorry."

He cleared his throat. "So what were you thinking about?"

"You don't want to know."

"Try me."

She swallowed hard. "The fact that all my fantasies about you weren't half as good as the real thing."

"You've...fantasized about me?" His voice sounded hoarse.

She propped on an elbow to look down at him, giving him a lopsided grin. "Mmm-hmm. Ever since I saw that calendar picture, you've starred in many of my—"

He mumbled a four-letter word on a sigh and closed his eyes.

"Sorry," she whispered. "You asked." As she settled back in the crook of his arm, she placed a light kiss on his chest, intending to keep the contact brief, chaste. But his warm skin against her lips was better than anything she could imagine. She opened her mouth and kissed him again, tasting him with the tip of her tongue.

Reyn moaned, a feral sound rumbling like thunder from his chest. She peeked up at his face, an apology on her lips. But before she could speak, he caught her chin, rolled on top of her and brought his mouth crashing down on hers. His kiss was deep and dark and dangerous. He ground his lips against hers with an urgency that kicked her pulse into a frantic rhythm. His teeth scraped hers, his mouth bruised hers, and his tongue plunged inside to tangle with her own. For long, shattering moments, he kissed her, being neither gentle nor polite. And she answered his need with her own desperate hunger.

Finally he pulled away and fell back on the bed. He gulped in oxygen, his head sinking back in the pillow, and his eyes squeezed closed. She watched him while she fought to control her own fractured breathing. When he finally opened his eyes, his gaze was a smoldering, smoky gray. "If we're gonna do this, we might as well do it right."

She blinked her confusion at his cryptic statement as he rolled away from her and climbed off the bed. Reyn crossed the room to the bureau and dug in the shaving kit sitting on top. Pulling out a small box, he ripped open the cardboard and extracted the contents. He tossed the handful of foil packs—condoms, she realized—onto the pillow by her head and threw the box in the trash.

"Only twelve in the box." He met her gaze with a hot, hard stare. "Think that'll be enough?"

A rush of heat washed through her, scalding her cheeks and tingling in her breasts. She drew a slow breath, searching for a retort that would mask her jangling nerves. She didn't want him to know the intensity in his eyes caused a quiver in her gut.

"Well," she drawled. "I don't know. I have more than twelve fantasies about you."

In the pale light from the window, she saw him hike up one eyebrow. "Oh, yeah?"

Holding her gaze, he hooked his thumbs in his waistband and stripped out of his shorts. The lighthearted quip she'd been forming died on her tongue. Every inch of him was resplendent male perfection. Corded muscle and sinewy strength. Wide shoulders and lean hips. Hard planes and harsh angles. And the expression in his eyes that said he knew how to use that body in ways she had never dreamed possible.

He stalked toward the bed and stopped at the foot.

"In any of your fantasies, did I ever..." he wrapped long fingers around her ankle and raised her leg, "...kiss you here?"

His warm lips pressed against the curve of her instep while his thumb massaged the sole of her foot. She squirmed as a crackling bolt of desire raced through her, left her weak.

He lifted a gaze that said he wanted an answer. She tried to speak but couldn't find her voice. When she shook her head, he twisted his lips as if her response disappointed him.

"What about here?" He slid his hand along her calf and dipped his head to kiss her behind the knee. Another flood of sweet sensation spun through her.

"No," she whispered.

"Pity." His lips ghosted over her inner thigh, and she tensed, her whole body humming, certain he was headed *there*.

Instead he released her leg and moved over her, bunching the borrowed T-shirt up in his hands and stopping to dip his tongue in her navel. "Here?"

Her belly filled with liquid fire. Her breath hitched.

"M-maybe."

Splaying his large hands at her hips, he skimmed his fingers upward, past her waist, over her ribs, stopping when his fingertips grazed the bottom of her breasts. Her nipples beaded in anticipation, yearning for his touch, and a strangled sound of frustration vibrated in her throat.

He raised his head and met her gaze. The corner of his mouth twitched, and amusement sparked in his eyes. "What is it, sweetheart? What do you want me to do?"

She scowled at him, and his smug grin grew. With a quick, easy motion, he slid the shirt off her and bent his head to catch a nipple in his lips. He tugged gently, and pure pleasure exploded inside her. She whimpered and arched her back, offering herself and begging for more. He moved to the other nipple and teased it with his tongue.

"Reyn." She sank her fingers into his hair, holding his head at her breast, greedy for more of the sweet torture.

When he looked up at her now, all teasing had disappeared from his eyes. "You like that, don't you, Olivia?"

She nodded.

"Say it."

Licking her lips, she rasped, "Yes."

He moved higher, letting his body slide across hers with a slow sensual stroke. "What about this?" He nipped at the curve of her shoulder, the arch of her throat, then tugged her earlobe with his teeth. "Do you like that?"

"Reyn," she sobbed, her body trembling. The coil of arousal wound so tight inside her she thought she might burst. He'd barely touched her, yet he'd electrified every nerve ending, awakened every cell of her body.

"In your fantasies," he whispered, his breath hot in her ear, "do I ever do this?"

Her heart thundered as he pressed butterfly kisses to the corner of her mouth, the bridge of her nose, her eyelids. His exquisite tenderness wrenched the tangled passion inside her in a new direction.

"Oh God," she breathed.

"Because in the last few days, I've fantasized about kissing you all of those places...and a whole lot more."

When he gripped her shoulders, turned her onto her stomach, she felt limp. Her bones had become useless jelly, and her blood flowed like molten lava in her veins.

Reyn's fingertips skated over her back, then he stroked his hands over her bottom and squeezed. Something warm and wet touched the small of her back, and she sucked in a sharp breath. Feathering his tongue along her spine, he worked his way back to her nape, and kissed her with an open mouth, hot and hungry against her skin.

"Please, Reyn..." she gasped. She was dying. Her body quaked and throbbed. She could barely breathe.

He caught a lock of her hair and rubbed it between his fingers. "So beautiful," he murmured, then plowed his hands deep in the damp tresses. "Your hair was the first thing that attracted me to you. I always was fascinated with fire..."

She heard more in his statement than he probably intended, and with effort, she found the strength to roll onto her back and gaze up at him. He propped on one arm, hovering over her, then reached for her thigh with his free hand. Pulling her leg up, he settled in the cradle of her hips, nudging the center of her heat with his erection. She jerked at the intimate contact, and a fiery jolt shot through her.

"Easy," he crooned, sinking slowly against her, fitting his steely length intimately against her. "Kiss me."

He captured her lips with his, but he didn't simply kiss her. He made love to her mouth with his lips and his tongue. When he rocked his hips against her, she rose to meet him, begging him to give her what his body promised. She ached for the fulfillment that was just beyond her reach. He covered her breast with his palm, rolled the straining peak between his finger and thumb.

Then he was gone. Cool air replaced the heat of his body on hers. She whimpered her protest and blinked rapidly to clear her blurry vision. Beside her, Reyn ripped open a foil pack, sheathed himself and turned to face her.

When he straddled her again, he gripped her chin and angled her head up, forcing her to look at him.

His eyes were the color of storm clouds, dark and turbulent, and his gaze penetrated deep into her soul. He held her with that piercing stare as he entered her with a swift, sure stroke.

Pleasure and pain roiled together as he filled her, and her head lolled back. A cry wrenched from her throat, and Reyn muffled the sob with a deep, plundering kiss. He laced their fingers and raised her arms over her head. For several seconds, he didn't move, giving her a chance to accept his invasion.

Finally, he pulled out. Slowly. When he glided back inside her, a low growl of satisfaction rumbled in his chest. She felt his groan as much as heard it. The vibration echoing through her body with ripple effect, spreading sweet sensation through her.

He kept the tempo slow at first, milking every bit of pleasure from the friction of her body gripping his. She read the burden of his restraint in the tension tightening his jaw, the tremor of controlled power in his muscles, the lightning in his eyes.

With a deft hand, he reached between her legs and rubbed her gently. Just a few strokes of his fingers sent her over the edge. She clung to him as she entered the maelstrom. Dizzying sensations and blinding light caught her up and battered her with wave after wave of pulsating bliss.

With a roar, Reyn plunged deeper and shuddered as he joined her in release. He collapsed on top of her, panting and trembling. Or maybe she was the one shaking. Twined with his body, still filled by his heat, it was hard to tell where he began and she ended. He rested for a minute before he lifted his head to look down at her, his expression inscrutable. Sighing, he cradled her head between his hands and kissed her.

Fiercely. Deeply. Thoroughly.

Her heart took wing, and she knew she was lost.

"Damn it." His harsh tone startled her.

"What?"

His face was a mask of sincerity as he grumbled, "We only have eleven condoms left."

Relief bubbled from her in a laugh. "Damn."

He smiled at her then, and her heart nearly stopped. She loved him. She knew it for certain when he gazed at her like he was, with devotion and tenderness glowing from his eyes.

"Wait here," he told her and kissed the tip of her nose. Carefully disengaging himself from her, he crossed the floor to the bathroom, and she savored the view of her lover's naked body.

Her lover. A thrill swirled in her gut.

She heard the water running and snuggled down in the sheets to rest, totally sated, and at the same time aching for more.

Loving Reyn was a little bit scary. She still had a long way to go to get him to open his heart and soul to her, to share his deepest self with her. And he had an apartment, friends and a job in Atlanta that he'd return to in a matter of days. But the sexy fireman of her fantasies had managed to steal her heart.

Olivia sighed and pushed the nagging thoughts aside, remiss to spoil the blissful moment. She'd worry later about the repercussions.

Chapter Thirteen

The squawk of a blue jay outside his bedroom window woke Reyn early the next morning. Though not particularly well rested, he felt more relaxed than he had in days. He squinted the morning into focus and discovered a fan of red hair under his cheek, his arm draped over a slim waist. Awareness brought him fully awake and fully aroused in the blink of an eye.

Olivia. He'd made love to Olivia last night. Not just once but many times, in many ways, each time better than the last. Damn, just remembering made his body ache for her again.

He forced the scintillating thoughts aside long enough to recall the events that had led her into his bedroom and had weakened his resolve to stay away from her. Wet clothes. Her tears. Her body trembling with fright.

Someone had tried to kill her.

Reflexively, his arm tightened around her, a protective response to the idea he'd almost lost her. He pulled her closer, snuggled his body behind hers so that her smooth, silky skin touched his from cheek to toe.

With a sexy, contented purr, she roused, stretching her lithe body like a cat. Glancing over her shoulder at him, she flashed him a sleepy smile. "Mornin'."

"Hey."

She turned to face him, nestling against him and stroking a hand over his chest. "What time is it?"

"Early."

"Good. Then there's still time before I need to go."

"Go where?"

She grunted as if the answer should be obvious. "To work, of course."

"Not today. Not with a killer after you."

She stiffened and raised her eyes to meet his. Her expression said everything she didn't. For a short time, she'd forgotten the horror of the night before. And as much as the killer's attempt on her life scared her, neither did she want to stay away from work. The conflict inside her played out on her face, and he shared her frustration.

"I'm getting close to figuring this whole mess out. Until then I want you to stay here, where I can protect you."

She groaned. "As nice as it would be, staying here in bed with you all day, I won't hide. I have a job, and I—"

"Call in sick."

"Reyn, I—"

He silenced her with a kiss. His intent had only been to distract her from her argument, but the minute his lips touched hers, he was lost. Heat slammed into him like a backdraft, knocking the breath from him, scorching him. His body remembered too well the incredible things they'd done together the night before, and he wanted more.

Olivia wrapped her arms around his neck, wove her fingers into his hair and pulled him closer, deepening the kiss.

Sliding on top of her, he parted her lips with his tongue, and she welcomed him inside. Her legs twined around him, and his naked body pressed against her heat. Rational thought fled, and within seconds he drove himself home, sinking into her with a moan. He couldn't get enough. Even as many times as they'd done this last night, he still needed more.

He tried to move slowly, to be gentle, certain that she must be sore this morning. But she set a quicker pace, urging him on. In the early morning light, he watched her face, something the dark room had all but hidden from him last night. Her face was free of makeup, flushed with passion, beautiful. *His.*

Oh God. He hadn't had sex with her last night, he'd been branding her. Staking his claim to her. He was her first lover, and that honor filled him with a sense of pride and possession. The emotion that swelled in his chest sharpened his senses, heightened his pleasure, intensified every nuance of their joining.

Sex had never been this good with any other woman. But he'd never made love to another woman as he had with Olivia. With every fiber of his being. With more than his body. With his whole heart and mind and soul. He wanted her again. He wanted her forever.

And it scared the hell out of him.

Coward.

He pushed aside the taunt hissing at the edges of his mind and roared his satisfaction as he climaxed. Thoroughly spent, he shifted as he sank back toward the bed so that he didn't crush her. Exhausted but sated, he lay motionless, catching his breath, trying hard to ignore the little voice that wouldn't be silenced.

You can't make her happy. You'll let her down. You're still a hopeless coward.

Olivia's fingers massaged his scalp then glided down his nape to his back. She sighed contentedly.

"Wow," she murmured. "What a way to start the day."

"Mmm."

She remained silent for another moment. The only sound in the stillness was the whisper of her breathing in his ear, the gentle patter of the continuous rain out his window.

Then she stirred, pressed a light kiss to his cheek, and spoke. "I'm falling in love with you, Reyn."

His heart slammed against his ribs, and icy fingers clawed him inside. Every muscle tensed. Every nerve screamed.

The demon cackled and sneered. *Now what are you going to do, coward? She's falling in love.*

Panic surged through him, seared him. He rolled away from her with a jerk, lurched off the bed. He needed distance. He needed to think. What had he done? He'd let his guard down. Let her get close. He'd slept with her, for crying out loud!

"No," he groaned, pressing the heels of his hands to his eyes.

Way to protect her, moron. Now you've set her up to be burned. Now she'll be hurt. Now she'll hate you when you prove yourself unworthy, when you fail her like you failed your mother.

"Reyn? What—"

"No." He spun to face her, aimed an accusing finger. "I told you not to fall in love with me. I warned you not to get too close."

"I-I know, but...that was before last night. Before we made love."

He saw fear flicker in her eyes, and his chest tightened. He should have known, should have seen what was happening last night. He should have stopped before things went too far.

Maybe, just maybe, it wasn't too late. If he could somehow undo some of the damage, break some of the bonds that had formed. He drew a shaky breath and growled, "We didn't make love. We had sex. It was just sex."

She shook her head. "Not for me. For me it was more. So much more."

"No! It can't be any more. It changes nothing." Even as he said the words, he knew he was lying. It had meant more to him too. Being joined to her had rocked his world. That was perhaps the scariest part. But looking too closely at the truth of his feelings toward her was like staring at the sun. It hurt too much, blinded him to the reality that he could never be what she needed. He had no right to love her, to ask her to love him.

Because you're too big of a coward to let her in, too scared to do the right thing. You don't deserve her.

He bit out a vile curse, and she flinched. Somehow he had to regain the distance that would protect her from his failure. He had to convince her they had no future, squelch her dreams, stomp her feelings before they had a chance to grow.

Hurting her now would kill him, but it would save her the deeper, more bitter disappointment sure to come if he let things between them progress.

"I let things get out of hand and that was a mistake. I'm sorry."

The look on her face flayed him open, left him raw and bleeding. He scrubbed a hand over his face, hating himself for letting things get out of control, leaving him no choice but to break her heart this way. He had to be convincing, could leave her no room for doubt. The break had to be clean and complete. Even if she hated him for it.

"I can't be what you need me to be, Olivia."

She stared at him with tears hovering in her bewildered gaze. Her stillness raked him with razor-sharp tines.

Hurting her, rejecting her this way ripped him apart. But it was for the greater good. Wasn't it?

He could see her trembling, and he ached to take her in his arms, soothe her, beg her forgiveness. But he couldn't. He couldn't risk failing Olivia and letting her see how miserably he fell short of her expectations.

"Why are you doing this?" she asked, her voice thready, heartbreaking.

"I'm not doing anything I didn't warn you about. I told you I couldn't be what you wanted. I don't want to hurt you, but I can't—" He huffed his frustration and scrubbed his jaw.

She pressed her lips together, obviously trying not to cry. He felt his own throat constrict, and before he broke down in front of her, he headed for the bathroom.

"I'm going to take a shower. I think you should go home now. I-I want to be alone."

She gave a harsh, humorless laugh. "What happened to 'I want you here so I can protect you'?"

Reyn slapped the doorframe and bit out a curse. "I'll still come down to the pharmacy later, but I have some things to do first."

She climbed off the bed, fire leaping in her eyes. "You're *so* gallant. Well, don't bother yourself on my account, Mr. Macho. I'll take care of myself."

"Be careful, Olivia. Have Hank take you in to town. I couldn't stand it if anything happened to you."

She tossed her hair and scowled. "I absolve you of any responsibility if I get killed. Heaven forbid you should *feel* anything where I'm concerned."

He tried not to look at her sleek, beautiful body as she snatched her clothes off the chair where she'd draped them last night. Her hurt and anger wrenched inside him. *Don't leave. I'm sorry. So sorry.*

"I trusted you."

"And I told you I was no hero. I can't live up to your fantasy." Without waiting for her response, he headed into the shower. He turned the water to the iciest setting and stepped into the punishing spray, clenching his teeth. He tipped his face up so that the chilling spray could wash away the sting of tears from his cheeks. Silently he prayed she'd be there when he got out. In his heart, he hoped she wouldn't give up on him. He clung to the hope that she'd see through his brutal tactics. That she'd have the love and strength he lacked to face down his fears.

Don't go, Olivia. I need you.

But when he stepped back into the bedroom, dripping cold water from the shower, she was gone.

Olivia stomped down the stairs, angry tears blurring her vision. She'd been a fool. Why had she thought her love, her faith would be enough to save him from his demons? People didn't change just because she wanted them to. She couldn't make him open his heart to her, couldn't force him to share his soul. All of her optimism and encouragement couldn't fix the things from his past that haunted him any more than she could undo the terrible mistake she'd made crawling into his bed last night.

Stupid, stupid! She'd given herself to a man who'd told her he couldn't commit, warned her not to fall in love, given her every out. But she'd let her blind belief in his caring nature, his integrity and protectiveness cloud the truth. He didn't love her, didn't want commitment, wasn't looking for anything more than a tumble in the sheets.

I can't live up to your fantasy.

She'd wanted her vision of what *could* be so badly, she'd ignored reality. She had only herself to blame. She'd made love to him without thinking about tomorrow, without considering his warnings, without...

...a condom.

Olivia's knees buckled as she reached for the brass knob of the front door. It rattled as she sank to the floor with a whimper. They hadn't used a condom this morning.

Mentally she tried to calculate where she was in her cycle, how likely it was that she'd conceived. But her mind froze. All she could think about was the emotionless tone of Reyn's voice. *I told you I was no hero.*

She considered leaving. She wanted to go home and put last night and this morning behind her. But Reyn needed to know about their slip-up, needed to be prepared for the possibility that she could be...

A sharp ache curled inside her, tightening her throat. She wanted to have a family of her own. But the idea of having Reyn's baby was bittersweet. Because he didn't love her.

On weak legs, she stumbled into the kitchen and dropped into a chair to wait for Reyn. When he came downstairs and spotted her sitting at the pine table, he hesitated in the doorway.

"I thought you'd gone home."

A fresh wave of pain washed through her, and she had to fill her lungs before she could speak. "And I will. But we have to talk first."

"I have nothing left to say."

"Well, I do."

He walked past her to the coffee machine and began fixing the pot to brew, presenting her with his back.

Olivia stood and continued, undeterred by his rudeness. "We messed up this morning."

"I'll say."

"I mean...this morning, when we made lo—" The words caught in her throat. "When we *had sex*—" Her tone was as hard as the bands squeezing her heart.

She watched his back as he continued setting up the coffee maker without looking at her.

"Reyn, we didn't use a condom. I could be pregnant."

His hands stilled, but he didn't turn. For long moments, he was quiet. Too quiet.

"Reyn?"

"Damn it, this is just the kind of problem I knew I'd cause for you."

She staggered back a step. More than the self-reproach in his tone, his word choice crashed into her like a physical blow. Her breath backed up in her lungs, and for several seconds, she couldn't speak.

"Whatever you decide to do, I'll give you money, help pay—"

"Keep your damn money! I don't consider a child to be a *problem*—" Her voice caught on a sob, and finally he turned.

His eyes reminded her of granite. Cold, hard, lifeless.

He truly didn't care that she could be carrying his baby. Family meant so little to him that he'd rather part with money than be part of his child's life.

Hurt, rage, disillusionment mingled and swelled inside her. She wanted to throw up, to lash out. She felt the world tilt.

Mustering her strength, she looked him in the eye, his cold gray eyes that stared back at her with no sign of remorse.

"Goodbye, Reyn," she whispered, then spun on her heel.

She ran for the door, blinking back her tears. She would not cry for him. She was through with Reyn and his distance. Family meant nothing to him. How could she have ever imagined building a life with him? How could she have been so blind?

As she ran for the woods, for home, the gray clouds reflected the bleak fog in her soul. And the sky wept for her.

I could be pregnant.

Olivia's announcement paralyzed his body while his mind raced with the implications.

What had he been thinking, making love to her without protection? He'd been so swept up in the moment, so intensely focused on her and his bone-deep need to be inside her, to claim her that he hadn't given a thought to precaution.

Damn. Damn. Damn!

He clenched his teeth so tight in self-censure that his jaw ached. His gut revolted with an acid bite.

Because he'd gotten so lost in what he was feeling for her, he'd screwed up royally. He'd done exactly what he'd been trying to avoid most of his life. Because he'd gotten too close, too attached, he'd hurt someone else he cared about.

And she hated him now. One more innocent life he'd ruined while he battled his inadequacies and ran from his demons.

He could be a father. He could have created a life, another innocent who'd suffer because of his failure. He'd thought he'd sunk as deep into his despair and fear as he could go.

He'd been wrong.

With a trembling hand, he grabbed the coffee pot and tried to pour himself a cup. The hot liquid sloshed out, burning his hand and splashing on the counter.

I don't consider a child to be a problem!

With a roar of frustration and self-disgust, he hurled the glass carafe across the kitchen. It shattered on the wall where his calendar picture hung, splattering his image with coffee, littering the floor with shards of glass. His chest squeezed with warring emotions, and he dragged in a labored breath. He'd been so careful, building walls to protect himself from this pain, yet his world had still collapsed around him. The walls had caved in on him. He was trapped in the rubble, suffocating, and only he could rescue himself. If he had the courage.

Coward.

The way he saw it, he had two options. He could go back to his anesthetized existence in Atlanta and bury the past again. He could run from the heartache and hide from the truth, try to escape his feelings for Olivia.

But what about his responsibilities to her and their child, if she was pregnant?

Olivia's bitter reaction to his offer of money replayed inside his head. He hadn't handled that well at all. Another mistake. Another painful blow to a woman he cared about. Deeply. So what did he do? How did he rectify the mess he'd made?

His only real option filled him with an icy dread. How could he stay in Clairmont? How could he live with the daily reminders of his failure and the pain of his losses?

The demon snickered and taunted him. *Coward. Take the easy way out. Walk away. No pain.*

But what about the agony he'd suffer if he walked away from Olivia? Losing her was an option he didn't want to consider. Losing the chance to be a father to her child left a bleak emptiness inside him. He groaned and scrubbed his face with his hand. He had only to think of the way she'd felt in his arms, the soul-piercing connection he'd experienced when their bodies were joined, to have his answer.

He wanted her, *needed* her in his life. She'd breathed hope and life into him with her optimism, chased away his gloom with her sunshine and warm smile. Her touch, her love gave him something he'd searched his whole life for.

Peace. Contentment. True joy.

But before he could think of a future, of children with Olivia, he had to settle the past. He couldn't give her the love and commitment she needed with his demons still haunting him. He still had so many doubts and unanswered questions holding him back, and he wouldn't give Olivia less than his best.

He had to redeem himself for his mistakes, earn his right to love her. He had to find out what happened to his mother, had to unlock the doors to his history that he'd kept firmly locked for so long, shutting out the demons and pain of loss.

His father was the key.

Driven by the need for closure, a need for long-overdue peace, he headed upstairs to finish dressing and get the keys to his truck. He knew just the person he needed to see. He had questions for Hannah Russell, and he was finally ready to hear the answers. Lancing the wounds of his past made entering a blazing house seem like a day at the park.

But Olivia was worth it.

Chapter Fourteen

Reyn knocked on the motel room door where his mother's best friend was living while her house was rebuilt. When Hannah Russell answered his knock, she didn't seem surprised to see him.

"I was wondering when you'd be by. I don't suppose this is a social call either."

"No, ma'am. I need answers."

Hannah's shoulders drooped, and she nodded her resignation. "So be it. Come on in."

Her apparent reluctance to talk stirred a fresh quiver of doubt in him, but he stepped inside and let his eyes adjust to the dim light.

Sara slept in one of the double beds, and Reyn hesitated. "Maybe we should talk outside. I don't want her to hear—"

"It's okay. She won't hear. A freight train couldn't wake her. School mornings are a real challenge at our house." Hannah gave him a weak smile.

Nervously wiping his damp palms on his jeans, Reyn sat on the corner of the second bed and met Hannah's eyes. "I need to know about my mother. Can you think of any reason someone would want to kill her?"

He prayed she'd give him something, some name other

than his own father. But he knew he was grasping at straws.

"There were always people who talked bad about her, gossiped about her because she had a child out of wedlock."

Another wave of guilt swept through him. His mother had endured so much for his sake.

"Plenty of the wives in town were jealous simply 'cause she always drew the men's eyes when she walked in a room. She was so pretty," Hannah continued and sat on a stained, stuffed chair beside the bed. She sighed and shook her head. "They justified their feelings toward her by spreading rumors about her flirting with every man in town, trying to seduce their husbands. The talk hurt your mother, but she didn't deny it or dignify the lies with a response."

"I remember the talk. Got in plenty of fights at school because of it."

Hannah gave him a melancholy smile. "I know. She worried about you. Hated the fact that you heard that kind of talk about her and felt you had to defend her. At the same time, it made her proud that you'd stick up for your family." Hannah sighed. "God, she loved you. She'd have done anything for you."

A knot of emotion rose in his throat. He had to cough to loosen the stranglehold before he could speak. "Lou told Olivia and me that in high school my mother dated...your husband."

Hannah looked away, drawing a deep breath and straightening her spine. "She did. They were right serious too. I tried hard not to envy her, seein' as how she was my friend and all. But I'd been in love with George forever, and all I could do was watch from the sidelines, so to speak. Then Claire got pregnant our senior year." She turned a meaningful glance toward him. "With you."

A current of apprehension flowed through him. They were getting close to the truths he'd avoided for years. "And?" he prompted when she hesitated.

"And George broke up with her. He wouldn't even speak her name. Asked me out to spite her." Hannah furrowed her brow. "I jumped at the chance, even though I really should have had more compassion for Claire's feelings, but...funny thing was, she encouraged me to go after George. Said she wanted me...and George...to be happy. I got pregnant with Billy a few months later, and George offered to marry me, to give our baby a name."

A strange niggling left Reyn feeling off balance. "I don't mean to sound rude, but...why did he marry you when you got pregnant and not my mom when she did?"

"I offered, but she turned me down."

Reyn jerked his head toward the door. He'd been so involved in Hannah's story that he'd not heard George come in. Hannah blanched, telling Reyn she hadn't noticed her husband either.

"You never told me that." Hurt colored Hannah's tone.

"Water under the bridge now." George strode into the room, scowling at Reyn. "Why don't you get to the question you came to ask and get on out of here, boy. You want to know if I'm your daddy, don't you? Or maybe you think I killed your mama 'cause of some old grudge or lovers' spat?"

Hannah gasped and pressed shaky fingers to her lips. "Did you, George? Oh, God...did you kill Claire?"

He turned his glare on Hannah. "No, damn it." He faced Reyn again. "No on both counts. I ain't your daddy 'cause I never slept with your mama. But she was givin' it to someone, 'cause she got knocked up while *we* were datin'. Still, I loved her and was willin' to marry her and give the baby a name, even if the kid weren't mine."

A mixture of relief and frustration swirled through Reyn. He

211

eyed the older man with a cautious gaze. "Then who is my father?"

"She wouldn't tell me." George swiveled his head toward Hannah.

"But...but I always assumed..." Hannah bit her bottom lip, and a soft, sad noise escaped her throat.

"You thought he was mine?" George asked. "So did everyone else in town, I suppose. Guess that's how Reyn's real daddy got away with his secret."

Hannah nodded meekly. "Claire never told me who Reyn's father was, and I never asked, 'cause I thought...well, it was just something we let lie, seein' as I thought my husband..." She huffed and rubbed her temple. "I'm sorry, Reyn. If I knew I'd tell you, but she protected her secret so well. Because of you. She didn't want you subjected to any more town gossip or comparisons or...or you to know which man in this town had...had not been willing to claim you. She thought it was better you believe he was just...gone."

"I'd wager she wasn't talking 'cause the poor sap was married." George stalked toward the back of the motel room.

Reyn tensed. "Why do you say that?"

George grunted as if the answer were obvious. Reyn's thinking was on the same track, but he wanted to hear George confirm his suspicions.

"Think about it," George growled. "She had to be protectin' him, if she wasn't telling who he was. He never stepped forward to claim either her or his kid. That had to be the reason why."

"What if he lived out of town? Or went to college and she didn't tell him?" Even as Reyn spoke, George was shaking his head.

"Naw. He was married."

Reyn's mind raced forward. "Gram said Mom was ready to tell. She was going to confront my father, and tell me about him but that she died before she could. Gram thinks whoever he is, that he killed Mom to keep her quiet. And if he *was* married..."

"It all fits." Hannah nodded slowly.

"That still leaves a lot of possibilities. Are you sure you don't have any idea who—"

"I never said I didn't know who he was. Just that she never told me. I figured it out. When he started killin' people—your mom, the sheriff—"

"The sheriff?" Adrenaline shot through Reyn's veins. "Olivia's father?"

George nodded. "Made it look like a hunting accident, just like he burned your house to cover your mother's murder. But Crenshaw was onto him, so he killed the sheriff before his investigation could uncover the evidence needed to make an arrest."

A moment passed before Reyn broke the silence. "Who? Who is my father? Who killed my mother?"

"Horton." George grimaced. "I know I should've said something when I figured out it was him but, hell...he'd already killed twice, and I had a family to protect. So I kept quiet."

An odd combination of icy grief and blazing fury tangled inside Reyn.

"George," Hannah whispered, her eyes wide and full of tears.

The older man turned to her now. "I'm going to turn myself in, Hannah. I can't live with the guilt anymore. He's gotta be stopped." George pinched the bridge of his nose. "I'll try to make a deal with the D.A., but I might have to do time, even with my testimony. I hid knowledge of two murders."

Hannah bent her head, and her shoulders shook as she cried.

Reyn's chest squeezed. Logically, he knew he wasn't responsible for Hannah's grief, yet he still felt the pull of guilt for having stirred up this hornet's nest.

"Hannah, Reyn saved our little girl. I owe him this." George Russell's voice broke, and Reyn glanced away, struggling to keep his own composure.

"When you and Crenshaw's daughter started askin' questions, I tried to warn you things could get nasty. Knew you were pokin' into somethin' that could get you killed, but you wouldn't let it rest."

"He killed Olivia's father too. She deserves to know."

George nodded. "On my way to the sheriff's office, I'll stop by her place and tell her."

"No, I will." Reyn stood and started for the door. He stopped with his hand on the knob. "Thank you. For telling me the truth."

Russell shook his head and looked at the little girl asleep on the bed. "No, thank *you*."

As Reyn cracked open the motel room door, George's fire department pager started beeping. He sighed. "Duty calls."

Olivia jolted when Hank's pager went off on the kitchen counter behind her.

Katy giggled at her sister's nervous gasp. "It's just Daddy's beeper, silly."

She forced a grin for Katy's sake as she scooted her chair back and headed from the kitchen to find Hank. "Yeah, silly me. Finish your breakfast, squirt. Gloria will be here soon."

Silly me, thinking I could save Reyn from his ghosts. Silly

*me, thinking my love was enough for him to open his heart or
that he'd care about his own child. Silly, stupid me.*

Olivia blinked back the moisture creeping into her eyes and
swallowed hard to wash away the ache of tears rising in her
throat. She knocked on Hank's bedroom door but got no
answer. Hearing the shower running, she let herself in and
went to the bathroom door. "Hank?" she called in through the
tiny gap that she opened the door. "Hank, your beeper went off.
You've gotta go on a call."

"My beeper?" he answered over the whoosh of water then
added an expletive. "All right. Thanks, Liv. Oh, and when I get
back, we're gonna talk about where you were all night."

She rolled her eyes. "No, we're not. I'm an adult, Hank. I
don't answer to you anymore."

The shower cut off. "Olivia."

She didn't respond. She didn't want to talk about last night
to anyone. She didn't want to think about the colossal mistake
she'd made, Reyn's cold rejection of her, the deceptive warmth
in his eyes last night when they'd made love. No. Had sex. It
was just sex to Reyn.

A fist of despair clutched at her lungs. Who was she
kidding? *She'd* been making love. She *loved* Reyn. She couldn't
imagine her life without him. But she had to go on without him.
He'd made that perfectly clear. On shaky legs, she headed to
her room where she sat on her bed, staring blankly at the
firemen's calendar on the opposite wall. She felt sick. Sick with
disappointment in herself. Sick with the possibility of facing
motherhood alone. Sick with bitter pain for the loss of what
she'd believed she had.

I can't be what you need me to be, Olivia.

Rising on trembling legs, she began changing clothes for
work. While she stared into her mirror, absently brushing her

hair and remembering Reyn's avid passion as he joined their bodies, Hank pounded on her door.

"I'm gone on a call, and Katy's yelling for you. She can't find her other shoe."

Olivia sighed. "Okay. Be right there."

"You all right, Jelly Bean? I was worried about you last night."

"I'm fine," she lied. In truth, she was bone tired and heartsick, but her family needed her. She couldn't let them down. Jamming her feet in a pair of sneakers, she headed out to the living room to look for Katy's missing shoe. "Where'd you leave it, squirt?"

"I don't know." Katy gave her a dramatic shrug and turned her hands palms up.

The doorbell rang, and Olivia groaned. "Coming." To Katy she said, "Try the laundry room."

Katy lumbered toward the back room, calling, "Here, shoe."

Trudging over to the door, Olivia glanced at her watch. She had to get the lead out if she wanted to be on time to work. When she opened the door, she blinked her surprise at finding Vance Horton on her porch. "Mr. Horton? What—"

"Is Hank here?" the man interrupted. He seemed agitated. Could it be about the call that came in on Hank's beeper? Horton should have been paged too.

"He just left on a fire department call. Why aren't you—"

"Good." Horton gave her a strange, crooked smirk.

"Is something wrong, Mr. H—"

He grabbed her arm and yanked her outside.

"What are you doing?"

He dragged her behind him as he lurched down the front

porch steps. Her pack of strays jumped to their feet and barked at the visitor. "We have some unfinished business, Claire."

Olivia stumbled along behind him, splashing through large puddles and trying to free her arm from his vise-like grip. His strange behavior puzzled her. "Claire? My name's Olivia. I—"

Then it clicked. Olivia's heart rose to her throat. Ice sluiced through her veins. *Unfinished business. Claire.*

"You killed Reyn's mother! You think I'm..." Panic swelled in her chest, and she fought wildly for release. "No!"

"Shut up." He jerked hard on her arm, almost pulling it from the socket. "I won't let you tell the world our secret. You've been nothing but trouble from the day I laid eyes on you, you Jezebel."

They were at the door of a white sedan now.

Just like the one that had run her off the road last night.

The dogs, reacting to her distress, were in a frenzy, nipping at Horton's heels and barking wildly. Rain poured from the dark clouds, soaking her clothes and chilling her to the bone. Terror washed through her as she met Horton's cold gaze.

"Get in. We're going for a little ride." Horton's face was a hard mask of hostility.

"Stop!" Olivia screamed as she fought him.

He shoved her into the front seat with a hard thrust and followed her inside the car. He held her arm as he pushed her into the passenger seat. Olivia tried to open the passenger-side door. It was locked, and the lock release button by the window was broken off. Her mind scrambled for another means of escape.

But before she could do more than say a silent prayer, Horton threw the car in gear and raced out of the driveway, spraying gravel behind them.

Chapter Fifteen

Vance Horton was his father.

Reyn squeezed the steering wheel as he drove his truck over the rain-drenched roads toward Olivia's house. Knowing the truth should make him feel something, yet he was numb. Stunned. Too busy examining all the angles and implications as the pieces of his history fell into place.

Vance Horton. The man who'd dogged him all through his years in elementary school, as if waiting for him to screw up. The man he'd watched arguing with his wife on several occasions. The man who'd come by the house the same afternoon his mother died.

It made sense now. Why hadn't he seen it sooner? Horton had been the last one to see his mother alive. Obviously their meeting had been confrontational, between Horton's report of Reyn's latest infraction at school and his mother's intention to tell the world about Horton's paternity. And Horton, as a volunteer fireman and knowing Reyn's penchant for playing with matches, would know just how to set a fire that would look accidental.

Finally, the numbness began to wear off, and a white-hot rage filled his veins. Horton had neglected him, his son. Horton had killed his mother. And Horton had led the campaign to drive Reyn out of town, condemning him for the fire that killed his mother. Perhaps it was just as well he hadn't known his father growing up. Knowing how the man had rejected and hounded him cut a deep swath through his soul. How could a man spurn his own child so coldly?

Immediately he thought of his own cruel words to Olivia that morning when she'd told him she could be pregnant. But he'd been shocked, confused, wanting to push her away. Well, he'd succeeded. Too well. He'd probably lost any chance of making things up to her. But he would try. He had to try.

A large white car, weaving wildly in the oncoming lane, whizzed past him, nearly hitting him, and Reyn released his frustration and pain in a string of obscenities directed toward the reckless driver. Careless driving like that, especially in this downpour, was a surefire way to get someone killed. He'd been on the scene of too many accidents to not know that much.

Pulling into Olivia's driveway, he tried to shake off the grip of anger. He needed to compose himself before he told Olivia his news. He had to rein in his emotions or risk losing control, breaking down in front of her. That was unthinkable.

As he approached the house, Katy clambered off the porch, lurching toward him on her tiny, braced legs. She waved her arms wildly, near hysterics. Panic grabbed him by the throat.

"Katy, what's wrong? What are you doing out in the rain?"

"'L-livia. H-help, 'Livia." Her teeth chattered, and her body shook. She could barely speak through the tears that racked her small body.

"What happened to Olivia?" he nearly shouted, grasping Katy's shoulders firmly.

"Mr. Horton took her. She s-screamed."

Dread snaked through his veins. "He took Olivia? When? Which way did they go?"

"Wh-white car. Went that way." Katy pointed down the driveway and gulped for air between sobs.

The white car he'd seen drunkenly weaving as it raced down the road. He muttered an oath through gritted teeth.

Firmly, he turned Katy to the house and nudged her toward the door. "Go back inside. Call 911 and tell them what happened. Then lock the door and don't let anyone in. I'll get Olivia, Katy. I promise."

A flash of metal caught his eye, and he stooped to pick up the object lying in the puddle near his feet. Olivia's ladybug pendant. The hair on his nape stood on end.

His heart in his throat, he jumped into his truck. He made a sharp turn on the front lawn and wheeled out of the driveway. Fear for Olivia knotted his gut and pumped adrenaline through his body. He'd only passed that white car a couple minutes ago, but even a couple minutes could be too many. His gut told him Horton intended to kill her.

Olivia had to think of something quickly or Horton would kill her. She had no doubt. His eyes lacked the lucidity that would indicate he was thinking rationally. He'd called her Claire and that alone spoke for the man's lost grip of reality. But if she could snap him out of the delusional state, maybe she could talk some sense into him, convince him to let her go.

"Mr. Horton, do you know who I am?" she asked, watching the man's face.

He jerked his gaze toward her, and in doing so caused the car to swerve on the slick road. Olivia fastened her seatbelt, then squeezed the armrest, holding on for dear life.

"Of course I know who you are. You're the bimbo who's trying to ruin me. You want to tell the town that I had sex with a student. You want to destroy my career. But I won't let you.

You want to tell everyone I'm that boy's father and rip my marriage apart. I've worked hard to get where I am, and I won't let you spoil everything for me."

Olivia's breath backed up in her lungs. "You're...Reyn's father?"

"Don't pretend you didn't know. You know about Reyn, and you know what I did to Claire."

Olivia stifled a gasp. "You killed her."

A muscle in his jaw twitched, and for the first time she noticed the similarity in the hard line of his mouth and Reyn's. "She was going to talk. Going to tell the boy everything. But then the town would find out. My wife, the school board. I had to shut her up. I never planned to kill her, but she started giving ultimatums. *No one* tells me what I have to do!"

Olivia tensed. If she could keep him talking, could she get enough information to have him convicted? "What did happen that day? Why *did* you kill her?"

He hesitated, his face grim. "She called the school. Said she had to see me. Then she started in on me about my obligations to my kid."

Olivia noted that he referred to Claire as she, not you. Maybe he had some clarity about the situation now.

"Stupid girl thought that I'd toss my family, my job, my reputation out the window and claim her brat? Ha! What a joke."

Horton glanced at her, drummed his fingers on the steering wheel. "She called me the worst mistake she ever made. Me! I was probably the only *real* man she ever had, but she called *me* a mistake. *She* was the mistake. She was the Jezebel." He huffed and gritted his teeth. "Then she said Reyn was the only good thing to come from her error in judgment."

Error in judgment. Olivia could relate with that. But Claire had obviously never loved Reyn's father. She, on the other hand, had fallen heartbreakingly in love with Reyn.

"She told me to do right by Reyn or else," Horton continued to rant. "She threatened to call Helen, tell her everything, so...so I hit her. She fell against the edge of the table and didn't get up. For a minute I thought she was dead, and I panicked. Then I realized how much easier my life would be if she was dead, so I carried her to her bed and..."

When he stopped, Olivia whispered, "Lit a candle in Reyn's room. Held it up to the curtains."

He didn't deny it. She was right. Oh Reyn, all these years he'd blamed himself, wondered if he'd left the candle burning. Her heart felt heavy, and tears pricked her eyes.

"And now...you're trying to destroy me too." The bitterness and accusation in his tone chilled her to the bone.

Stay calm.

"No. Mr. Horton, nobody's trying to destroy you. If you turn yourself in, I'm sure you could get a reduced charge and—"

"Never! I've come this far without anyone knowing what that wench did to me, what she made me do, and I won't go to prison for it now." He glared at her with a wild expression, like that of a trapped animal. An animal was always the most dangerous when cornered. Fear sat like a rock in her stomach and dampened her palms. She took a deep breath, trying to clear her mind and deciding how to reason with an irrational man.

"If you let me go, it would be a sign of good faith on your part, and I'm sure the sheriff would—"

"The sheriff?" He squinted a chilling look at her. "The sheriff is dead. I made sure of that after he started poking around and asking questions."

An icy shiver crept up her spine. "You...you killed Sheriff Anders?"

Horton scowled. "Anders? Hell, no. His name's Crenshaw. But no one knows I did it, 'cause I made sure it looked like an accident."

Olivia gasped. *Oh, God. Her father?*

The noise drew his attention, and he glared at her with dark speculation in his eyes. "He was getting too close to the truth. I had no choice."

Horrified shock rendered her mute. Surely she'd heard him wrong.

"You should have left well enough alone, girl. Now I have to make sure you can't talk either."

An odd buzzing rang in her ears, and she thought she might throw up. Her father. Claire. And she would be next if she didn't think fast. She forced her voice to work, strained though it was. "If you kill me, Reyn will figure out what happened. He's already on to you. He'll go to the police and—"

His bitter laugh cut her off. She felt the tires slip as he took a curve too fast, and she grabbed the door handle tighter.

"Reyn? That's who the town will think killed you. A lovers' spat gone bad."

Olivia swallowed the panic that threatened to choke her. She had to stay calm if she was going to have a prayer of getting away. The man wavered between past and present, clearly confused, obviously desperate, definitely deadly.

"Who are they gonna believe?" Horton asked, a smirk twisting his lips. "A known arsonist, or one of their own? I'm on the town council. I've run their kids' school without incident since I got rid of that trouble-makin' boy twenty years ago."

"Please, Mr. Horton, don't make things worse for yourself.

Think about your family, and what they—"

"My family!" Horton glared at her again, the vein at his temple throbbing with his fury. "My family will never find out. You and your bastard son will not ruin me, Claire. So don't you threaten me."

Claire. Oh God, he thought she was Claire again. Olivia pressed her lips together and focused on keeping her breathing under control. He continued to stare at her with a menacing glower, and she realized he wasn't watching the road.

"Mr. H-Horton," she rasped, turning to peer through the driving rain out the windshield. They'd crossed the center line, and she prayed that no other car came down the road at that moment. "The road, Mr. Horton. Watch the r—"

He jerked the wheel, and the car fishtailed before righting itself. Her heart thundered, and she slipped a protective hand over her belly. Knowing she could possibly be carrying Reyn's child gave her strength. She would survive this if only for her baby's sake. A baby she desperately wanted and would protect at all cost.

A thought occurred to her, gave her a ray of hope. "Mr. Horton, if you kill me, your grandchild will die too."

His head whipped around to face her. He stared at her from under thick, furrowed eyebrows. "What are you talking about?"

"Reyn's baby would be your grandchild. I'm carrying your son's baby." She didn't tell him that her pregnancy was still just a small possibility. An unconfirmed chance.

Again the man stared at her instead of the rainy road. She tore her gaze away to look ahead of them. "Mr. Horton, please watch the road."

"You're pregnant?" he roared. "How could you be so careless? You have to get rid of it. My wife cannot find out."

Olivia gulped in a deep breath. He still thought she was Claire. *Oh God.* Peering through the gray mist ahead of them, she struggled to keep her voice calm. "I'm not Claire. I—"

Ahead of them, leaping out of the murkiness of the fog, a raging flood swamped the road. Clairmont Creek had overflowed its banks and swept across the highway.

"Mr. Horton, look out!"

Her cry came too late.

The car careened forward, into the rushing current of the rain-glutted creek. She braced herself as their momentum carried them forward and the force of the water pushed them sideways. The front end of the sedan ran up the sloped guardrail, and the wheels lost purchase at the edge of the bridge.

Olivia screamed. The car flipped and dove over the side of the bridge, propelled by the rushing water. They landed upside down in the swollen creek, brown water raging outside the car windows. Knowing they were going under, she unbuckled her seatbelt, lowering herself awkwardly to the roof of the car, which was now their floor. Slowly she rolled down her window a crack. The outside water poured in and began filling the car's interior, equalizing the water pressure inside and out.

She glanced at Horton who hadn't moved since they crashed. He lay crumpled at an odd angle on the roof. A trickle of red ran across his forehead into his hair. "Mr. Horton."

She knew better than to move someone who could have a neck injury, but the other option was letting him drown. Grabbing his arm, she tugged, trying to move him upright so his head would stay above the water as long as possible. The man weighed a ton and barely budged. She tried again. "Come on, Vance. Help me."

The car was filling quickly, water creeping upward,

depleting their supply of air. Using every ounce of her strength, Olivia dragged Horton upright. She propped him against the driver's side while she groped for the passenger-side door handle. Locked. Damn, she forgot. She'd tried it earlier.

With the passenger's side downstream, it was the only option for escape. Opening Horton's door against the current would be next to impossible. The passenger window was their only out.

The water had reached her chin and continued to rise. Groping in the dark, cold water, she found the window handle and rolled the window down the rest of the way. The water rose faster now. She fumbled to grab Horton again and choked on a mouthful of the water. Panic gripped her as she coughed and sputtered for a last precious breath of air.

Holding her breath and ducking under the water, she caught Horton under the arms and pulled hard. He moved slightly, but not enough. With a sinking sensation in her heart and the sting of oxygen depravation in her lungs, Olivia accepted that she couldn't save both Horton and herself. She had to get out. Now.

Reyn drove as fast as he dared on the rain-puddled road, scanning the highway for any sign of the white sedan. Anxiety dried his mouth. The thought of Horton hurting Olivia made him crazy.

If anything happened to her, it would be his fault. He hadn't protected her like he should, even knowing someone wanted to kill her. And the bastard had darn near succeeded twice.

Spurred by guilt and worry, Reyn pumped his Sierra with just a little more gas. *Please, let her be all right.*

He didn't think he could stand losing someone else he

loved. Because of his own screw up. Because of his failure to take care of them. Because of his cowardice.

When he felt the truck hydroplane for a moment, Reyn gripped the steering wheel tighter.

Yes, his cowardice was why he'd let Olivia walk out of his house this morning. His fear of what he saw happening between them. *I'm falling in love with you, Reyn.* He'd freaked. He'd let his demons convince him he couldn't give her all that she deserved. That he couldn't live up to the fantasy she'd created, the hero she believed him to be. Maybe the demon was right.

Why else would he have sent her away, knowing she could be carrying his child? But he'd needed some distance, some time to think, and he cruelly pushed her away. *Coward.*

If not for him, she wouldn't be in danger now. If he hadn't sent her away, she'd be safe. But he'd failed her. Oh God, he'd failed the woman he loved more than his next breath.

His pulse jumped as that thought reverberated in his head. Yes, he loved her. And it took the threat of losing her to wake him up to that fact. He wanted Olivia. And what's more he wanted her baby. Their baby. He wanted the family he'd lost years ago.

But first he had to earn the right to have her, to have his family around him, to have their love and respect. *Please don't let me lose her. Please give me another chance*, he prayed silently as he scanned the foggy road for the white car.

Overflow from the ditches along the side of the road crept onto the highway, making the driving even more treacherous. But he plowed on through the pouring rain, cursing the veil of water that hampered his view of the road ahead.

The mist stretched accusing fingers toward him as it roiled and swirled in his headlights. His windshield wipers hissed a condemning *tsk-tsk* in the stillness of his cab.

Coward. The demon laughed, and tears stung his eyes.

In the murky gray of the fog and rain, a flash of color caught his eye. He strained to see through the downpour and made out the rush of water where the Clairmont Creek bridge should have been. Then he saw the bottom side of the white car. Terror flooded his veins.

He stood on his brakes, and with a screech of tires on the wet pavement and a sideways slide, his truck stopped inches from the raging stream. Being the low point in the parish, the place where much of the rainfall from upstream collected, the creek was swollen many times larger than normal, to dangerous proportions.

Wiping his windshield with his arm, he scanned the swirling eddies and briskly flowing current for the color that had caught his eye. From under the rushing water, a head of flaming-orange hair rose out of the brown torrent. Olivia.

Throwing his door open, Reyn dashed out of his truck and to the edge of the water. "Olivia!"

One arm flailed as she struggled against the current. With her other hand, she clung desperately to the overhanging limb of a willow tree at the edge of the rushing stream.

Stream? Hell, she was contending with a river. A death trap. A current stronger than a person could swim. Floating limbs and debris that could knock her unconscious.

Reyn flew into action.

As close as Olivia was to the edge of the water, he hoped he could reach her without going into the current himself. Sidling up to the bent willow, he grabbed the thin trunk and leaned out as far as he could toward Olivia. "Grab my hand!"

Her startled gaze found him, her eyes wide with fear. "Reyn!"

Between fighting the current and the din of the water and rain, she'd clearly not noticed his arrival.

"Grab my hand, and don't let go for any reason."

She tried, stretching her fingers as far as she could, but the current kept pushing her back.

"Damn it," he growled, realizing this approach wouldn't work. He straightened and whipped his shirt over his head. Twisting it, he tied a knot in each end. Rain dripped in his eyes as he stretched out over the water again, holding tight to the willow for support. Olivia batted at the shirt knot, narrowly missing each time. "Come on, Olivia. Grab it."

Risking losing his balance, Reyn stretched another couple inches toward her. He heard the branch he clung to crack under his weight. Finally her fingers closed around the knot in his shirt, and he hauled her toward the bank of the swollen stream. She let go of the branch that had saved her life and wrapped that hand around his wrist. As soon as he could reach her armpit, he dragged her from the water. She half stumbled, half crawled onto higher ground, falling against him as he fell on his rear end.

"Reyn." She burst into tears and wrapped her arms around his neck. "Oh, thank God. I was so scared!"

"Are you okay?"

She nodded, her silky wet hair brushing across his chest, and he knew he'd never felt a sweeter sensation in his life. Olivia was alive. Safe. He held her shivering body close and glanced back at the upended sedan. A prickle of dread washed through him.

"Where's Horton?" he shouted over the din of rushing water and drumming rain.

She pulled back, blinking at him as rain drops splashed in her face. "How did you know—"

"I'll explain later. Where is he?"

She turned to look at the mostly submerged car, and he knew. His sense of duty kicked in. Duty and something else. Something stronger and more compelling. A desperate need for redemption, for justice, for the chance to right a wrong. He pushed her away and hurried up the bank to assess the situation.

Olivia splashed through the wet grass to catch up with him.

"You're not going in after him, are you?" Her voice reflected her horror.

"I have to."

"Don't be crazy! You can't go out in that." She flung her hand toward the swift, deadly water. "He's probably already dead anyway. I tried to get him out, but he was unconscious and—"

Rope. He needed some kind of rope.

He turned and hurried back to his truck, not letting her finish her sentence. Every second counted.

"Reyn, listen to me! The current is too fast. Going in there is suicide."

Opening the long tool box across the back of his truck bed, he scooped out a chain he'd left in the truck after he'd used it to help a buddy take down a dead tree in the guy's yard. Not a rope, but close enough.

"Reyn, don't do this. You could be killed. It's just not worth the risk!"

"I have to try. It's my responsibility to save lives, not sit back and do nothing."

She dogged his steps as he wound the chain around a secure spot on the truck frame and secured the attached hook.

He tugged hard to make sure it would hold. Then, untangling the chain, he stretched it upstream from the submerged car.

"Reyn!" Olivia screamed. The fear in her voice brought his head up. Her eyes were red, and she trembled as she stared at him, pleaded with him. "*Please* don't do this. Think of Lila and what it would do to her if anything happened to you."

He held her gaze as he wrapped the chain around his waist and fed it through the belt loops of his jeans. "When I was a kid, I stood in the door of our burning house and let fear decide my mother's fate. I was too cowardly to save my mother when I had the chance, and I've lived with that on my conscience ever since. Now I have another chance. A chance to save my *father*."

He kicked off his shoes and tossed them to her. "And once I save him, he can pay for murdering my mother. She'll finally have justice. It's the least I can do for her."

Olivia stepped up to him, her gold eyes piercing his soul. "Please, Reyn. You don't have to prove your courage to anyone."

Emotion tightened his throat. "Yes, I do. I have to prove it to the demon."

Her brow wrinkled with confusion, but he didn't stick around to explain himself. He had work to do.

"The passenger's window is open," she called to him as he moved further upstream. Nodding to her, he took a deep breath.

And dove into the rushing water.

The current carried him downstream while he swam as hard as he could to move out toward the vehicle. The combination of current and manpower took him to the upended car in a matter of seconds. He grabbed the frame of the sedan and held on tightly, working his way, hand over hand, pulling himself to the level of the passenger's window.

After filling his lungs with a deep breath, he ducked under

the surface. Pulling on the frame of the car for leverage, he propelled himself, feet first through the open window and out of the main current. The water was murky and dark, but he made out the man in the driver's seat. Seizing the front of Horton's shirt, he pulled the man toward the window. His father's limp body floated toward the tiny escape hatch, and quickly Reyn tugged the slack in the chain over Horton's head and around his body. Clenching the ends of the chain in his fist, he held it in place under the other man's armpits and pushed back through the car window.

While he battled to guide the large man out the small window, Reyn's lungs screamed for air. The chain bit into his hand, and the current tried to sweep him downstream. But he refused to release either the lifeline to his father or his grasp on the car frame. And the real test was still to come.

The swiftly moving water would pull on Horton's limp body, and he'd have twice the fight against the current to get the man to the creek bank. His hand burned where the chain cut into his skin, and his arm muscles strained to pull the deadweight through the water.

An image of his mother flickered in his mind. Summertime. Learning to ride his bike. Her smile. *You can do it, honey. Don't give up.*

The memory sent a fresh flash of determination through him. He'd ridden his bike that night long ago, because he refused to let his mother down. And he wouldn't let her down now either.

Finally he squeezed Horton through the car window, and the battle with the water began. He gasped for air as he broke the surface and began swimming for safety. They were floating downstream rapidly, and he felt the chain at his waist jerk when they reached the full length of the links. He tried to swim with one arm while he hung tightly to the chain wrapped around Horton.

It was a lost cause. The current was too strong. Horton was too heavy.

"You little brat. Didn't your mother teach you respect for your elders?" The steely eyes of the elementary school principal focused on him, and he felt them drill into him like icy spikes.

Reyn shook his head, clearing the ancient memory from his mind. His muscles ached. The hand gripping the chain securing Horton grew weak, trembling with exertion.

Let go. Save yourself. No one would blame you, the demon taunted. *Walk away. Just let go...*

For a moment he considered giving in. The chain slipped in his hand, and he loosened his fingers a bit to ease the sting.

Suddenly bright lights blinded him, and he heard a roar of an engine. Blinking, he glanced toward the bank. The headlights of his truck glared at him through the mist.

The truck tires spun in the mud and then slowly the Sierra rolled backward. He felt himself being pulled through the water toward the bank.

Olivia. Knowing she was there, helping him, working with him, sent warmth coursing through his water-chilled body.

Despite the pain of the chain cutting into his hand, the force of the current pulling against his arm as he dragged Horton with him, he held on tightly. He wouldn't walk away. Not this time.

In a matter of seconds, they were pulled out of the current and onto the higher ground. Reyn coughed, clearing his lungs and catching his breath. He loosened the chain around Horton and rolled the man onto his side. Water flowed from Horton's mouth and nose. When the water stopped trickling from

Horton's lips, Reyn flipped the man on his back and felt for a pulse. Finding none, he started chest compressions and tipped Horton's head back to breathe into his mouth.

"Reyn." Olivia scrambled up beside him. "Thank heavens! I never—"

"Do you know CPR?"

She nodded. "I learned it when Katy was born, and we thought we might have to—"

"Start chest compressions," he interrupted.

She hesitated.

"Come on, go!" he shouted.

She inched into place, and together they worked on his father, fighting for his life. When he looked into Olivia's eyes between breaths he saw her doubt, her concern.

"He can't die," he growled.

"Reyn…"

Just then Horton sputtered and coughed. Another mouthful of water gushed from his lips. Reyn pressed his fingers to his father's neck. A faint pulse fluttered there. With another cough and a gasp, Horton opened his eyes and peered up at his rescuers.

"Welcome back, Dad, you sonofabitch," Reyn muttered darkly. "Now you can spend the rest of your life rotting in prison for murdering my mother."

Chapter Sixteen

Reyn stepped off the hospital elevator at the ground floor and headed back to the emergency room. He found Olivia sitting in a molded plastic chair in the waiting room. "Any word yet?"

Olivia looked up from contemplating her wet shoes when he spoke. She shook her head, her expression somber.

Helen Horton and her daughter sat waiting for the doctors to bring news of Vance's condition, and Olivia glanced at them before dropping her gaze toward the floor again. "I hate this for them. Their lives have been ripped apart."

"Horton brought this down on them. Not you."

She raised her chin to meet his gaze once more. "I know that, but still..." She paused. "How did Lila take the news?"

He shrugged. "Mixed emotions. About what you'd expect. She's glad Horton has been caught, relieved to hear it's over. But sad, too, about the people he hurt, the way things ended. She wants to see you later, by the way. Wants to see for herself that you're all right."

She hummed an acknowledgment and looked away.

An awkward silence fell between them, and he took a seat in the chair beside her, fumbling for a place to start apologizing for his abhorrent behavior.

"Who's with Katy?" he asked instead of broaching the more painful topic of his cruelty.

"Hank. Turns out the fire call was a false alarm, probably called in by Horton to get Hank away from the house so he could get me."

The reminder of Olivia's brush with death sent a wave of nausea through him, and he muttered an obscenity. "I owe you an apology."

Beside him, Olivia tensed, straightening her back. She stared down the hall, not looking at him.

"If I'd stayed with you, like I promised, Horton wouldn't have had a chance to—"

"You're not my keeper."

He sighed. "But I should have been there. I knew you were in danger, and I didn't protect—"

"Look. Reyn...just forget it. Okay?" She turned and met his eyes then, her own swollen from crying and shadowed with fatigue. "You were there, at Clairmont Creek, when it counted, and for that I'm grateful. So let's just call ourselves even and quit while we're ahead. Deal?"

Her tone was curt, wounded, and her gold eyes lacked the bright glow that always warmed him in the past. It was as if a light inside her had gone out, as if her joy for life had been extinguished. He knew he was to blame for the grief in her eyes. And he'd give anything to repair the damage he'd done.

"About this morning..." he began, his heart in his throat.

"Don't." She turned away and bit her bottom lip. He saw the moisture welling in her eyes and watched her battling the tears. His chest ached with regret for having caused her this pain. Damn it, why did he always hurt the people he loved most?

"I'm sorry for the things I said," he continued, knowing his words were completely inadequate to erase the scars he'd caused.

"I said *don't.*" Anger vibrated in her tone. "I don't want your apologies. You warned me not to fall for you, and I did anyway. I'll deal with it."

"Olivia..." He reached for her hand on her lap, and she jerked her arm away.

She stood quickly and whirled to face him. "And if I am pregnant," she said in a low voice, "I won't make any demands of you. You're free to go back to Atlanta, no strings, no obligations, no regrets. Okay?"

Lunging to his feet, he plowed a hand through his hair and gritted his teeth. "No, it's not okay. Because I do have regrets. I hate like hell that I hurt you. The things I said this morning were hateful and cruel, and I'm sorry."

She sighed and ducked her head, but her jaw remained clenched tight. "Fine. Apology accepted. Now will you please go. I really don't want to talk about this any more."

He raised a hand in surrender. "All right. You're right. This isn't the time or place. When *can* we talk?"

She shook her head, frowning. "You don't get it, do you?"

Cold fear slithered through him. He narrowed his eyes on her, and his voice sounded gravelly when he spoke. "No, I guess I don't."

She put her shoulders back and lifted her chin. "I don't want to talk later. I don't want to talk *ever*. I made a mistake trusting you, falling in love with you, sleeping with you. But I'll deal with it and move on."

He felt the blood drain from his face, felt the room spin, felt her slipping away. "No. Olivia, listen..."

He reached for her, and she stepped back, out of arm's length. "No, I've thought about everything you've said, everything that's happened, and I understand now that it could never work between us. I should have seen it before, but I was blinded by the fantasy I created in my mind about you. I wanted you to be someone you aren't, and there's nothing I can do to change who you are."

Pain like a hot poker stabbed his chest. "And who do you think I am? Why won't it work?"

She squeezed her eyes closed and pinched the bridge of her nose. "You're just different from me. We have different lives, different priorities, different needs."

Desperation and grief choked him, but he forced words through his tight throat. "Tell me what you need, Olivia. I'll give it to you."

A tear broke free from her auburn eyelashes and trickled down her cheek. With his heart flayed open, his pain a living thing, clawing him inside, he stepped toward her and caught her tear with the pad of his thumb.

She gasped when he touched her and opened her eyes. The heartache and longing in her gold eyes tore him apart.

"I want your demon. But you can't seem to give it up."

Reyn took a step back from her, staggering drunkenly as if pushed. He tried to take a breath, but his lungs, his heart felt paralyzed.

His demon? He wasn't sure what he'd thought she would say, but it wasn't that. He remembered telling her by the raging creek that he had to prove himself to his demon. That had to be how she knew his name for the pain and guilt that haunted him.

But he hadn't told her, hadn't told anyone about the memories and recriminations that fed the demon and kept his wounds raw. Now she was asking him to give her his demon. What the hell did that mean? What did she expect from him? Didn't she understand that he had no control over the demon? That he couldn't change the past?

"I...I don't know how to do that," he whispered, his voice hoarse.

She gave him a weak, sad smile. "And that's why we have no future."

Olivia turned, took a step, then faced him again. With two quick steps she closed the distance between them and caught his lips with hers. He tasted the salt of her tears and the agony of another loss in her kiss.

"Goodbye, Reyn," she whispered. Then she spun away and fled down the hospital corridor.

Numb with shock from Olivia's rejection, Reyn sat in the emergency room waiting area for long minutes after she left, desperately trying to understand the turn of events. Somehow he had to repair the damage he'd done to their relationship, had to figure out how to give Olivia what she needed to believe in him again.

He looked up when a doctor emerged from the exam room where Horton was being treated. He listened as the doctor told Helen Horton that her husband would recover and had sustained no apparent brain damage during the brief time he was clinically dead. "But," the doctor continued, "he's lucky to be alive."

Helen turned a meaningful glance toward Reyn.

He turned away. He didn't want her gratitude. He'd saved Horton for selfish reasons, because he wanted justice for his mother's murder.

"Can I see him?" he heard Helen ask.

"As far as I'm concerned you can but I think the decision is up to the sheriff. Your husband is facing serious charges, and Sheriff Anders is waiting to question him."

Having already given his statement to the sheriff earlier and having the report on Horton's condition that he wanted, Reyn surreptitiously headed for the elevator to go to Gram's room.

An untouched lunch tray sat beside Gram's bed when he entered the room, and he met his grandmother's anxious gaze with the best smile he could muster.

"Horton will be okay, and the sheriff has him in custody. I think this mess, for my part anyway, is finally over." He sighed as he dropped into the chair beside Gram's bed.

"Does that mean you'll be leaving town?" The wistful note in her voice poured acid into the bleeding wounds Olivia left inside him. He winced and rubbed a hand down his face, thinking of all the times he'd excused the melancholy in Gram's voice as a bad phone connection. He had a lot of fences to mend before he could face himself in the mirror.

"I won't leave until I know you're okay. And...and then I'll come back as often as I can to check up on you."

Gram gave him a half-hearted smile, as if to say, *Yeah, I've heard that before, pal. But I don't buy it.*

"I mean it this time, Gram. I'll be back to see you."

The light of hope glowed in his grandmother's eyes. "And to see Olivia?"

He turned away, his jaw clenched in self-reproach. "Probably not for Olivia. She's not speaking to me."

"What? But why? I thought—"

He shook his head.

"Reyn?"

He struggled for his composure before he met her gaze. "I've hurt Olivia, and I don't know how to make things right."

"Do you love her?"

He took a deep breath, calming a strange fluttering inside him before he answered. "Yeah, I do."

Gram squeezed his hand and drilled him with a no-nonsense gaze. "Then don't give up until you make things right. Love is too precious to lose."

"But how do I fix things?"

She smiled. "Who do I look like? Dear Abby?"

"Gram, I'm serious. I don't know what to do."

She stroked his hand lightly. "You'll think of something. I've never known you to walk away from a challenge."

Reyn tensed. *If she only knew.*

He'd walked away so many times. Too many times. He'd let so many people down. His mom. Liz. Now Olivia.

He'd let his demon rule his life, hold him prisoner for years. He'd—

His breath caught. *I want your demon.*

Something inside him shifted. For the first time, he saw himself, his actions from a different angle. As his thoughts took off in a new direction, Reyn flopped back on the chair beside Gram's bed. His mind reeled, his heart drummed erratically.

He thought back to the day he'd gone into the Russells' burning house to find Sara. Facing the smoke and fire that day, he'd resolved never to let someone get hurt because he'd walked away, because of his cowardice. But wasn't that what he was doing now? Even though he'd thought he was protecting Liz, protecting Olivia when he'd held them at arm's length, in truth keeping them away *was* what hurt them. Withholding his heart was how he'd let them down. Maybe he'd really kept the distance in his relationships to protect himself. He'd let his demon convince him that by *not* loving someone, he could avoid the hurt and the guilt of failing them in the end. Yet that mindset had made failure a self-fulfilling prophecy. By denying himself the love they wanted to give him, he hurt them and hurt himself more.

"Reyn, honey? Are you all right? You're pale as a sheet."

He wet his dry mouth and raised his eyes to Gram. "I, um...something you said just...I've spent my whole life walking away from what mattered. Hiding."

"Hiding? From what?"

"The demon."

His answer clearly confused and unnerved Gram, and he quickly tried to explain. "That's what I call my...my..." What was it? He had to answer that question for himself as well as for Gram. For Olivia. Reaching deep into the past, his memories, his heartache, he came up with the word. "My...guilt."

Saying the word, putting a name to the pain and doubt that had plagued him, made so many things fall into place. His guilt over his mother's death fed his fear of failing the people he loved.

"You were right." He glanced at Gram, whose face reflected fathomless understanding and love. "I couldn't forgive myself for hurting the people I loved. And because I couldn't see it, I kept repeating the same mistakes."

And as long as he listened to the voice of the demon, he would go on doing the one thing he wanted most to avoid.

Reyn groaned and buried his face in his hands, knowing the horrible mistakes he'd made, all in the name of protecting the people he loved.

"Well, at least now you know what *not* to do. Hmm?" Gram's expression brightened. "You have a chance to do things the right way with Olivia. And if you're smart, you won't let that darling girl get away."

A spark of hope flickered to life deep in his soul, a feeling much like the refuge, the peace he'd known with Olivia in his arms. "I need to go, Gram. I have to find Olivia."

"That's my boy."

He leaned over and placed a kiss on Gram's cheek. "Thank you."

She framed his face with gentle hands. "Good luck, honey. I love you so."

Emotion clogging his throat, he nodded and smiled then hurried out of the room. Though he better understood his own actions and defense mechanisms now, he still had to convince Olivia he would and could change.

The one thing Olivia said she needed from him was his demon. She wanted him to give up his fear, his guilt and to close the distance between them. He had to figure out a way to show her that he wouldn't let his doubts and uncertainty come in the way of giving her his whole heart, all of his love and commitment.

When he arrived at her house, he still had no specific plan, but he wasn't above begging if it meant convincing Olivia how much he loved her and needed her in his life.

Hank answered the door with a frightened-looking Katy in his arms. The little girl's face brightened when she saw her visitor, and, looking into the girl's wide brown eyes, Reyn had his answer. He knew what Olivia wanted, knew where he'd made his colossal error with her. He knew what he needed to offer her to win her back. Family. He'd seen how much her family meant to her, seen her volatile reaction to his misguided reaction to her possible pregnancy. The idea of starting a family with Olivia flowed through him and felt so right he thought he'd burst with joy.

After greeting Hank, Reyn gave Katy an encouraging grin. "Hey, cutie, how're you doing?"

"I was really scared before."

"I know. But you were very brave, and everything's going to be okay." Even as he said the words to Katy, he prayed he was right. Olivia had to listen to him. He had to win her back. Somehow. He met Hank's wary gaze. "I need to talk to Olivia. Is she here?"

"She was. But she said she needed to do some thinking and took off a little while ago."

Reyn's heart sank, but when he scanned the front lawn, wondering what message to leave, he noticed Olivia's battered car parked at the side of the house. She couldn't have gone far.

She needed to do some thinking. His spirits rose.

"Thanks," he told Hank. "I think I know where to find her."

Chapter Seventeen

Olivia gazed out over the still bayou, a hollow ache inside her. She sat with her legs bent in front of her, her arms propped on her knees and her heart in tatters. But it was her own fault. She should have known she couldn't make Reyn change if he didn't want to, that he wouldn't open himself to her and share his deepest, truest self until he was ready. Not when he had years of practice shutting people out.

Hearing the hollow thud of footsteps on the dock behind her, Olivia dashed the tears from her cheeks and glanced over her shoulder to see who was there.

"Hi," Reyn said, giving her an anxious smile. "Mind if I join you?"

Her heart constricted. "As a matter of fact, I do. I've said all I have to say to you. Please don't make this harder for me than it is."

"It's hard for me too, Olivia. Please just hear me out."

She buried her face in the crook of her arm. "What?"

"For starters, I know what it's like growing up without a father, and if you are pregnant, I want to know about it. I want my kid to know me."

She blinked at him, not sure she'd heard him correctly. "I thought you didn't want—"

"I know what I said." He cut her off quickly then frowned. "I panicked 'cause things were going too fast, and I was...well, scared of loving you and the idea of being a father."

She scowled, and he hastened to add, "But I've realized some things since then, and I wish I could take back those horrible things I said. If you are pregnant, I want to be part of our child's life. All right?"

The thought of sharing a child with Reyn, having a tie to him that would keep her wounds open and festering, made her head light and her heart heavy. But how could she deny him such a basic, honorable request?

"Yeah, fine. If I'm pregnant, I'll let you know, and we'll work out some kind of visitation schedule."

She heard his harsh, humorless laugh and raised her head.

"A visitation schedule? Olivia, I don't want some damn visiting rights."

She rubbed the spot at her temple that had started to throb and fought to keep her temper. "Then what do you want? Christmas cards? Sunday phone calls? Maybe you'll stop by in twenty years or so?"

She could tell by the shadow that darkened his eyes that her remark had cut him, and she regretted her jibe. But it was too late to take it back. It was too late for a lot of things.

"No, I want..." He squatted beside her, an earnest appeal in his eyes. "I want to marry you."

She stared at him, unable to respond for a moment, wishing with every fiber of her being that she could say *yes*, praying just as hard for the strength to say *no*. "We can't get married just because I could be pregnant, Reyn. We wouldn't—"

He grabbed her hand, surprising her, interrupting her.

"Then marry me because you might *not* be pregnant."

A startled laugh bubbled up from throat. She shook her head. "What?"

"Marry me and give me the chance to get you pregnant. Please, Olivia. I love you, and I want to spend the rest of my life building a family with you."

A dragonfly buzzed by her head and lit on Reyn's sleeve. She stared at the water bug, uncertain for the second time in minutes that she'd heard Reyn right. She knew, even if she had heard correctly, it still solved nothing between them.

She struggled for a breath, felt a fresh ripple of pain wash through her. "Reyn, I can't—"

"Wait. Don't answer me yet. First, I want to give you my wedding present." He squeezed her hand and licked his lips nervously. "I want to give you...my demon."

Her breath caught, and her heart tapped an expectant rhythm.

He looked down at their joined hands, laced his fingers with hers and held onto her hand as if his life depended on it. His seriousness caused an anxious quiver in her chest.

"I've spent the last twenty years believing I was to blame for my mother's death." His eyes told her how painful that admission was.

She opened her mouth to contradict his assumption, but he plowed on with his explanation.

"The fire started in my room, with the candles I was notorious for experimenting with, while I hid in the woods, fearing a whipping for taking matches to school. By the time I realized my house was burning, the fire was out of control. I only made it as far as the front door before the heat drove me back. The heat and...my fear." He drew a deep breath, clearly struggling to lay out his tragic past to her. "I knew my mother was inside. I knew I needed to go in and try to get her out, try to help her, but…I didn't. I couldn't. I was too scared to do what I knew I needed to do to help my mother. And because of that, she died. I've lived with the guilt of letting her down, of letting my cowardice decide her fate ever since." His voice cracked, and he swiped away moisture from his eyes.

Her heart ached for him, and tears stung her eyes. He was letting her inside his walls, she realized. Sharing his soul, his emotions, despite what it cost him. She absorbed the significance of his confession as he continued, her heart swelling with pride for his sacrifice to her and shared pain for his grief.

"Since then, I've been afraid to let anyone close, afraid that I'd fail them the way I failed my mom. But mostly I've been afraid to love anyone for fear of losing them and going through this pain all over again." He scowled and clenched his teeth before finishing. "Rather than face my fears, I've walked away from love time and again. And I avoided any reminders of my guilt, of my loss, even when it hurt people I loved."

"Like staying away from Clairmont so long?" she asked, her throat raw and tight with tears.

"For starters." He sighed. "Being back in Clairmont, facing everything I've been running from for years has been a real wake-up call to me. Learning the truth about Horton and my mom's death has helped put some things in perspective. She'll finally have justice, and by helping get her that justice, I think I can finally begin to forgive myself for my inaction before."

She stroked his cheek and struggled to speak. "Oh, Reyn, surely you see now—looking at your mom's death through the eyes of a fireman rather than the eyes of a small boy—that there was nothing you could have done without losing your own life in the process?"

"Probably so. But guilt doesn't always listen to reason." He covered her hand with his, brought her fingers to his lips. "What I do know is that I'm tired of letting the demon, my guilt and my fear, rule my life. Gram says real courage is doing what you know you must despite your fear." He looked deep into her eyes and said resolutely, "I will not walk away from love again. And I love you, Olivia. I want to be with you. For always.

"I can't undo the mistakes I've made, and I can't promise that I won't let you down sometimes in the future, but I swear on my life, I will do my best to make you happy and to be the best husband I can be. I want to stay in Clairmont. My home is here. My family is here. And I want to raise my children here. With you. Please, give me another chance."

Olivia couldn't breathe, couldn't speak, couldn't believe her ears. He wanted to share her life, build a family, give himself to her. She stared into his expectant gaze. Gone were the storm clouds that had shadowed their depths for the past weeks. Instead, a shimmering love, a warmth and joy smiled back at her from his clear gray eyes. This was the Reyn she'd been searching for, the man she'd made love to, the grandson Lila had bragged on. Her fantasy. And he wanted to make her dreams come true.

"Olivia?" Reyn's tone was worried, and she realized how long she was taking to answer.

Laughter welled from deep inside her, and she launched herself into his arms. "Yes! Oh, absolutely yes!"

She kissed him hard and sank against his muscled chest. His kiss answered her fervor with love and passion that were unmistakable. She grinned and whispered seductively, "I'm burning up with a fire only you can put out, Lieutenant Erikson."

A spark of mischief, a flicker of desire heated his eyes. "Oh, yeah? Bring it on, Red. I'm ready for it."

Reyn wrapped his sweaty hand around the cross-shaped door handle and steeled himself with a deep breath. The October sun warmed his face when he tipped his head to soak in its rays.

He couldn't have asked for a prettier day. Of all days to be late, why the morning of his wedding? Olivia was going to kill him. Nervous tension tightened his chest as he opened the door and waited for his eyes to adjust to the dimmer light inside the sanctuary. He forgot to catch the door, and it banged closed, drawing all eyes to the back of the church.

Reverend Halmon grinned. "I thought the bride was supposed to make the grand entrance."

"Sorry. I saw Mrs. Skinner's car on the side of the road, and I stopped to help her change a flat." Reyn adjusted the tie of his dove gray tuxedo and smiled sheepishly.

"I knew it was either heroics or another woman. In this case, it was both." He heard Olivia's wry tone, but the morning sun streamed in the side windows and blinded him from a clear view of his bride. As he started down the aisle, a flash of color called his attention to the saints and angels in flowing robes gazing down from the stained glass. He remembered seeing condemnation and censure from these faces just a few months ago. He waited for the demon's voice to spoil his happiness, his wedding day. And waited.

Instead, as he stared at the artfully crafted faces in the colorful glass, he heard his mother's voice, an echo of the day he mastered riding a bike. *I knew you could do it, honey. I'm so proud of you.* Today, the saints and angels smiled their approval. A sense of peace and closure flowed through him. Redemption for his mistakes.

"Sometime today, fireman. I thought you guys knew how to

hustle." His bride's voice pulled him out of his thoughts.

He turned toward the altar and stepped out of the bright beams that blinded him. And caught his breath.

Olivia's fiery hair spread on her shoulders, and her heavenly face radiated love and joy. In the flowing satin wedding dress and with baby's breath in her hair, she looked like an angel. Until she sent him her wicked, lopsided grin. A devilish promise of sensual pleasures awaiting him.

He slid his gaze over her curves, still slim and sleek since she'd not gotten pregnant...yet. But he'd correct that soon enough. Imagining Olivia's belly swollen with his child flashed heat through his body. He couldn't wait. He had to look away or risk becoming embarrassingly aroused in church.

Hannah Russell, with Sara at her side, gave him an approving nod. George was serving an abbreviated sentence for concealing knowledge of a felony in exchange for his testimony against Vance Horton. Meanwhile, Horton awaited trial for his numerous crimes including two murders.

Lou sat next to his wife, beaming like a proud father, while Hank stood next to Olivia, waiting to serve as Reyn's best man.

Hank nodded to him. "Glad you could make it, boss."

Boss. Reyn smiled, still getting used to the idea of being the town's new Fire Chief. He'd been assigned the duty of reorganizing the volunteer fire department and made the first permanent, paid member of the new Clairmont Fire Department and Rescue Squad, which would include other neighboring towns.

He glanced to Olivia's left where Katy and Gram, back on her feet again and ambulatory with the help of a walker, served as attendants to the bride. They flashed him dual grins of affection, which he returned. A warmth spread through him, while he scanned the faces around him, knowing the wealth of love and support the citizens of Clairmont held for him and his bride.

He took his place beside Olivia, once again stuck by her beauty and reveling in the joy that she would be at his side for years and years to come. After a long absence and years of heartache, he had finally come home.

About the Author

Georgia native, Beth Cornelison received her bachelor's degree in public relations from the University of Georgia. After working in public relations for more than a year, she moved with her husband to Louisiana, where she decided to pursue her love of writing fiction.

Since that time, she has won numerous honors for her work including the coveted Golden Heart awarded by Romance Writers of America. She made her first sale to Silhouette Intimate Moments in June 2004 and has gone on to publish several more books with Silhouette. She has also had releases from Five Star Expressions, Sourcebooks and Samhain Publishing. For more information, visit www.bethcornelison.com.

A terrorist plot puts their lives—and hearts—on the line.

Under Fire
© *2008 Beth Cornelison*

When Jackson McKay and his daughter are kidnapped, their captors demand his research files on a devastating chemical weapon—or they'll kill his little girl. Jackson searches desperately for a way to save his daughter and also protect his country from the terrorists. No risk is too great. His daring escape sets in motion a deadly game of cat and mouse.

Arriving at the scene of a wildfire, smokejumper Lauren Michaels and her crew are caught in the crosshairs of Jackson's nightmare. Lauren is the only one who can lead Jackson off the burning mountain and to the police. In order to prevent a national crisis and save a child's life, they embark on a treacherous journey—one step ahead of a sniper!

But more than their lives are at risk, because an unexpected heat flares between them that may cost them their hearts...

Warning: This title contains sex, strong language, some violence, smart men, courageous women, and heart-pounding action. Possible side effects of reading include racing pulse, missed sleep, and nail biting.

Available now in ebook and print from Samhain Publishing.

HOT STUFF

Discover Samhain!

THE HOTTEST NEW PUBLISHER ON THE PLANET

Romance, fantasy, mystery, thriller, mainstream and
more—Samhain has more selection, hotter authors, and
everything's available in ebook.

Pick your favorite, sit back, and enjoy the ride!
Hot stuff indeed.

WWW.SAMHAINPUBLISHING.COM

LaVergne, TN USA
22 December 2010
209796LV00004B/2/P